# ANGEL
# OF THE ABYSS

## BY ED KURTZ

GORDIAN
KNOT
BOOKS

Footsteps sounded on the wooden stairs behind me. I turned to see a small woman coming up on the landing. When she saw me standing there, she gasped, "Oh!"

I said, "Ms. Wheeler?"

The woman laughed. She was short and bony, her iron gray hair pulled back into a girlish ponytail. She stretched her thin mouth into a smile and said, "No, I'm Barbara Tilitson. You must be Mr. Woodard."

Another member of the sewing circle, I decided. She walked slowly toward me, digging a jangling keyring from her knitted purse.

"That's me," I told her.

"Is she not in? I'm surprised. Probably stuck in traffic. I can't imagine the traffic in your neck of the woods can best ours."

"I tried her cell phone and heard it ringing inside," I said. "That is, I assume it was hers. Could be a coincidence, I guess ..."

"Well, let's just see," Barbara said with a pleasant lilt. She jabbed a bronze key into the doorknob and pushed the door open. I followed her into the dark room and waited for her to switch on a light. When she did, I squinted and looked at what was once probably a pleasant room, furnished with antiques and decorated with framed reproductions of classic one-sheets for silent pictures—but the place had been smashed up by someone who knew about smashing. There were turned over chairs, broken glass, and the rug on the floor had been pulled up and tossed into a pile in the corner. All of the posters had been ripped out of their frames, like somebody was looking to see if there was anything behind them. In one, America's Sweetheart Mary Pickford knelt reproachfully in a nightgown beneath the title *A Good Little Devil*. Beside the poster, a plump woman with short salt-and-pepper hair slumped in a faux leather club chair.

Barbara Tilitson screamed.

I knew then why Leslie Wheeler had been giving me the slip since my arrival. She was dead.

# PART ONE

## GRAHAM

# 1.

## BOSTON, 2013.

I was in the lab, working on a digital scan of an obscure Monogram musical from the mid-Thirties, when the call came in. Freddie Garcia, one of the interns, poked his head through a crack in the door and said, "Phone for you."

I left the print running through the scanner and followed Freddie out to the front office. The receiver was sitting on a mess of papers. I picked it up.

"This is Graham Woodard."

"Mr. Woodard," came back an unfamiliar voice, "my name is Leslie Wheeler—with the Silent Film Appreciation Society?"

She left it off on that lilt. I hadn't heard of them, so I waited for her to continue.

"We were contacted recently by a lady who seems to have found something quite rare, a 35 millimeter reel dating from the mid-Twenties."

I sighed quietly, casting a glance back at the door to my lab. The scan was going to take another forty-five minutes at least, but I hated not sitting there with it. Leslie Wheeler gently cleared her throat, snapping me back.

"Well," I said, "it's not necessarily rare. Depends on what it is."

"Mrs. Sommer—that's the lady who found it—certainly didn't know. That's why she got in touch with us. But I've had a look at the reel, Mr. Woodard, and I'd have to say it's terribly rare, indeed."

I rolled my eyes, glad I wasn't talking to this lady in person.

Truth was, I fielded calls like this fairly often: people who were damn sure they'd stumbled across the find of the century when it was only some great aunt's home movies or, at best, a modern dupe of a perfectly ordinary film. Just a few weeks earlier I heard from a guy in Needham who paid a hundred dollars for a stack of cans at an estate sale, believing he'd tricked the seller into parting with a lost Martin and Lewis picture. Turned out it was only *Bela Lugosi Meets a Brooklyn Gorilla* with Martin and Lewis clones Mitchell and Petrillo. Not only ordinary, but public domain. I nearly strangled the guy when I found out.

"All right," I said, "I'll bite. What is it you think you've got?"

"The reel is in terrible condition, of course," she went on. "Cellulose nitrate, you know."

I knew. Highly degradable—and flammable—film stock they used back in the good old days. More than fifty percent of the films made before 1950 were lost forever because of that stuff, but occasionally something turned up. But that still didn't make it the find of the century.

"Careful with that," I advised. "The heat from your projection lamp could ignite that like it was gunpowder."

"The thing is, I didn't recognize the actress," she said, ignoring my warning completely. "If you knew me, Mr. Woodard, you'd be surprised. There isn't very much about the silent film era I don't know."

"Bully for you," I said.

"But of course I'd only ever seen Grace Baron in still photographs."

That stopped me cold. I sputtered for a minute before managing to speak English again. "Did you say Grace Baron?"

"The one and only."

"That's impossible," I said. "Grace Baron only made one film …"

"I know. *Angel of the Abyss.*"

"Which was destroyed almost a century ago."

"The El Dorado of lost films, Mr. Woodard. One of the great enduring stories of old Hollywood."

I rubbed my forehead and longed for a cigarette. I was on quitting attempt number three of the year so far and hadn't had one in days.

"Ms. Wheeler," I said as calmly as I could, which wasn't much, "are you telling me you have *Angel of the Abyss* in your possession? Right now?"

"Only part of it, the one reel that was found."

"An original print?"

"It would have to be. No copies were ever made to my knowledge. After all, it's been considered lost since 1926."

From the lab I could hear the cut-rate, Poverty Row chorus girls warbling away, their off-key voices in the process of being saved for posterity by champion of cinema, Graham Woodard. I cradled the phone between my ear and my shoulder and leaned over to pull the door shut. I couldn't have cared less about the musical I was working with if what Leslie Wheeler was saying was true. It was almost too incredible to believe.

"Ms. Wheeler," I said, "please understand that in this line of work, I come across a great many people who, in their excitement over a find like this, make mistakes with regard to identifying the film in question. And since no one has actually *seen* Grace Baron in motion since Calvin Coolidge was in office, I'm sure you can understand my skepticism."

She gave a soft laugh and said, "Yes, I was forewarned of your … curmudgeonly outlook, Mr. Woodard."

It figured someone had passed my name along. I wasn't the first guy anybody called about something like this—not even in Boston—so I paused at that, wondering who exactly was doing the forewarning. Before I could give it much thought, she asked me for my email address. I rattled it off to her and she said, "Give me just a second, please. I'm sending you something I think you'll like very much."

Her fingers clacked over a keyboard on the other end, and I waited with the ever-familiar constriction in my chest from the nicotine fit I was experiencing.

"There we are," she said after a minute. "Sent."

I pursed my mouth and sat down at Freddie's computer, where I brought up the browser and logged onto my account.

There at the top was a new email from Leslie Wheeler, which I clicked open. She had sent it so quickly there were no comments, not so much as a hello—just an attached file. A video.

I double-clicked it and held my breath as it opened.

The set was magnificence in simplicity—intricately painted backdrops mimicking old world buildings lining a cobblestone street. All studio, of course, the effects more akin to live theater than film. Low stagelights penetrated the otherwise dark, misty air between canvas shops and restaurants, creating floating will-o'-wisps that silhouetted the figure emerging from the middle distance. As the figure moved closer, slowly, to the camera, it was revealed to be a woman, dressed in an archetypal babushka costume, shawl and headdress and all. She carried a rotting basket in her small, white hands, and shot wary glances around at the mist and fog as she stepped lightly up the street. When she reached the middle of the set, she stopped, canted her head to one side as though listening for something. She reached beneath the cloth covering the basket and withdrew a jagged table knife with a shaking hand.

The film jumped here. I presumed it was placement for an intertitle, some dialogue to be inserted or translated for foreign markets. Next thing on screen was a stock brute character creeping up from the shadows: heavy five o'clock shadow, rumpled cap on his sweaty dome. His eyes made up all black and menacing. The woman stepped back, threw a hand up to her mouth and in the process dropped her basket. Apples rolled down the street. She stuck out the knife as if the brute would impale himself on it, but he only seized her wrist and knocked it from her hand. She screamed—silently—and her attacker whipped both shawl and head-wrap from her like they were performing a choreographed dance number. She spun, milk-white breasts heaving, her then-fashionable bob all raven's wing black.

Her eyes went wild then, extraordinary eyes, bigger than Theda Bara's. The brute lunged behind her, grabbed her by the shoulders and pulled her in close. His face like a slavering wolf, right up against hers. She drew in an enormous breath, her eyes widening still ... and then just sighed it out. Defeated. Her expression died there on nitrate stock, heavy-lidded eyes and her formerly full mouth forming a thin, straight line. She slumped, and the brute relaxed his grip, nodding as he grinned.

Together they walked back into the mist until they were subsumed by the shadows. There the video ended.

The only film of Grace Baron, or at least a part of it. And I'd just watched it by way of a close-shot cell phone video. My mouth hung open like the hinges were broken. I was transfixed, partly because of the insane Indiana Jones moment in front of me, but mostly because the few surviving stills of Grace in her short prime did little justice to her haunted beauty.

She was extraordinary.

"Well, Mr. Woodard?"

I still held the receiver to my face, but until she spoke I'd managed to forget it was there. I cleared my throat and tried to focus. All I really wanted to do was hang up the phone and watch the reel again. And then again after that. Instead, I closed out the window and sucked a deep breath into my lungs. I wished it was infused with nicotine more than ever.

"This isn't bullshit," I said. That elicited a small laugh.

"No, it certainly isn't," she said.

"But listen: this is a major find. I mean, it's a *really* major find. I know it's the wrong end of the continent, but somebody like UCLA would probably be the place to take this. And the lady who found it—she's here in Boston, too?"

"Oh no, Mr. Woodard," she said, "I've never even been to Boston, I'm sorry to say. I'm right in the heart of old Hollywood, as a matter of fact. UCLA would be a skip and a jump for me, but I'm not entirely sure that's the route I want to take just now."

"Well, why the hell not? This is bigger than *Convention City*." Classic MGM comedy; offended the Catholics, so the studio boss ordered all the prints destroyed. I could always feel it in my gut that there was still a print out there somewhere.

"It's the Holy Grail," Ms. Wheeler agreed, "or one of them, at least. But I want to know more, and while I'm trying to figure that out, I want you to restore the one reel we have so far."

"God, I hope you're keeping it in a cool, dry place," I said breathlessly.

"I am, don't worry. I know a thing or two about film preservation too, Mr. Woodard."

"Of course you do," I came back, a little worried that I'd offended her. "I'd be glad to dupe the reel, though I won't sleep a minute until it arrives. Shipping something that fragile ..."

"Again you misunderstand me," she interrupted. "I prefer not to ship the film. I would prefer you came here to do the work. I can provide you with all the equipment you need, all the software, to ensure an excellent negative dub and digital copy can be made. I'll expect you to work on the grain and decay of the print, of course ..."

I sat down in Freddie's chair, slumped.

"You want me to come out to L.A.? Ms. Wheeler, I'm afraid that's impossible; I have a job to do here on the right coast, you know. Two jobs, as a matter of fact—I teach, too, when school's in—but neither of them affords me the luxury of skipping off to California for God knows how long."

"All of that will be taken care of," she insisted. "You'll have a hotel room, a decent one, and free rein of a lab to work in. And with some luck, we'll turn up the rest of the picture while you're here, increasing your workload—and your pay—tenfold."

When I first started talking to Leslie Wheeler I pictured some old maid with too much time on her hands and a chunk of dough left to her by some relative or another, enough to set her up sipping tea and talking about old movies to all of her old maid friends. Now I wasn't so sure. More and more she was starting to sound like someone with some kind of stake in finding and restoring *Angel of the Abyss*, though I couldn't for the life of me see what that was. Still, money was money, and the opportunity was undeniably golden even if I'd be a lot closer to my ex-wife than was comfortable to me. Last I'd heard from her, she'd jaunted out to Southern California with the Neanderthal she'd left me for. But hell, L.A. was a big town, easy to miss folks, and I'd be hunkered down in the lab all the time anyway.

And more than that, I'd be a part of history and one of the very first people to see a lost treasure in nearly a century.

"I'll tell you what," I said. "Let me talk to my boss here in Boston. Guy's the biggest old movie nut in the world, so when I tell him what we've got ..."

"No, you can't tell anybody about the film," she said suddenly. "Not now. Not yet. Not until we have a much better grasp on what it is we've got. Surely you can understand that."

I didn't. But I said, "Sure, I understand. But that still leaves my day gig."

"Tell them it has to do with Helen, family drama. You are coming to Los Angeles, after all."

My fingernails dug into the chair's upholstery.

"Hang on a minute—how do you know about my ex-wife?"

Leslie Wheeler chuckled softly.

"Who do you think recommended you to me, Mr. Woodard?"

# 2.

## HOLLYWOOD, 1926.

At the sound of the telephone, Grace Baronsky rolled over on the thin mattress and pulled a lumpy pillow over her head. The bells jangled across the whole bungalow like she was sleeping in a belfry, and she silently cursed Saul for installing the damned nuisance in the first place. She had never lived with one before and hardly understood why she had to start doing so now. If Saul wanted to talk to her, she was only a taxi ride away. And if he needed her at the studio at a certain time, there was plenty of time to tell her before she left for the day. So she rebelled, punishing her boss by ignoring it entirely. Or at least not picking up the receiver; no one could ignore such a hellish racket, even if they were stone deaf.

After eleven infuriating rings, the bungalow fell silent again. But Grace could still hear the bells echoing inside her skull.

"Oh, for Christ's sake," she groused, and she threw the pillow across the room. Her hopes of sleeping a little longer were dashed, and the throbbing behind her eyes from last night's gin came on full. "Damnit, Saul."

The head of Monumental Pictures may have been the savior who pulled her from the hard work and obscurity of vaudeville, but he was also a relentless taskmaster—both on and off the set. Late fifties and built like a teapot, Saul Veritek never tired. He drove cast and crew like a lion tamer from nine in the morning until six at night, and when the stage lights dimmed and the camera stopped rolling, it was time to hit the gin joints. And when Saul Veritek asked you to join him, he wasn't asking.

Grace sat up and threw her slender legs over the side of the bed. The cold floor met the bottoms of her feet and she hissed through her teeth. The place was sweltering by noontime, but then she was almost never home between the start of the workday and last call. How a fat, middle-aged man who smoked half a dozen cigars every day could outlast her was anyone's guess, but she knew for a fact Saul wasn't hurting this morning.

The Sonnig watch she never wore shone at her from the nightstand, informing her that she had about fifteen minutes until her driver pulled up out front. She groaned, rose tremulously, and padded naked to the wingback chair in the living area, over which the gown she wore the night before was slung. *Let the ladies in hair and wardrobe fuss,* she thought. *Whose picture is this, anyway?*

She laughed at her own momentary audacity. "Saul's, of course."

A horn sounded outside. The driver was early. Grace slithered into the gown, smelling strongly of tobacco and spilled booze and dance-floor sweat, and stepped into a pair of heeled court shoes. She then fumbled for her bag, found the flask at its bottom, and took a belt to get her started. It was a big day, after all.

Today, Grace Baronsky was scheduled to die.

Jack Parson sat in his canvas-back chair with the tattered shooting script in one hand and a smoldering butt in the other. He was in his shirt sleeves, no collar, and sweating through the tan vest slung over his sloping shoulders. A few feet away stood Saul Veritek, immaculate as always, sucking on a cigar and trembling with silent laughter. He was enjoying his director's agony. He always did.

"Look, Parson," he said in a condescending manner, "you got your nutty Kraut sets, didn't you? The place looks like Picasso puked all over it. Have I cried about it? Didn't I give the go-ahead to this nightmare here?"

He gestured broadly toward the sharply angled set jutting crazily in every direction before them. A set painter stood frozen in the middle of it, staring wide-eyed at the plan he held like it was the lost Mormon tablets.

At the far end of the studio, Grace Baronsky stood in her dressing robe worrying her earrings and taking in the set.

"It's the sex, Saul. The devilishness of this whole thing. The denouement is … well, it's ghastly."

"You wanted to make a European picture. Here it is."

"I'll probably get arrested. Did you think of that? There are obscenity laws, you know."

"There are hardly any laws when it comes to motion pictures. The legislature is thirty years behind the times, if not more."

"There was that case in Ohio …"

"This ain't Ohio. Christ, this is hardly even America. They'll want to throw you in the pokey, sure, but they won't have a leg to stand on. And think of it—this picture will be like nothing anybody's ever seen before. It will be a sensation. You, Jack, will be a sensation."

"I'll be a goddamned pornographer is what I'll be."

Saul chuckled through a blue-gray cloud of smoke. He then raised his chin and looked across the open warehouse studio at his nervous star-to-be.

"Grace, darling," he called to her. "Come on over here for a minute, will you?"

With a strained smile, she stepped lightly on her bare feet, bouncing almost rabbit-like. Jack avoided eye contact with her. He sucked a final drag from his cigarette and crushed the end on the floor beneath his heel.

"Grace, honey," Saul wooed, "you've read the script, haven't you?"

"I have," she said. "Of course I have."

"And what do you think of it? I mean your general impression."

"I think it's marvelous, Mr. Veritek."

"Saul, honey. It's always Saul."

She laughed lightly. Jack shook his head, patting his vest pockets in search of another smoke.

"Saul," Grace agreed. "It sure beats the Keystone Kops, doesn't it? I mean, this isn't just a gag, is it? This is—I don't know—*art*."

Stabbing the cigar between his teeth, Saul rocked back on his heels and presented both palms to the director.

"Do you see? Art, my boy. Let Warners bore them to death with whatever thing Barrymore's doing this year. We're going to give them art."

"If by art you mean tits, ass, and fucking the devil, fine. We'll all agree to call that art."

"You're being difficult, Jackie," Saul complained.

"You had the script changed. I get difficult when I get the wool pulled over my eyes."

"Only sheep got wool. You're no sheep."

"No, but you're sure a wolf, Saul."

It was an insult, but Saul smiled. Between the two of them, Grace fidgeted with the hem of the robe. Saul placed a gentle hand at her elbow and took the stogie from his mouth.

"Now Grace here, she gets it, don't you Grace? She knows a sensation when she sees one."

"It'll sure knock them over," she agreed, hesitantly.

"Indeed it will," he agreed. "What's Paramount got? *Aloma of the South Seas?* Christ. Fox is doing another war melodrama. It's a bum year for the picture business, Jack—but you're gonna cinch it. And you know why?"

Jack just smoked and sweated. Saul sucked a deep breath into his lungs and pinched at the hem of Grace's robe. "Do you mind, dearheart? It's for art."

He gave the fabric a tug for emphasis. Grace swallowed, turned her eyes to the director, but he wasn't looking at anyone. For a moment she froze, an ice sculpture in flesh, but the unwavering gaze of the studio head made its point. With a crooked smile and a silent sigh, Grace opened her robe and let it fall to the dusty floor at her feet. Beneath it she wore nothing but a sapphire ring on her right hand.

The few crewmen loitering around the studio stopped what they were doing to stare, slack-jawed, at the nude woman in their midst. Grace heard a throaty chuckle and fought against the urge to snatch up her robe and run.

"Audrey Munson did it," Saul said to Jack. "Annette Kellerman did it. It's not unheard of, nude women on film. But this, Jack—*this*. And in the context of that script ... Jack, you're not looking."

"For Christ's sakes, Saul ..."

"You'll need your eyes to direct this picture so *look at her*, goddamnit."

Jack muttered, "Damn you, Saul."

Grace tried to force a laugh, but it came out more like a honk. She knelt down and hurriedly shrugged back into her robe. Saul ran a hand over his mostly bald pate and patted her on the behind with the other.

"There's a good girl," he said. "Now run along and get into costume. We've got a picture to make, haven't we, Jackie?"

"Yeah," he said in a half-whisper.

With that, Saul dropped what remained of his cigar to the floor and walked triumphantly out of the studio, head high. Jack and Grace exchanged a brief glance. She then turned and hurried back to wardrobe, clutching the robe tightly closed with both hands.

# 3.

## BOSTON/L.A., 2013.

I got married at 23; Helen was only 19 then. It was a stupid move on both our parts and just about everybody told us so, but I didn't listen. Twenty-three year olds don't listen to much. At least I didn't.

Eight years went by, most of them sullen and crabby, and then after a week of the old silent treatment she brusquely informed me that we were done, she'd met someone else, and I was expected to move out by the end of the week. I did, and I hadn't been in the same room with her since. No kids, no pets to squabble over. I signed a waiver agreeing to whatever she wanted in front of the judge so I wouldn't have to appear in court. That was what they called an amicable divorce. I didn't feel particularly amicable about any of it, but I was glad when it was over. I tried dating a little in the aftermath, but nothing stuck. A year later I landed the lab gig and decided to marry that, instead. I'd been holed up in front of my scanner pretty much ever since.

Except for when I wasn't, and when I wasn't I was usually habituating the back end of Bukowski's, a neighborhood pub in Back Bay, nursing something dark and working my way through a peanut butter burger. I thought they sounded downright blasphemous first time I saw it on the menu, but curiosity got the better of me and I'd been a believer from that moment on. That's what I was doing within an hour of hanging up the phone at the lab, washing my heart-clogging repast down with a pint of the black stuff and wondering how the hell Helen managed to creep back into my life.

I hadn't gotten quite that far into the conversation with Leslie Wheeler. Once I'd agreed to the job, she told me she'd get everything arranged and get back in touch. I didn't really think Helen was so evil that she wouldn't recommend my skills to somebody looking for what I do, but I still couldn't get past the fact that there were experts better equipped than I who weren't three thousand miles away. I appreciated the commission, but it just didn't make a lot of sense.

I was halfway through swallowing the second-to-last bite when a shadow intercepted the setting sun glaring through the window. I glanced up as Jake Maitland sat down across from me.

"Guya, Gake," I said with a maw full of peanut butter, white bread, and beef.

"Didn't your mother ever tell you not to talk with your mouth full?"

I shrugged and swallowed the rest. Rinsed my gullet with the rest of my Guinness.

I said, "Why don't you rustle me up another one?"

"One on you?" he asked.

I shrugged again. He traipsed off to the bar.

Jake Maitland was tall and rangy with a pitted face and short-cropped hair. Sort of an Ed Gein lookalike, almost. He was in the same class of failed screenwriter as I was; we'd both gone out to L.A. in the Nineties to make good on the so-called Indie boom and both came back to the East Coast inside two years with our tails between our legs. You could say one of my lousy scripts got produced, unlike old Jake, though by the time they were done with it none of my words were left intact. I got a "story by" credit and enough scratch to leave town with.

We hadn't known each other out there, but I'd met him at some lame party around 2001 or 2002. An okay guy, talked too much. Still had visions of grandeur. I'd lost mine somewhere between Albuquerque and Little Rock on the drive back home.

When he came back, Jake set my pint in front of me and took a long draw from his own. It left an off-white mustache across his top lip.

"How's the old movie business?" he asked.

"Picking up."

"I couldn't do it, man. Hell, I can hardly watch films anymore. I always think I could've done better."

Like I said: visions of grandeur. I let it pass.

Jake sat down and said, "So what's new?"

"Heading out to L.A., looks like."

His eyes popped wide. "L.A.? What's doing out there?"

"Nothing half as good as you're thinking," I said. "A restoration job, sort of."

"What, they don't got people for that on the left coast?"

"They got plenty. It's kind of a weird deal."

"Does it pay?"

"Sure, it pays."

"Gift horse and all that, then," Jake said.

"Sure," I said. "And all that."

We finished our pints, ordered another pair, and chatted aimlessly about everything from the resurgence of South Korean cinema to whether or not Ken Russell would ever be appreciated enough in the U.S. After I paid—for all of it—I made my excuses and started to leave. Jake grabbed my wrist as I started to walk by him, stopping me dead.

"This hasn't got anything to do with Helen, does it?"

I groaned some, pulled my wrist free.

"Yeah," I said. "A little."

Jake screwed up his mouth and shook his head.

"Nothing half as bad as you're thinking," I said. "At least, I don't think it is." Truth was I didn't really know. Not yet, anyway.

"How you planning to get out there?"

I glanced at the time on my phone, making a bit of a show out of it.

"Flying, I guess. Folks I'm working for are covering everything."

"Forget that," Jake said, killing off his beer and standing up from his chair. "I'll drive you. I miss the old town, it's been years. And besides, we've never been there together, have we? Powers combined, right?"

I laughed awkwardly, avoided eye contact for a minute.

"Look, I'm not going out there to do anything but work on an old print," I said. I didn't know if Jake had ever heard of *Angel of the Abyss*, but I wasn't going to press my luck. "I'll be in the lab all day and sleeping all night. Besides, driving there would take half a week. They'll want me there sooner than that. Sorry, buddy—can't do it."

I patted him on the shoulder and gave an apologetic smile. Jake smiled back, and as I finally got past him he said, "Okay … see you there, Graham."

"Yeah, sure," I said with a laugh on way out. But I sort of knew he meant it.

While the lead attendant went over her safety speech in a droning, half-asleep voice, I leaned over the one book I brought for the trip: *Lives of the Silent Film Stars*. I was proud to possess an impressive library of texts on film history, criticism, and theory, though the volume in my lap wasn't one I'd spent much time reading. It was structured more or less like Butler's *Lives of the Saints*—I used to be Catholic, so I couldn't help but make the comparison—but these were saints of the silver screen, almost all of them actually sinners. The one chapter dealing with Grace Baron dedicated only two paragraphs to the subject. I read them three times over before the plane started down the runway.

She was born Grace Baronsky in Boise, Idaho in June of 1901 (exact date unknown), though some sources listed her year of birth as 1904. She moved to Hollywood with an aunt in 1922 and, upon being discovered by Monumental Pictures head Saul Veritek, began production on her only film, *Angel of the Abyss*, in 1926. She was either 22 or 25 at the time. Production lasted ten weeks, and the picture premiered at the Domino Theater in Hollywood on August 15. It was an instant sensation—of the bad kind. A pair of nude scenes scandalized a packed house of Hollywood elites, while the subject matter drove them from their seats. No script, footage, or stills were known to exist, but the first and last picture to star Grace Baron, as the studio rechristened her, reportedly dealt with such taboo topics as rape and a graphic occult ritual that depicted Baron's character giving herself to an anthropomorphic goat.

Not long after, according to my reading, Monumental shuttered. Saul Veritek was ruined. The director, Jack Parson, skipped to Europe and ended up making expressionist pictures in the Weimar Republic until Hitler took over. After that, he went to England, then Canada, and eventually back to the States where he fathered a future minor movie exec and melted into obscurity. And Grace Baronsky vanished from the face of the earth. Extensive searches were made for her in both California and Iowa for over a year, but in early 1927 she was officially declared dead by the County Coroner's Office of Los Angeles. Rumors persisted to the present that she had gotten mixed up with some sort of underground communist cabal that had something to do with her disappearance and, possibly, her death. But no one really knew.

The plane lifted off from Logan and I closed the book. I had six and a half hours to kill and I spent it nodding on and off, half-thinking and half-dreaming about a forgotten starlet who was notorious for one night before the worst kind of fame swallowed her whole.

I landed at LAX fifteen minutes early and spent another twenty waiting for my suitcase at the baggage claim. After that I traipsed over to where all the drivers stood around holding signs for specific pick-ups among which, according to Leslie Wheeler, I was supposed to be one. I glanced at each sign in succession from right to left, but none of them had my name on it. My next glance was through the glass doors leading to the sidewalk outside and the myriad of taxis and vans and limos crowded next to it. A couple of guys were out there smoking, so I rolled my suitcase out to them and asked to bum a smoke. The taller and wider of the two knocked a Camel out of his pack and lit it for me, and I stood there smoking with them until I was done. It tasted like heaven.

When I returned inside the group of drivers had thinned some, but there still wasn't one designated for me. I loitered another half hour, bought a coffee at a stand and wished there was someone else to beg a cigarette from, which there wasn't. No soap. I grumbled and found a quiet corner to dig out my state-of-the-art-in-2002 mobile phone to call the number Leslie gave me. Straight to voicemail. Naturally.

Outside I hailed a taxi. The driver didn't pop the trunk so I dragged my suitcase into the backseat with me. When he asked me where to I told him the hotel Leslie set me up with, the Wilson Arms. It ended up being a forty-five-minute ride that made me as poorer in dollars as it had in minutes.

The hotel was right in the heart of old Hollywood, a once glamorous town gone to seed and now on its way back up thanks to regentrification. My old apartment building was only four blocks south, though I wasn't feeling sentimental. I rolled my case into the narrow lobby, took in what looked like a recently refurbished atmosphere, and then told the clerk my name. He said my room was ready and paid for, and he handed me a key. Not a keycard, an actual key. Some old things still stuck around. I rode the elevator up to the third floor, found 325 around the first corner in the hallway, and went inside.

It was a smallish room, but big enough. A few framed glossies of dead movie stars on the walls. Maybe they'd stayed here, and maybe even in this very room. Maybe the place was haunted. I sat down on the edge of the double bed and had a staring contest with David Niven. He won.

On the credenza there was a white envelope with my name on it. Gratified that at least something did for once, I picked it up and ripped it open. Inside was a check for two thousand dollars, signed by Leslie Wheeler. A sticky note on the back of the check read: *For the third reel. More if we find them. Start tomorrow? LW.*

I folded the check in half and slid it into my wallet. Then I opened the mini-fridge next to the credenza, found a $10 bottle of beer, and drank it. I wanted a cigarette and thought about roaming down to street level to find one or twenty, but instead I lay down on top of the comforter and dropped into a deep sleep, still in my clothes. When I woke up the clock beside the bed told me it was three in the morning. I washed my face in the bathroom with cold water, dug my book out of my travel bag, and read the paragraphs on Grace Baron again. The hazy photo next to the text still failed to compete with the footage I'd seen from *Angel of the Abyss*. After I set the book down on the bed, I closed my eyes and replayed the reel in my head. Then I waited for dawn.

The unimaginatively named Silent Film Appreciation Society was housed in a narrow postwar building on a side street of Hollywood Boulevard, several blocks east of all the action. There wasn't anything resembling a guide to the offices in the dusty entryway, so I wandered up the stairs and examined the doors on the second floor until I found what I was looking for. Masticating savagely on a flavorless piece of nicotine gum, I knocked on the door. When a few minutes crawled by and no one answered, I knocked again.

"Ms. Wheeler? It's Graham Woodard."

Still nothing. I tried the doorknob. Locked.

I muttered something I wouldn't say in front of anybody's mother and wandered back downstairs and out to the sidewalk. I'd passed a cluttered little souvenir shop on the way here that was just up at the corner, and I remembered a sign in the window advertising their ridiculous prices for cigarettes. Six minutes later I dropped eight bucks on a soft pack of Pall Malls and had one in my mouth before I left the shop.

So the elusive Ms. Wheeler failed to have me picked up at the airport and she wasn't in the office when I expected her to be. She'd paid me—if she hadn't, I'd likely be en route back to LAX by then—but I had no idea if or when I'd start earning my keep. I was starting to get a little grouchier than usual and entirely unsure how to proceed. For want of a better idea, I returned to the door on the second floor of her building and knocked again, louder and longer. Nothing, as I expected, so for a last-ditch effort I called her number again.

On the other side of the locked door, a mobile phone chirped with its preset ringtone. I jumped a little.

I took the phone down from my ear, but I let it ring and listened to the sound coming from inside. It kept going until I pressed END. I supposed people left their phones behind all the time—I knew I'd done so on many an occasion—but it didn't gibe well with me. Not with everything else amounting to her total absence since I'd landed in Los Angeles. I felt a small tremble in my knees and knocked again, softer.

"Ms. Wheeler? Leslie?"

Footsteps sounded on the wooden stairs behind me. I turned to see a small woman coming up on the landing. When she saw me standing there, she gasped, "Oh!"

I said, "Ms. Wheeler?"

The woman laughed. She was short and bony, her iron gray hair pulled back into a girlish ponytail. She stretched her thin mouth into a smile and said, "No, I'm Barbara Tilitson. You must be Mr. Woodard."

Another member of the sewing circle, I decided. She walked slowly toward me, digging a jangling keyring from her knitted purse.

"That's me," I told her.

"Is she not in? I'm surprised. Probably stuck in traffic. I can't imagine the traffic in your neck of the woods can best ours."

"I tried her cell phone and heard it ringing inside," I said. "That is, I assume it was hers. Could be a coincidence, I guess …"

"Well, let's just see," Barbara said with a pleasant lilt. She jabbed a bronze key into the doorknob and pushed the door open. I followed her into the dark room and waited for her to switch on a light. When she did, I squinted and looked at what was once probably a pleasant room, furnished with antiques and decorated with framed reproductions of classic one-sheets for silent pictures—but the place had been smashed up by someone who knew about smashing. There were turned over chairs, broken glass, and the rug on the floor had been pulled up and tossed into a pile in the corner. All of the posters had been ripped out of their frames, like somebody was looking to see if there was anything behind them. In one, America's Sweetheart Mary Pickford knelt reproachfully in a nightgown beneath the title *A Good Little Devil*. Beside the poster, a plump woman with short salt-and-pepper hair slumped in a faux leather club chair.

Barbara Tilitson screamed.

I knew then why Leslie Wheeler had been giving me the slip since my arrival. She was dead.

# 4.

## HOLLYWOOD, 1926.

The abduction took twice as long to film as Jack anticipated, putting the production a few hours behind schedule. The heavy, a character actor by the name of Billy Terence, kept fumbling awkwardly over Grace when he was supposed to be exerting villainous force, afraid to offend the lady. Jack alternately whined and bellowed, commanding Billy to grab her, dominate her, own her. At first Billy blanched, beside himself in spite of his rough looks. Only when Grace touched him gently on his rocky, weathered face and told him it was all right, that they were only performing, could he get the scene right.

By then, it was well past one in the afternoon and there were still five pages left to finish. Jack leapt from his chair, ordered the take golden, and screamed at everyone to move quickly to the next set. Cast and crew scuttled, moving equipment and changing costumes en route to the other end of the stage. There, an avant-garde cemetery replete with angular tombstones and a high black fence stood in shadows, waiting to be illumined by stage lights. Once the light spilled down in sharply angled slats, Jack lighted a cigarette and directed the players to their positions.

Also smoking was the barrel-chested youth who shadowed the chief electrician, Horace, like a lost pup. As Grace floated over to her director, now dressed in a semi-transparent gown with a plunging neckline, the young man smiled awkwardly at her. She ignored him and paused at the edge of the set to talk to Jack.

"Ready to die, pretty thing?"

His starlet feigned an awkward grin and nodded, once.

Behind her, hurrying to form a semicircle around a flat tomb, were six day players in long brown robes tied at the waist with frayed ropes. Grace turned slowly to face them. The half dozen faces regarded her with deference, as though she was already a star, equal to Lillian Gish, Clara Bow. Anyone. The tops.

The director said, "Let's get the scene done today if we can. No sense in wasting Mr. Veritek's time or money."

Grace took her place, lying on her back along the length of the faux tomb. Her tormentors shuffled in close. The one at the head of the tomb fingered a stage dagger jammed in the rope at his middle.

It was time to bring the Angel to the Abyss.

Jack growled, "Action."

*They guide her down, flat as an ironing board, upon the cold stone slab. She is pliant. They work in tandem, hands exchanging her silken flesh until she is, at last, in position. Like a well-oiled machine. Her eyes are open—wide, glassy—but she does not see. Above her, torches flutter flames and pale, angular faces change shapes in the dancing shadows of the light. At the head of the slab, in front of a narrow gray monument, stands one taller than his brethren—the chief minister, perhaps, if such groups have ministers—and he stretches his long white fingers out over her, snatching at air. The others sway slightly in a measured rhythm, join hands. The head man's hands vanish into the folds of his robe and a pair of disciples, one on either side of her, whisk away the thin fabric that barely conceals her goose-pimpled form. The torches play havoc with the contours of her naked body and the minister produces a strange dagger, shaped like a serpent, and he strikes …*

"A specter!" cried Saul Veritek, his right hand concerned with a tumbler filled to the brim with gin while his left played with some blonde bit player's hair. "Risen from the grave!"

Grace Baron stood in the foyer of the suite, resplendent in her peach crêpe gown. Lace at her neck, beneath the pearls that glittered in the chandelier light. If she imagined she heard a gasp, she wouldn't have been wrong.

The band, all Negros except the pianist, played "Rhapsody in Blue." Gowned and tuxedoed party-goers danced drowsily in pairs scattered throughout the suite, most of them clutching their drinks more desperately than their partners. Prohibition, it seemed to Grace, had only made liquor flow more freely in Los Angeles.

"Come," said Saul, releasing his blonde and taking Grace by the elbow. "Have a libation. It isn't every party that has a virgin sacrifice among its throng."

His pink pate gleamed with sweat as he led her to the bar, where a Filipino barman was shaking up a martini for a tall, handsome man with a craggy face. Grace squinted at him, then whispered to Saul, "Isn't that William Hart?"

Saul chuckled. "In the flesh. On his way out, the old cowboy. He's been pumping everybody he sees for cash, trying to make his own last hurrah. *Tumbleweeds*, he calls it. Can you imagine? With Tom Mix filling movie houses he wants to make some drab old bore called *Tumbleweeds*?"

"I saw him in *The Scourge of the Desert* when I was a girl. We got a lot of oaters back in Idaho."

"Folks liked that sort of thing back then," Saul said. "What, you're starstruck? Come now, I'll introduce you."

He guided her to the bar and extended two fingers to the barman. "A couple of gin and tonics, would you Manny?"

Manny nodded and got to work. Saul turned to Hart and tapped his shoulder. Hart sipped his martini and looked down with a tired smile.

"Oh, it's you, Saul."

"Hart, you old horse," Saul boomed, shaking the tall man's hand. "I'd like you to meet my new star, Grace Baron. Turns out she's a fan of yours."

"You don't say," Hart said, widening his eyes at her. He took her hand and pecked the back of it. "I'm always glad to meet a fan, and a new star of the screen no less."

Grace's face filled with blood and she smiled. Saul heaved a laugh.

"She's still fresh. Once people see the new picture and she's on the cover of *Picture Play*, you'll be blushing to meet *her*."

"I'm certain of it," said Hart. To Grace, he said, "Tell me about it. The picture, I mean."

"Well," she began, "it's …"

"Secret," Saul cut in. "You're just going to have to wait, pardner."

"Heavens," Hart said with a grin. "I'll wager it's a corker."

"You'd win that bet."

"Say, have I said much to you about *my* new picture? I'm doing it independently, you know."

"And I wish you the very best of luck with it, Hart. Really I do." Saul patted the tall man condescendingly on the shoulder and took up Grace's elbow once again. "Look, Gracie—there's old Jack. Let's say hello, shall we?"

Quickly he led her away, and as she went she craned her neck and said, "Nice meeting you, Mr. Hart."

The fading cowboy nodded and drank, his face fallen and colorless. He looked like the grandfather of the star of *The Scourge of the Desert*, though only eleven years had passed.

"*Tumbleweeds*," Saul snickered as they approached Jack Parson, seated alone on a windowsill with his eyes on the band. Jack sucked at a cigarette and slouched so that his back curved.

"Not bad, these fellows," he said absently. "I think I've seen the saxophonist in some clubs."

"Who knows?" Saul said. "One looks the same as another to me. Say Jackie, where's your drink?"

"Don't you know there's an amendment against that sort of thing, Mr. Veritek?"

"The law's against making and selling the stuff—there's no law against drinking it. Hell, I'll get something from that Oriental over there." He gestured broadly at Manny, the bartender. "What'll it be, old boy?"

Jack sighed. "Scotch, I suppose."

"There's a man's drink," Saul opined. "Pleased to see you've some balls left, Jackie."

The fat man giggled and waddled back to the bar, sloshing his gin on the carpet.

"He's even worse when he's in his cups," Jack said to Grace.

She sat down beside him on the windowsill and took his cigarette from him, drew deeply from it, and then handed it back.

"Saul's all bark," she said.

"Some dogs bark too much."

"Maybe it's what got him where he is."

"That's just fine," Jack said with a pained expression. "If this picture doesn't send him back from wherever the hell he came from."

"Gee, you're tough on that," Grace said. She sipped her drink and crossed her long legs. Jack noticed. "I never heard of a director hating his own movie so bad."

"Happens all the time. First time for me, though. And anymore I don't think of the damned thing as mine. It's all his." He pointed his chin at the bar, where Saul was guzzling something brown and ogling a plump brunette. "So what's your story, anyhow? Wait—let me guess. You're from some no-name town in the middle of the country and you came out here with an aunt, only to be discovered in a department store."

"It was vaudeville for me, actually, but the rest is pretty close. How did you get all that?"

"It's a very old story, Ms. Baron. I think Scheherazade knew that one."

"I guess she knew them all," she said with a wry smile.

"All the good stories were already told before the Lumière brothers filmed their first frames."

Grace raised her eyebrows and sighed. She scanned the suite, glancing at red faces hovering above starched collars and gleaming necklaces, but none of them appeared to belong to Saul. A few she recognized from pictures she had seen, though the gin worked diligently at clouding her memory. The band laid into something slow and hypnotic and she closed her eyes for a moment, taking the music in. When she reopened them, Jack was rising to his feet.

"I don't think Saul is coming back with that drink," she said.

"It's just as well. I'd rather be clear-headed for tomorrow's scenes."

"You may be the only one."

He ran his fingers through his thick black hair and heaved a sigh.

"Good night, Grace," he said. "Don't let the devils here keep you from the devils tomorrow."

With his head down and shoulders jutting forward, Jack went past the band and melted into the sweating throng. Grace watched him disappear and downed the rest of her drink while she pondered what he'd said. Something from Shakespeare buzzed in her head, half-remembered: *All the devils are here.*

She squinted at the glass in her hand, then went tipsily back to the bar for a fresh one.

# 5.

## L.A., 2013.

I sipped at a mug of tepid black tea prepared and given to me by Barbara Tilitson. It was bitter and needed sugar, but I didn't say anything about it. There was a squat guy with red hair bearing down on me where I sat, his necktie crooked and shirt spotted with sweat. Said his name was Shea, and that he was a police detective. I didn't say much to him either, because he was a policeman and I didn't have a lawyer present. That much I told him. He said I watched too much TV.

"You're from Boston," he said, droning as though he was bored. I agreed that I was. "Got a couple of parking tickets for you here in Hollywood, date back to the Nineties."

"I lived here for a year. Went back home."

"To Boston."

I sighed. "Yes."

"All right. Explain to me again your relationship with Ms. Wheeler."

"There wasn't any relationship," I said. "I never met her, not in person. She hired me over the phone to do a job out here. I was just showing up to work when I—when Ms. Tilitson and I—found the place like this."

"And Ms. Wheeler. Like this."

I said, "Yeah."

A couple of blue shirts were tip-toeing around the place, wandering from room to room like they were thinking about renting it. Poor Leslie Wheeler remained where we found her, slumped dead in her chair. In the kitchen on the other side of me

Barbara paced and wrung her hands. I wasn't sure how much more of this she could take.

"Okay," Shea said, rubbing the back of his neck and looking annoyed. "Let me go talk to Ms. Tilitson some more. Looks to me like you just stumbled onto a real bad scene, Woodard."

"At least I already got paid up front," I groused.

The detective gave me a sideways look.

"That right? You gonna keep that without doing anything for it?"

"No," I said. "I plan on doing what I came here to do, actually."

"I doubt that very much, Mr. Woodard," Barbara said as she shuffled slowly into the room. Her eyes were red and swollen. "The reel is gone. Whoever killed Leslie must have taken it with them."

"Reel?" Shea squeaked. "What kind of reel?"

Barbara and I locked glances. I reached for the pack in my pants pocket.

Between the two of us, Barbara and I told the policeman as much as we knew, starting with a primer on *Angel of the Abyss*, a few biographical details concerning Grace Baron from me, and how Barbara and Leslie's club got their hands on the reel. I then explained how I got roped into it, remembering along the way that I still wasn't one hundred percent sure how I did. That was when the little redhead managed by some miracle of modern science to make my day even worse.

"We'll want contact information for this Florence Sommer," he said to Barbara. And then, to me: "And for your ex-wife, Mr. Woodard."

"Do you have to drag her into this?" I whined. My voice rose a few octaves. I sounded like a petulant adolescent.

"She's already in it, if she tipped Ms. Wheeler to your skills," he said. "And like you said, it doesn't make a whole lot of sense to bring a guy in from the East Coast to do something a hundred guys can do right here in Los Angeles."

"She wanted to keep the whole thing under wraps," I said. "This film really is a big hairy deal, detective. Apart from the people in this room and a few others here in L.A., everybody else in the world thinks it's lost—gone forever. Ms. Wheeler wanted to keep it that way for a while."

"Awful secretive for an old movie," he said.

Barbara snorted. "First of all, it's not just some old movie. It's a lost classic, a treasure. Secondly, Mr. Woodard—forgive me, Mr. Woodard—paints the thing like Leslie was trafficking in state secrets or something. It wasn't like that at all. She just wanted to maintain control over this discovery until we had all of our ducks in a row. A thing like this will explode in a hurry, Detective Shea. You may not care much about it, but there a great many people who do. And there aren't—*weren't*—very many people with a greater knowledge of silent cinema than Leslie Wheeler."

"I can believe people care a lot about this stuff," the detective said sourly. "Looks a bit like Ms. Wheeler lost her life over it, doesn't it?"

"God," Barbara moaned. Her lips trembled and her face squashed up, palsied with anguish. "My god. Poor, poor Leslie."

One of the blue shirts chauffeured me back to the hotel. It was just past one o'clock but I felt like I'd been awake for days, so I crawled under the sheets and tried to catch a nap. No dice. Not after what I'd seen, which was in fact the first and to date only dead body to ever cross my path. Though I'd never laid eyes on the woman, I had spoken with her and I couldn't help but feel a great deal more involved in her death than I liked. And every time I tried closing my eyes, all I could see was her.

So I got up, withdrew another ten-dollar brew from the mini-fridge, and flipped through channels until I came to Robert Mitchum tearing up the backcountry byways in *Thunder Road*. I watched it to the end and stayed tuned for the follow-up, *The Sundowners*. I didn't make it all the way through that one; somewhere around halfway through I crashed, hard. When I woke again, the sun was setting behind Hollywood and there was something with Irene Dunne playing on the television. I switched her off, stepped into my trousers, and dragged myself down to the street for a smoke.

Along the way, I got to philosophizing. It occurred to me that, though I agreed with Barbara about the film's importance, there was something to Shea's incredulity, too. Just how important was an old silent movie, anyway? Everyone involved in its production, from the star down to the kid who delivered sandwiches to the set, was long dead by now. More than that, even the most essential contributions to our culture didn't seem that important in the long run, at least not while I leaned against the hotel's façade with a cigarette dangling from my mouth and my eyes on the weirdos and tourists shambling up Hollywood Boulevard like zombies. The whole damn world was going to come to an end someday and when that happened, who would be left to give a damn about Shakespeare, or Dostoyevsky, or Van Gogh? Never mind *Angel of the Abyss*. I doubted more than a thousand people alive even knew it ever existed. Only cinema geeks like me and the late Leslie Wheeler could possibly be bothered. Us, and whoever found it necessary to murder her in order to get their hands on one eleventh of the film. There were more pointless reasons to die, but I couldn't think of many.

Dark thoughts like this consumed me and I started to lose focus on the whole nasty situation that enveloped me. I decided I needed a drink, so I stamped out my smoke and went back in to find the hotel bar. Despite the years I'd had to get used to it, I still hated the idea of a bar I couldn't smoke in, but I swallowed it down and ordered a Dewar's on ice. Almost as soon as the bartender set to getting it for me, I felt a hand on my shoulder.

"There you are," Jake said. "I've been looking for you, pal."

*For Christ's sake*, I thought. I said, "Man of your word."

"Mama taught me not to lie," he said, pulling up a stool beside me. The bartender came back 'round and set my drink in front of me. Jake said, "One of those for me, too."

With a sharp nod, the bartender got to it. Jake slapped his hand on the bar, startling me a little, and grinned ear to ear.

"Back in Cali, man!" he boomed.

I winced. I absolutely hated it when people said *Cali*. The only thing worse was *La-La-Land*.

"Probably not for long," I said. He cocked his head to the side as I sipped my scotch.

"Job fall through?"

"You could say that."

"Well, dish. What's the story, Graham?"

"Went to meet with the lady who hired me this morning," I began.

"Yeah?"

"Only she was dead when I got there."

"Jesus," Jake said. "Are you serious?"

"Serious as an Eisenstein picture, bud."

"What, she was old or something? Heart attack, something like that?"

"Not so old. Cops think she was murdered." They *think*. It was pretty damned cut and dry, actually.

I killed my drink and signaled for another.

"Holy shit. That's terrible, Graham. That must have been a hell of a shock."

I chuckled morosely. "You've got that right. My old man dropped dead in the living room when I was in high school, but I never saw the body. Fact is, this is my first, and it wasn't at a funeral or anything nice like that. She was just crumpled up in a chair, dead as disco. Place was trashed, too."

I didn't know why I was being so candid with Jake of all people, but my mouth just ran away with me. Probably I just needed somebody to talk to after everything that happened and he was handy. Nonetheless, I was starting to feel a bit queasy thinking about it and decided to change the subject.

"What about you? You flew out here?"

"Borrowed some cash, got a decent deal on the ticket."

Figured.

"How'd you find me here?" I asked.

"Made sense you'd stay in Hollywood, so I started calling around. Got this dump on the fourth try."

"Regular Hardy Boy."

"Sure," he said. "Maybe I'll open my own agency. Take pictures of cheating husbands and shit."

That would probably be the most work he would have ever done in his life, but I kept that to myself.

"Where are you staying?" I asked him.

"Not far. Little motel with questionable morals. I don't have a sugar mama funding *my* vacation." The words had barely passed his thin lips before his face pinched and he dropped his eyes to his lap. "Ah, crap. Sorry, Graham."

I waved it off. The waving hand was a little uncoordinated. The scotch was doing its job.

"Forget it. Listen, maybe I'll stay on another day or two. I'll ask how far ahead my room is covered and cash the check I got. Tomorrow we'll do something, you know, Los Angelesy. Make the best of it."

"Hey, that's the spirit," Jake beamed.

"Damn," I drawled, simultaneously tapping the rim of my glass at the barman. "Why let a little murder ruin a perfectly good trip? We'll go to Disneyland. Get a goddamn star map. Maybe we'll run into Brad Pitt and get a fucking autograph."

Jake pursed his mouth and absently stirred his scotch with the little black straw the barman put in it. I laughed and grabbed his shoulder as the guy brought me number three, which I grabbed and clinked against Jake's glass. After a deep slug from my hooch, I sighed with gratification and said, "Forget it, Jake—it's Chinatown."

An old joke we'd once shared, the line from the Polanski film, and enough to break the ice I'd formed by being a morbid ass. Jake grinned, and I slapped him on the back before excusing myself for a smoke outside. It was damned curious how much more I liked the guy when I was in my cups.

Outside the city was brighter in the night than it was in the daytime, lit blindingly with streetlamps and glaring neon signs. Traffic had picked up, transporting sight-seers and party-goers, though all the characters in cartoon costumes seemed to have gone home for the night. They had been replaced by the same transvestite street walkers I remembered from my time there in the Nineties. It was great knowing how things didn't change.

I fired up a cigarette, dragged deeply on it, and suddenly remembered what the cop had said about getting in contact with Helen. The thought sent me crashing to half-sobriety and I started to worry that I'd end up in a room with her in some grimy police station, my past never quite willing to give me up to the future.

Such were my unhappy thoughts as I worked my way down a smoldering Pall Mall and the brick wall burst in a cloud of dust about six inches from my ear. Without giving it much thought, I dropped to a crouch and another shot cracked the night, this time hitting the wall where my head had been seconds earlier. Pathetically, I was still clutching my cigarette between two fingers.

A set of tires squealed, peeling out, and I looked up in time to see a late model Saab speeding down Hollywood in a cloud of exhaust and burned rubber. I couldn't see who was in the car, but I knew damn well that whoever it was, they'd just tried to shoot me dead. I collapsed on my ass and sat there on the sidewalk, half-drunk and dumbfounded, trying to convince myself it was just another one of L.A.'s notorious, mythic, random drive-bys.

But as I finished my cigarette and people came bursting out of the hotel lobby and from both sides of the street, I knew perfectly well that wasn't the case.

*Angel of the Abyss* was catching up to me.

# 6.

## HOLLYWOOD, 1926.

Though there was a tremendous panic about it at first, Jack's failure to arrive on set was eventually chalked up to a severe hangover—the man was simply sleeping it off at home. Upon this pronouncement, several members of the crew and some extras got to shuffling in either direction, whereupon Saul Veritek took up the director's bullhorn and bellowed at everyone to remain where they were.

"This is no recess, you ingrates," he hollered. "Time is money, for Christ's sake. We have five pages need shooting and by God we'll shoot them."

Grace, barefoot in her ethereal, postmortem silk gown, floated beside him and whispered, "Saul, surely we shouldn't go under Jack's nose."

The producer lowered the bullhorn slowly and turned to flash a dry grin at her.

"Dearheart," he cooed, "when I want to hear you speak, they will be words I have written. Do you understand?"

She stiffened. Her lip trembled.

"Of course," she said, softly. She added, "Mr. Veritek."

With that, Grace Baron swept up the length of the cloudy gown and padded across the cold stage floor to the lot outside, where she lighted a cigarette and groaned with frustration.

"Trouble in paradise?"

She started, coughing on the smoke and moving her arms up to cover her bosom, and spun on her heel to find a lean youth leaning against the façade of the stage, a metal flask in his hand. He was in his shirtsleeves, rolled up to the elbows, with suspenders keeping up his sagging brown trousers and a rumpled cap on his head. The handsome youth assisting Horace with the lighting. Grace comported herself, stepping back and sucking deeply from her smoke.

"Drinking on the job?"

"Whatever gets you through the day."

"Can't think but Mr. Veritek wouldn't like it much."

"That old rummy? You're kidding."

"Most fellows can't carry it like he can."

"I do all right."

He smiled, took a pull. Grace raised an eyebrow.

"Lighting man?"

"Apprentice electrician. I'm working under Horace."

"Hope he's making me look good."

"Shouldn't be hard," he said.

Her cheeks, high on her otherwise pale face, pinked.

"I'm Grace," she said, offering her hand.

He accepted it, said, "You don't say."

"Now don't be smart."

"Who, me? I didn't even finish high school."

"What'd they call you when you quit?"

"Dummy. These days I call myself Frank. Frank Faehnrich."

"Used to know a Frank," she reminisced. "Back home."

"Where's home?"

"Idaho, if you can believe it."

"Sure, I believe it."

"Does it show?"

"Not so's you'd notice."

She finished her smoke, dropped it on the ground. "Where's headquarters for you, Mr. Electrician?"

"Uh-uh. First tell me who's Frank."

"Which Frank?"

"Idaho Frank."

"A nobody. Probably still making ice cream sodas at the drugstore on Chance Street."

"It's a job."

"Spill, mister."

"Not far from here. A little town called San Domingo. What's so bad about a soda jerk?"

"I've known loads of jerks," she said. "A jerk's a jerk."

"And a man's a man, and a woman's a woman. What's it amount to? Ain't here but enough time to get confused about it all, anyhow. Hell, maybe all jerks ain't created equal, when you think about it."

"What sort of jerk are you, Frank?"

"Only the best kind," he teased.

"That a fact? And what kind is that?"

*"Grace! Set!"* Saul boomed from inside the set. *"Now!"*

"Maybe you'll find out," Frank said. "Best hurry along now. I've got to help shed some light on that pretty face of yours."

"A charmer," she pouted, fluffing her hair. "I've known loads of them, too."

She offered a sardonic wink and rushed back inside. Saul stood dead center, his fists planted on his broad hips and sweating profusely. His shaggy brown eyebrows were squashed together and the cigar in his mouth wasn't lit.

"Only in Hollywood," he groused. "Anyplace else and you'd be on the goddamn street."

"Don't strangle yourself," she chided him. "Only having a cigarette."

She bounced past him, back to the cemetery at the northwest corner of the sprawling stage, where a day player in a grave-digger's getup leaned on a shovel, half-asleep. Taking her position, Grace glanced over her shoulder at the lighting rig beside Jack's—now Saul's—chair. Horace was sweating worse than the boss beneath the white-hot lamp, cranking it up and playing with the shades. Behind him Frank stood with his hands behind his back, his eyes on Grace and the rest of his square face a cipher.

*Vacant and crawling with mist, the cemetery lies dormant, the once imperious stones now cracked and covered with lichen. Only a bright shaft of moonlight slices through the pitch, illumining the tomb upon which, some years earlier, a maiden's heart was pierced by the ritual blade. The heavy lid trembles, disrupting the blanket of mist, and then edges away, cattycorner to open a broad black triangle leading down into the cold finality within. From the grave, a lone hand slowly rises, its ashen, feminine fingers curling around the edge of the stone. She is risen.*

Grace emitted a stunted yelp upon pulling the chain on the lamp. The dim bulb threw a yellow haze across the bungalow that caused Jack Parson to sit up, cough, and smile wanly at her from the edge of her bed.

"Christ have mercy, Jack," she wheezed.

"I'm sorry," he said, standing and smoothing out his sport coat with his hands.

Grace lay her bag on the chair and shut the door. She then fumbled for a cigarette from the box on the dresser, lighted it, and frowned at Jack through a blue haze.

"Are you drunk?"

"I wish I was."

"Don't you dare touch my liquor."

He went over to where she stood, inspiring her to take a few steps back. Without asking, he took a smoke for himself and lighted it with her crystal lighter.

"Did you shoot today?"

"We shot."

"Brought you back to life, did he? *Saul*, I mean." He spoke the man's name like a foul oath.

"That's what it says in the script. Those are the pages for Tuesday, which is today, by the by."

"The son of a bitch is turning it into some sort of … horror picture."

"Hard to influence the course of events when you don't show up at the studio, Jack."

She puffed with exasperation, kicked off her shoes. Jack moved the bag to the floor and sat down in her chair.

"Why don't you go somewhere else for your next one?" Grace asked, the cigarette dangling from her lips as she struggled her way out of her dress. Jack fixed his eyes on the floor. "Or do like Bill Hart's doing—he's making a picture all on his own."

"Hart's washed up. A joke."

"Well, you're still a young man. Just make Saul's picture and put a lid on the sad sack routine. You're only making enemies, boyo."

"In this town, it's easy."

"Easier still when you do all the work."

Standing in her brassiere and bloomers, she crooked one foot behind her and pushed out a sigh at his boyish embarrassment.

"You've *seen* me stark, for Pete's sake."

"Talk to your boss—that was *his* scene, you know."

"It's art, remember? With a capital A."

"God, you're a lively one tonight," Jack said. He leaned forward to stamp out his pilfered smoke.

"Certainly I am," she answered, shrugging into a shiny robe. "I'm freshly resurrected, or didn't you hear?"

"Didn't you ever read Mary Shelley? Even the resurrected can get put on ice."

"I thought you had a beef with the ghoulish stuff."

"I just wanted to make a great picture, Gracie. That's all. Something to really lift the form."

"How much lifting does it need? You never saw a Griffith picture? I don't guess you've got anything up your sleeve to make *Intolerance* look rotten, or do you?"

"Don't be cruel to me."

"You're cruel to yourself," she spat. "Like I said, you're young yet. Everything won't go your way, not for a while, maybe not ever. You've got a lot handed to you on a gold platter and you act like you're dying in a trench."

"My brother-in-law died in a trench," he said low.

"And you didn't, brother—you're here right now in Hollywood in the picture business, surrounded by enough glut to make old Babylon drool with envy. Get out of here, Jack. I want to go to bed."

"I don't want to leave. I don't want to go anywhere."

Grace grimaced, dropped her smoldering end in the ashtray.

"You're a fool, and much too sober. Go find a tavern and drink them out of house and home. You'll want to crawl in a hole come morning, but I bet you'll thank me for it."

"I can't work like that."

She laughed. "Who's working? My director was a bald, fat man chomping on a cigar. Maybe you've heard of him."

Jack lurched forward, arched his right arm around her waist. Grace squirmed and planted her hand roughly on the center of his chest.

"Stop it, Jack."

"Let me stay. Just for tonight."

"I told you no already."

"I'm wounded, Gracie. My pride is. I don't want anything from you. Just let me stay here tonight."

"Get going, Mr. Parson. You've got a lot of self-pitying to catch up on and I don't want to play."

He relented, released her. Narrowed his eyes to slits.

"Cruel," he groaned.

"I didn't get this part in any back room, yours or anyone else's. And I won't do any back-room foolishness to keep the part now. Leave this instant, or Saul Veritek is going to hear an ugly little story tonight and I really will have a new director on this goddamn picture."

Jack marched for the door, opened it, and grumbled low and indistinctly.

Grace said, "Good night, Jack."

He slammed the door shut.

She dreamed of low, snowy hills and a gable front house with icicles on the eaves, daddy waving goodbye and somewhere her mother softly sobbing. Aunt Eustace would be along in the morning. There was going to be more for little Gracie than digging potatoes out of the cold earth. Much more.

*You get you some rest, Gracie, Californy is a long ways away.*

# 7.

## L.A., 2013.

The two policemen who took me the handful of blocks to the station on Wilcox didn't say much. They didn't seem involved, or like they wanted to be. Just a pair of well-armed chauffeurs. Inside, I was guided to a dimly lit office that still smelled like the cigarettes they used to allow in there, in the previous century. I sat down in front of an old metal desk and waited for ten minutes, looking at a framed photo of a redheaded cop, his wife, and their daughter. The wife had red hair, too. The kid was Asian.

When Shea came in, he had a Styrofoam cup steaming in each fist. He passed one to me on his way behind the desk, said, "Heard you were a bit stewed."

"Wasn't planning on getting shot at," I told him. He was about half right; I figured I was well on my way to sobriety before the second shot stopped ringing in my ears. I sipped at the coffee—it tasted like pencil shavings.

"Taxpayers' best," Shea commented, having noticed the sour look on my face.

"Nice family," I said, looking at the photo again. He ignored that, like it was meant to be an insult.

"Tell me some more about this job you're here for," he said, leaning back in his chair. It squeaked loudly.

"Nothing shady about it, at least not on my end. Look, I'm just a film geek. I teach a couple of courses about old flicks at a community college every year and spend the rest of my time digitalizing ones nobody really cares about before the celluloid dissolves. This lady—"

"Leslie Wheeler?"

"Yes. She called my office out of the blue a few days ago—"

"In Boston."

"Right. She told me her little club had come into possession of a particularly rare film. Well, part of one, anyway. A reel."

"How'd she get it?"

"Someone named Mrs. Sommer gave it to her. Them. Whatever."

"Her and Barbara Tilitson?"

"I guess. I only really knew about Ms. Wheeler."

"All right, go on."

"That's all there is, really. She offered me a gig to come out here and work on the reel. Good money in it, and she said they might even dig up the rest of the picture."

"From this Sommer woman?"

"I guess. I don't know."

"What's the movie?"

"It's called *Angel of the Abyss.*"

"Haven't seen it."

"No one living has. Not in its entirety. It's been lost for most of a century."

"But you have. Seen it, I mean."

"No, just the third reel. About ten minutes or so, twenty from the start."

"Tell me."

I washed the knot in my throat down with more of the terrible coffee, and then I told him. I told him about the scene I'd only seen by way of an emailed mpeg, its brilliantly stark lighting, Grace Baron's masterful performance done without the benefit of dialogue. It occurred to me in retrospect how much she reminded me of the French silent actress Maria Falconetti— Dreyer's Jeanne d'Arc—and I told Shea that, but he just shrugged and reprimanded me to stay on topic. He scribbled on a notepad the whole time, which made me chuckle. I'd have guessed an L.A. detective would have upgraded to at least a Blackberry by now.

"And how about the rest of the thing? What's it all about?"

"I can only tell you what I've read. It's a very dark melodrama, way I understand it. A peasant girl from a broken, abusive home heads to the city to improve her lot, ends up getting mixed up with a conman who arranges for her to be sold into a white slavery ring and, eventually, some kind of Satanic ritual where they sacrifice her."

"How sweet. You say this was a silent movie?"

"1926."

"Didn't know they made crap like that back then."

"Some people thought it was brilliant."

"Sounds like torture porn to me."

I snickered. "There's more—she makes a deal with the Devil, comes back to ruin the lives of the conman and his main lieutenants. So it's got this whole supernatural revenge thing going for it."

"I'm more of a Steve McQueen guy, myself."

"I'd never have guessed."

He gave me a look.

"All right, Woodard," he said like it was an effort, "So a woman you've never heard of calls you out of nowhere to fly all the way across the country to work on this old movie. You agree, get here, find her dead. Right so far?"

I shuddered, but not so he noticed. "Yeah."

"And the movie, the *reel*, is gone. Other valuable stuff left behind, but not this reel you're supposed to be working on. Which means the job's dead, so it's time for Graham Woodard to buzz back off to Beantown, am I correct?"

"That was my thinking," I agreed.

"Except maybe somebody would rather you didn't."

"You don't still have drive-bys in Los Angeles, Detective Shea?"

"On that stretch of Hollywood? Sure, it could happen. I'd be surprised, but it could happen. But you factor in how much trouble somebody's going to over this whole 'angels in the abbey' crap—"

"*Angel of the Abyss.*"

"—it does seem pretty damn coincidental to me, I got to admit."

I wasn't arguing. Simply thinking about it got my skin prickling all over again.

"So the way this goes," Shea went on, absently worrying his necktie, "is that you tell me whatever it is you haven't told me yet, because there are some awfully big pieces left out of this puzzle, Mr. Woodard."

Downing the foul dregs of the coffee I made a tight knot of my eyebrows and locked eyes with Shea. I hadn't said a word about Jake, though despite my diminishing liking for the guy concurrent with my rapid sobering up, I didn't think for a second he had anything to do with any of it. My ex-wife, on the other hand, was another matter entirely.

I said, "Helen."

"Yes," he said. "The former Mrs. Woodard."

"I haven't spoken to her in more than a year."

"But she got you the job, didn't she? She recommended you to Ms. Wheeler."

"That's what I was told."

"Are you not on good terms with your ex-wife?"

"I'd say not. She left me for another guy. I didn't take kindly."

"Then why would she want to help you out like this?"

"It's not that I need the help," I said. "I'm not hurting."

"She pulled for you."

"I don't know if she did. She knows—*knew*—Ms. Wheeler in some capacity. Dropped my name. Maybe she didn't even think about it first."

"Just slipped out."

"Like that," I said.

"For a gig a hundred people in Los Angeles could do without traveling."

"Probably a thousand. And a lot of them better than me."

"Isn't that just a little strange?"

"She said she wanted to keep the whole thing under wraps."

"Leslie Wheeler said that?"

I nodded. "She wanted to maintain control over the project. Over the film. I think she was afraid if L.A. people got involved it would get out of hand and it wouldn't be her baby anymore."

"Wanted all the glory, then?"

"Such as it would be, sure. Far as I know, nobody outside of me and that little knitting club knew a thing about it."

"Knitting club?"

I grinned. "My nickname for their group."

"I see," Shea said.

He tapped the tip of his pencil on the notepad and made a guttural noise in his throat. When he glanced up at me again, his sourpuss had softened to a look of concern, or close to it.

"Do you know where your ex-wife lives, Mr. Woodard?"

"Somewhere around here."

"In Hollywood?"

"In L.A.," I said. "I have no idea where, exactly."

"We had a recent address for her and a Ross Erickson—you know him?"

I frowned. "Yeah. That's the fu—the guy she ran off with."

"Well. A couple of officers went to have a word with her this afternoon, after we last talked at Ms. Wheeler's office."

"Fantastic." My hand contracted, splitting the cup.

"She wasn't there, is the thing. Nobody was."

The last few drops of room-temperature coffee dribbled down my wrist, but I paid it no attention. "What are you driving at, Detective?"

"Fact is, no one's seen her or Mr. Erickson for about a week. Far as we can tell, they haven't been at home at all. Their apartment doesn't appear to have been tossed like Ms. Wheeler's office was, and there was jewelry inside. A small amount of cash, too. No robbery, and no planned vacation in all likelihood. Folks don't usually leave everything behind when they're planning on going away for a week."

I mulled this over, unsure how to react. I wondered if they'd found anything approaching drug paraphernalia, and decided Shea wouldn't tell me if they had. All I could manage to say was, "I don't talk to her."

"You don't seem very upset."

"I don't know what I am. Today I've found a body, been shot at, and now I've just been told my ex-wife is—what, missing?"

"I didn't say that."

"You're suggesting it."

"Does she do anything with movies? Like you or Ms. Wheeler?"

I moved my jaw without a sound a bit, jarred by the change in topic.

"She—no. She's in insurance. Or she used to be. She couldn't care less about something like this."

"But she knew Leslie Wheeler."

"Apparently."

"Seem like strange bedfellows to you?"

"I couldn't say, as I never met Ms. Wheeler."

Shea grinned. "You have a point there. You want another coffee?"

"I'd rather drink crude oil," I complained. "Listen, how long am I going to have to stay in town?"

"You watch too many old movies, Mr. Woodard."

"It's what I do."

"You're not obligated to remain here. Of course I'll need to talk to you again as this comes together, but I can't keep you from going home to Massachusetts. I'd appreciate it, however, if you'll keep me apprised of your whereabouts."

Shea didn't have anything else to drill me about after that. He asked a few pointless questions, small talk about where I grew up and what I'd done when I was in L.A. last, but I sensed it was all devised to let me down gently after informing me that Helen was missing. He gave me his card for the second time in one day and told me they'd posted a couple of guys in an unmarked car in front of the hotel—a security detail, he called it. As he was walking me back to my dour chauffeurs, he patted me on the back in a fatherly way and said, "Don't worry about your ex, Mr. Woodard. I doubt it has anything to do with this mess."

I wasn't nearly as confident as he was, but I didn't say so. Outside, in the perfect Southern California night, Shea fired up a Parliament and offered me the pack. I accepted, delighting in the slight buzz I got from not chain-smoking all the time and getting used to it. We puffed in silence, waiting for the patrol car to come around, until he cleared his throat and narrowed his eyes.

He said, "Whatever happened to this Grace Baron, anyway?"

"She vanished," I told him. "She was declared dead less than two years later. Some folks say she ran off with a communist agitator, or that he killed her. It's probably just an urban legend born of the McCarthy era."

"So that's, what—ninety years ago?"

"Thereabout, yes."

"Before Black Dahlia," he mused.

"Yeah," I said, "but after Virginia Rappe."

"Good old Tinseltown," the detective mused. "Cold case capital of the world."

"Is that true?"

The patrol car pulled slowly up on Wilcox and idled in front of us. Detective Shea shrugged and dropped his smoke on the sidewalk, grinding it under his heel.

"I don't know," he said. "Go on back to your hotel, Mr. Woodard. Try and get some sleep."

"Too bad the bar's closed by now," I said, and I got into the back of the police car.

The conscientious hotel staff had, however, restocked my expensive mini-fridge, so I made myself a fifteen-dollar highball and sat back on the bed. I reflected on how surprised I was that the detective seemed to know who Virginia Rappe was—the aspiring actress whose mysterious death ruined Fatty Arbuckle's life and career—which led me to think about what a wild time the 1920s really were in Hollywood. Murders, drugs, prostitution, blackmail, organized crime … the modern movie business had nothing on them. Rappe died in '21, followed by the murder of William Desmond Taylor in '22 from being stabbed in the back. Plenty of grim tales of the like followed, from Thelma Todd to Elizabeth Short, but in the 21st century were they anything more than lurid stories from a bygone era?

Perhaps they all were, I thought. All except the disappearance of Grace Baron. Gone since the year after my maternal grandfather was born, but still stirring the pot. Whatever had happened to her, to her only picture, the perpetrators thought them both to be buried forever. Now the picture was resurfacing and with it, maybe, something somebody needed to stay in its grave. Leslie Wheeler knew enough to get her killed; hell, I knew next to nothing and they were taking shots at me. And since I strongly doubted there was a gang of supercentenarians gunning for me, I was more puzzled than ever. Puzzled, and more frightened than I cared to admit to myself. It was insane to think anybody could resort to murder over something older than almost anyone living, but insanity was the order of the day.

Lucky me, I was caught right up in the middle of it with one corpse behind me and god knew what ahead. I made a second highball with what remained of my cola and whisky and I downed it into two Herculean gulps. Somewhere beyond the marginally safe confines of my police-guarded hotel, somebody was washing Leslie Wheeler's blood from their hands—and making room for mine.

But I wasn't the only one. There was still Barbara Tilitson, Ms. Wheeler's colleague. Shea hadn't mentioned her, though he needn't have—it wasn't like I was *his* colleague. Still, I wondered what the police were doing to protect her. More than that, I wondered what she knew.

It occurred to me that she might also have been acquainted with my ex-wife, and that a supposed expert on the era of American silent films could also shed some light on what the hell was going on. I was already stepping into my shoes and rinsing my booze-infused mouth out with mouthwash before I'd made up my mind to go talk to her.

The clock radio on the nightstand told me it was a quarter to three in the morning. The black-and-white monster movie playing soundlessly on the television backed up its sentiment. I sat back down on the mattress and, like I'd done before I found Leslie Wheeler's body, I waited. While I waited, I zoned out, revisiting that reel in my mind, but subconsciously recasting Grace Baron's role with Helen …

I snapped out of it and looked out the window. The charcoal smog was settled over the tops of the buildings, obscuring antennas and bright neon signs and the distant Capitol Records tower, but the first orange light of morning was beginning to battle it back for another day. I snatched the room key from the dresser and headed out to find Barbara.

# 8.

## HOLLYWOOD, 1926.

*D*earest *Gracie* (began the letter in a florid hand),
  *How are things, my darling starling? Have they painted your portrait for PHOTOPLAY as yet? Just you wait, lovely child—in short time you shan't be able to walk to the grocer without a mob of fans accosting you. Miss Mary Pickford will never know what hit her! (Once I met Mary, a sweet if aloof woman.)*

  *Gracie, please do forgive your auntie for her silence—I haven't written in so long, and I am so close, but no excuses from me. It is unforgiveable! Here is the thing: I have made a great friend in a gentleman of the Valley. I call him Joe and he calls me his Old Girl. My Joe has a hand in the picture business himself, a distributor of sorts as I gather, and naturally he is positively dying to meet my niece, the soon-to-be-Marchesa of Hollywood. Won't you join us this Sunday for luncheon? We will lay out by the swimming pool and eat grapes and drink champagne, won't it be divine! Do say you will come, Gracie—in fact, don't bother writing back to me, but come!*

  *With all the Love in the World,*
  *Your devoted Auntie Eustace*

# 9.

## L. A., 2013.

"Here's one in Mission Hills," Jake said, his mouth half-full of syrupy pancakes. "Not sure it's spelled right."

He turned his smart phone around to show me the screen: a site called *Find 411* listed a Barbara Tilitson between blocks of ads in Mission Hills, in the San Fernando Valley.

"Is there an address?" I asked him. "Or a number?"

"You have to pay. These things are scams."

I grunted. The waitress swung by to refill our coffee cups. I'd barely touched my omelet, but Jack was nearly through devouring his breakfast.

He found me in the hotel lobby, poring over an old school phone book lent to me by the desk clerk, who was herself astonished to discover they actually had one. I was squinting at the sundry Tilitsons around Hollywood, none of them Barbaras, when Jack appeared at my shoulder with an offer to front me breakfast if I gave him the lowdown on the shooting. I obliged, we wandered a few blocks up to a greasy spoon, and now that I'd told him what little there was to tell, he was attempting to help me track Barbara down.

"Why don't we go to that office? You know, the knitting club."

"Crime scene, my man," I explained.

"Probably find a rolodex in there or something. Worth a look."

I ended up paying the tab.

The hall looked like something straight out of a television show, replete with flickering ceiling light and yellow police tape crisscrossing the door to the late Leslie Wheeler's office. When we'd exited the cab we saw no police cars, no cops on guard duty. Up on the second floor it was just as vacant. Jack went directly to the taped-up door and I followed closely behind. He tried the knob. It was locked.

"Better wipe your prints off that," I said.

He snorted. "Yeah, all right, Columbo." He did it anyway, looking a little embarrassed. "Pascal's wager," he said.

He shrugged and I grinned at his misuse of the phrase, and then we headed back for the stairs when the door clacked behind us and squealed open. Jake flattened against the wall like it somehow made him invisible, but I stepped forward and narrowed my eyes at the doorway. Barbara Tilitson poked her gray head out into the hall and raised her eyebrows at me. Her eyes were pink and swollen. She'd clearly been crying.

"Oh, it's you, Mr. Woodard," she rasped. "I thought I heard someone try to open the door."

"You did," I said. "We didn't expect anyone to be inside."

"No one is supposed to be. Not even me."

By then Jake had overcome his terror of the woman and slinked back up behind me. I stepped aside and said, "This is Jake Maitland."

"Barbara Tilitson," she said, limply shaking his hand. "Forgive the state of me. I really shouldn't be here. I was going through old newsletters, if you can believe it. The police took so much, but they left the newsletters. I didn't think anyone would mind. Of course, we do it all by email now. But Leslie handled all of that. I'm not very good with computers, Mr. Woodard. Not very good at all. With Leslie gone, I really don't know …"

She trailed off, hiccupped, and covered her mouth with her hand. Her eyes welled up and she turned so that I couldn't see her face. I touched her shoulder, softly, and waited for her to compose herself.

"Good Lord," she said with a breathless laugh. "The state of me. I swear."

"Is there still tea inside?" I asked, a bit impulsively.

Barbara nodded while wiping her eyes with her fingers. "And a kettle. Nothing criminally suspicious about all that, I suppose."

"Come on, then," I said. "Let's sit down in the office. I'll make the tea this time."

Again she nodded and waddled back through the tape, barely disturbing it with her small frame. I made it through with almost as much ease, but Jake tore it down entirely. I shot him a look, which he ignored. To my surprise, Barbara sat down in the chair we had found Leslie Wheeler in the previous morning. She sat nervously, her knees together and back hunched, like a school kid waiting to be scolded by the principal. At her feet on the bare floor—the rug was gone now—about a dozen crude newsletters were fanned out. The paper was yellow and crinkled, a hand-drawn legend photocopied at the top of each one: *The Silent Film Appreciation Society*. The issue on top, featuring a fuzzy publicity photo of Rudolph Valentino, was from Fall/Winter 1989. I decided she and Leslie must have been at this for quite some time.

"There are Typhoo bags in the cupboard above the hot plate, Mr. Woodard."

I found them, looked over to Jake who shook his head *no*. While I heated the kettle on the hot plate, I glanced over at a corkboard on the wall beside an old plastic telephone. On it several notes were tacked, containing movie titles, event reminders. A program from a Lillian Gish retrospective at the Cinémathèque. And a few photographs of Barbara and Leslie that looked to span a great many years. In each of them the two women held onto one another in a tight embrace, grinning broadly or looking at each other. I began to better comprehend Barbara's grief.

The kettle squealed and I poured two cups that I brought out to the front room. Barbara took hers with a pained smile. I sat at the table, next to Jake.

Barbara sipped cautiously from her cup and said, "I'm surprised you're still here. In Los Angeles, that is. I'm afraid you can't help us anymore."

"I'd still like to try," I said. "You see, Ms. Tilitson—"

"Barbara. Please."

"Barbara, we came around here hoping to find a way to get in touch with you. I hate to alarm you, but somebody tried to kill me last night."

"Kill you? Good god, that's terrible."

"You're telling him," Jake piped up.

Barbara said, "This damned town. Forgive my language, but really."

"I don't think it's just this town, and frankly the police don't seem to, either. I think it has something to do with what happened to Leslie. And with *Angel of the Abyss.*"

She seemed to hold her breath for a moment, her eyes focusing on something invisible in the center of the room like cats sometimes do. When she snapped out of it, she shivered slightly and heaved a deep sigh. Her face was drawn. Though only a day older than the last time I saw her, she seemed as though she'd aged significantly since then.

"Forgive me if I sound accusatory, Barbara," I said, followed by a protracted silence in the room, "but is there something you're not telling me? Something I should know?"

"Mr. Woodard," she began. "Graham. How much do you know about Grace Baron?"

"Not much," I confessed. "Whatever the available bios and websites have to say. It's not a lot. I don't gather anyone really knows that much about her."

"Some people do," Barbara countered. "Leslie did. She knew quite a great deal about Grace. And of course as long as she remained a distant memory and her only film remained lost, no one could really be bothered by anything she knew."

I pursed my mouth and breathed through my nose, frustrated and confused. It was the same aggravating question posed over and over again: how could something so old have riled up so many people?

"You're waiting for me to tell you everything," Barbara went on at last. "But I'm afraid I can't. We were close, Leslie and I. But she didn't tell me everything. In fact, ever since she came into possession of that damned reel—me and my mouth again, I'm so sorry. Honestly, I never talk like this …"

"What about the reel?" I said, cutting her off.

"It's just like she … closed off, I guess you could say. Shut me out, to some extent. That reel, and the promise of the rest of them, seemed to mean more to Leslie than anything else in the world."

"More than just her love of old movies?" Jake asked. I'd nearly forgotten he was there, but it was a good question.

"Oh, yes. Heavens, yes. We'd be involved with a few terrifically exciting projects over the years, and by god it was something we shared together. We found *Losers Weepers* together, at an estate sale in Sawtelle back in '92." She laughed girlishly at the memory. "It was our bond, our glue. Not this time. Not with the Grace Baron picture. That Leslie kept all to herself. She didn't really want me anywhere near the thing, or at least that's how I felt."

"And she brought me into it because of my remoteness from it all," I mused aloud. "From it, and the both of you. From Los Angeles."

"Apparently so, yes. I don't know why anyone would want to harm you over this, Graham. I really don't. But I'm sorry about it and I want you to believe me Leslie would never have asked you out here if she'd have thought for a second something like that could happen."

I nodded solemnly and sipped at my tea. It was going cold.

"Did you ever meet this Mrs. Sommer?" I asked her.

"You mean the woman from whom Leslie got the footage in the first place? Yes, I met her once, quite briefly. It was when Leslie picked the reel up—I went with her, though she tried like hell to put me off."

"What was she like? How did she end up with it?"

"Mrs. Sommer was fairly ordinary, I suppose. A bit awkward, socially. She told us the reel had belonged to her father, who died and left behind a small estate that included it."

"Did she know what she had?"

"Not at all. In fact she held onto it for more than a year before she stumbled upon a magazine article that mentioned *Angel* and she remembered it gathering dust someplace. After a little research, she realized she had a treasure and ended up finding us—well, Leslie—by our little website."

"I wonder," Jake muttered. I turned to him and raised my eyebrows. He lowered his and went on: "I was just wondering whether the cops have a lead on this lady. Maybe she decided the footage was too valuable and wanted it back? Like, real bad."

"Did you or Leslie pay her anything for it?" I asked Barbara.

"Not that I'm aware of. She agreed to let us take care of preserving it. I'm sure Leslie would have been quite clear that the reel would remain her property."

"What about the rest of the picture? I was told there might be more reels, in time."

"My impression was that Mrs. Sommer hadn't yet catalogued the entire estate. There were some other films—nothing rare or valuable—but the notion was there could still be more, maybe even other parts of *Angel.* Of course, that was all between her and Leslie. I had very little to do with it, I'm sorry to say."

She crinkled her eyes and touched her mouth. The moment passed as quickly as it came on.

I said: "Do you remember where this Sommer woman lived, Barbara? I think I'd like to pay her a visit."

"It was in the Valley. Sherman Oaks. I remember."

I made another couple cups of tea, but I didn't touch mine. We were all quiet for a while, but I still had one more question for Barbara.

"Do you know a woman named Helen Bryan?"

She canted her head to one side, thinking it over.

"No … no, I don't think. Who is she?"

"His worst mistake," Jake offered.

"My ex-wife," I specified. "She was the one who dropped my name to Leslie. I never quite got how they were acquainted."

"I'm sorry, but this is the first I've heard of her. Like I've said, Leslie kept me in the dark a lot over all of this. It doesn't sound like you're on very good terms with her, but perhaps she would be the one to ask?"

"Probably so," I said, "but she appears to be missing."

"What?" Jake crowed. "You didn't tell me that, Graham."

"Slipped my mind," I lied. His mouth hung open. "Later," I said.

I told Barbara that I was sorry to have bothered her so

much, and she said it was no trouble, though she looked mighty troubled to me. I offered her a hug, a bit out of character for me, which she accepted. I noticed she was clutching a small, crumpled photo in her left hand. It was of Leslie Wheeler, smiling toothily and wearing a pair of dark sunglasses. We had both loved and lost, I thought, but her loss was a hell of a lot worse than mine.

# 10.

## THE VALLEY, 1926.

Eustace piloted a 1918 Olds, a touring car, that sputtered as though it was dying all the way from Hollywood where she collected her niece. They were heading to the Valley, where Eustace now manipulated the contraption along narrow, winding roads with gloved hands and squinted eyes.

It was the crummiest automobile Grace Baronsky had ever ridden in, an enormous step down from the Twombly back in Idaho or the car Saul sent for her every workday morning.

"It is absolutely divine to see how well you're doing, Gracie," Eustace hollered above the wind and the motor. "*Divine*. And you look terrific. Better than I've ever seen you. To think what a skinny child you were before I whisked you away from nowhere. A transformation. A meta—what is it?"

"Metamorphosis," Grace said.

"You're a *butterfly*," replied her aunt.

The sun hung white and hazy, low in the sky but above the hills that surrounded the San Fernando like sentinels. Houses and bungalows were springing up all around, with filling stations and clothing boutiques and minor movie palaces to service the people who would live in them. Los Angeles never stopped spreading, growing. Grace felt like the whole of the country was spilling into the city and its environs, as if America had been upended by some great, massive god and all the people were helplessly rolling west. How many of them came in search of fame and fortune? How few were as fortunate as she, discovered within a few short years and primed to take the world by storm?

*How lucky ...*

"Just how did you meet this Joe?" she asked, eager to disrupt her own musing.

"Joe, Joe," Eustace sang. "Good, good Joe. The man is a prince, my child. Not too rich—not yet, anyway—but none too poor, either. And he knows *everyone* worth knowing. Well, everyone apart from you, of course. But aren't we just about to change that?"

Grace smiled, barely.

"He sells pictures all over the country; to theaters that want to show them, see. A lot of them are all connected up to the studios, but there are tons that aren't, and my Joe writes them and works it out. So if your old Ma sees *your* picture at the Boise Century, it might very well be Joe Sommer who got it there."

Her throat constricted slightly at the thought of her mother watching *Angel of the Abyss*—watching little Gracie die and come back, murder and flaunt and fornicate. It was far from the first time this waking nightmare stirred horror in her breast, but it had yet to relent in its intensity.

"Matter of fact," her aunt continued, "I might even bet on that. You see Joe knows Mr. Veritek, dearheart. Not extraordinarily well, mind you, but Veritek is an independent and Joe says the independents represent the prepon—prepolder ..."

"Preponderance."

"Of his business, yes."

"This one may be a tough sell in the heartland," Grace said low.

"What's that, Gracie?"

"Never mind. Are we nearly there? The motor is jangling my nerves."

"Spitting distance!"

"Grand."

The bungalow sat low and squat at the bottom of a gradually declining hill, surrounded by equally squat palms and crawling vines that struggled toward the windows. Eustace almost flooded the Olds easing the thing down to the bottom, where she guttered it and clapped her gloves together with an awkward squeal.

A stone path curved between the palms toward the front door, above which an open transom window coughed up a thin rail of pungent cigar smoke. Grace wrinkled her nose. Eustace knocked gingerly.

The man who opened the door revealed himself to be tall, a bit round around the middle, gray at the temples. He wore a thin black mustache just above his upper lip, which tightened around the end of his cigar. His eyes were gray, friendly but lingering. Grace felt blood fill her cheeks as her aunt planted a hand at the small of her back and pushed her forward.

"Mr. Sommer," she said. "Allow me to present my niece, the picture star Grace Baron."

"Oh, she's not a star yet," Joe Sommer said, spreading his lips to show short, squarish teeth. "But I reckon she will be. You can wager that."

"A gentleman of the highest order!" Eustace declared. Joe took Grace by the hand, a bit roughly, and brushed his mouth across the back of it.

"Champagne on the lanai," he said. "Olives and cheese. I have the cheese delivered."

"*La-nai*," Eustace mouthed to Grace.

They all went inside.

The bottle popped like a gunshot, causing Grace to flinch. Joe's mouth stretched into a lupine grin and he laughed at her.

"Let's see those glasses, ladies," he said.

They sat in slat-backed chairs on a concrete patio behind the bungalow—Joe's lanai—which was surrounded by more ratty palms and a new white fence. The sky looked like the ocean and a mild breeze picked up from the west. Eustace kicked off her shoes and giggled. Grace drank her champagne quietly.

"Saul Veritek," Joe said at some length, his mouth full of half-chewed olives, "is a friend of mine. He may be a small fry compared to the big boys, Paramount and United Artists and what have you, but the man's got a solid head on that flabby neck of his. You can trust me when I tell you if Saul Veritek says he's going to make a star out of you, that's exactly what's going to happen."

Grace's ears burned. Her aunt tittered and shook all over, sloshing her champagne around in the glass.

"Good god, Gracie," she said. "You're a long way from Idaho now."

"I suppose I trust Saul," Grace said with some caution. "It's Jack Parson I'm worried about. He's missed days, you know. And when I went home the other night he was in my place waiting for me. You'd have thought he was drunk as a lord, but he really doesn't drink much. He's getting a little, I don't know ... crazy."

Joe chuckled. "I know him too, a little. That Parson thinks he's an *ar-teest*. Our man Saul doesn't have the patience for that malarkey, not when there's money at stake—and in the picture business, money is always at stake. You want to be an artist, go paint a picture. This is industry, I always say. We're all cogs in the machine, but my *god*, what a beautiful machine."

"Alarming that he broke into your home, though," Eustace said. "What sort of man does that?"

"Feh," Joe groaned, waving his hand. "That one's harmless. Believe me. I probably shouldn't say this in the company of nice ladies like you two, but Jack Parson hasn't exactly fomented a reputation as a ladies' man in this town."

Eustace's face paled and her cherry-red mouth formed a broad O. "You don't mean ..."

"I don't know the old fellow *that* well," Joe said. "I don't have the hardest evidence here, but word gets around in Hollywood. You screw up and everybody knows it. And glory be, just about everybody screws up out here."

"Some worse than others," Grace commented, half to herself.

"How do you mean, Gracie?" Eustace leaned in, eager for something juicy.

"It's just a strange place,' Grace said, her eyes fixed on her glass. "You hear all kinds of things that make *Picture Show* look like a fat pack of lies. In the magazines, everyone is just so happy to be here. Playground of the gods, and all that. But I haven't met very many happy people, Aunt Eustace. Most of the people I've met seem ... broken, somehow."

"Half of 'em are dipsomaniacs, a quarter of them faggots," Joe grunted, shaking his head. "Sure, there's crime. A few bodies've been buried. But hell—pardon me, ladies—but seriously, my old man worked the iron mines in Michigan in the Nineties and you know what? The men running that show were a bunch of crooks, too. Like I said: *industry*. Just keep your nose clean, Gracie. You do your work and go home at the end of the day. Stay away from the vultures. You'll be fine, darling. Just fine."

*Just fine*, she mouthed. She didn't believe it.

# 11.

## L.A., 2013.

With one of my cigarettes clutched between his fingers and a thousand-yard stare ahead of him at the 101, Jake exhaled noisily and flicked his ash out the window.

"We could write a screenplay about this," he said dreamily. "You and me. It's some story already."

I was driving, a rental from the last century we'd picked up for a little more than twice what I expected to pay. Good old California. I turned the volume knob down on the ancient tape deck radio and said, "Have at it—you have my blessing."

"Sorry, man," he came back. "I guess you've got a personal line in all this."

I said: "Yeah, I guess I do."

He tossed the smoke out the window, and I glanced in the rear-view mirror, scanning for cops. Maybe Jake forgot how serious they were about tossing butts in Southern California, but I sure hadn't. They didn't screw around when it came to fire hazards.

"So tell me," he said, rolling the window back up. "What the hell happened?"

"When?"

"With you wife, man. What's the story there?"

"She left me. You know that."

"It's about all I know. What with all this shit, seems like there's more to it, you think?"

There was. Plenty more. Truth was, I'd been married to a sociopath for years and pretended I didn't know it. I did know it, though. I just didn't want to know it.

"She's out of my life," I said tersely.

"Not anymore she's not. I mean, she's out, but she keeps cropping up."

"We'll be in the Valley pretty soon," I said. "Traffic's not bad, considering."

"Yeah," Jake said, taking the hint. "Considering."

If there was a Knucklehead Hall of Fame back in Boston, I'd have a revered place on the wall. I was never a world class fuckup—that's a different hall of fame altogether—but I'd done my share of significantly stupid things over the years that knocked me down a peg or two to plain old knucklehead status. Marrying Helen Bryan was chief among them.

Maybe that's not fair. Marrying her I can forgive myself for. Sticking around? That's another matter.

After we made it official I worked on an impractical English Literature degree and she talked about all the things she wanted to do but never had the motivation to actually execute. After about six months up there, my wife clammed up on me. Stopped talking to me. Just shut me out. Then she started running around with a new friend, who happened to be male and liked to take her out to fancy restaurants and late-night movies. I complained about it, and she threatened to divorce me if I was going to make a big deal about it. I relented. See what I mean? Grade A Knucklehead.

Things went from bad to mind-bogglingly shitty from there. By then I knew damn well that I was being cuckolded, as they used to say, but I just swallowed that pill and immersed myself in my graduate work, knowing it would never amount to anything since I wasn't planning on continuing with it once they handed me a diploma. I tried to write a novel. It didn't go anywhere so I gave it up. I got to drinking a little more than I ought to have. Then I got to drinking a lot more than I ought to have. The booze drove me into a hole and it drove my wife even deeper into the arms of Mr. Wonderful. Then one night I got a call from the Norfolk County lockup. My bride was being held after her beau got pulled over in Brookline and the cops found a gram of blow in the trunk. A little while and a warrant later, they found an ounce in Helen's purse, too.

I bailed her out to the tune of five grand. The charges didn't stick. She literally begged me on her knees to forgive her, to put it all behind us. Knucklehead that I was, that's just what I did. And when it turned out she was pregnant and we both knew, given the coldness of our marital bed those last several months, that it couldn't possibly be mine, I turned a blind eye once again while my wife quietly took care of it. As they used to say.

The Other Guy disappeared from our lives and though things didn't exactly go back to normal, at least she stayed around. I quit drinking. I never asked about the coke and she never brought it up. We ate supper together, watched television. Went to bed at a reasonable hour. It was tense, though, the way so much was said without either of us ever saying anything. The way she'd recoil if my leg accidently brushed up against her in our bed at night.

And then, just like that, she was gone. She didn't take much, enough for a long vacation, but there was no note, no phone call. No warning. I got an email a week later. Helen had run off to California with Other Guy Number Two. I didn't even know about this one. She'd been a lot more careful. The divorce papers showed up in the mail within a month. I signed the waiver and sent them back, and then I went directly to the nearest package store to buy the biggest bottle of bottom shelf rotgut in the place. Inside six weeks they knew me by name there. *Good morning, Mr. Woodard.* Yeah—morning.

Goddamned knucklehead.

Destroyed by love and stupidity. I can't think of an older story than that.

Florence Sommer lived in a small postwar crackerbox house in Sherman Oaks with rotting shutters and stray cats lingering arrogantly in the small side yard. I pulled the crappy rental onto the side of the street in front and enacted that age-old L.A. tradition of trying to figure out whether or not I could legally park there. The signs all seemed to contradict one another and even on their own didn't make a whole lot of sense. I threw caution to the wind and left the car where I'd stopped. There wasn't a meter, but I didn't much care.

A doormat welcomed us by way of smiling cat faces and the legend HOPE YOU LIKE CATS! I didn't really have an opinion about them one way or the other but felt like it was about to swing sharply. Jake rang the bell. We heard shuffling feet and a hoarse voice politely asking someone named Mr. Kitty to move out of the way. A second later the door opened and there stood a heavyset woman, mid-sixties, with a terrible blue-black dye job and a hideous sweater more cat hair than wool.

"Yes?"

"Are you Mrs. Sommer?" I asked, channeling my inner Jack Webb.

"I'm Florence Sommer…," she began with no little caution.

"My name is Graham Woodard," I told her. "I work with the Silent Film Appreciation Society?" Came off as a question. Not very firm.

"Oh, Leslie and Barbara," Mrs. Sommer said. "Nice ladies. Well, come on in. Hope you like cats!"

Jake and I exchanged glances and he shrugged. We went on in. It smelled like cat shit and ammonia, a combination that wrestled my nostrils and won in nothing flat. Florence Sommer tottered from the door to the nearby kitchenette, where she hovered over the range.

"Tea?" she squawked. She sounded like Louis Armstrong's little sister. When she fired up a filterless Camel, I could see why.

"You got any beer?" Jake said.

I jabbed him in the ribs with my elbow. "Tea is fine, thank you."

He hissed in my ear: "I'm fucking sick of tea, man."

I jabbed him again. His eyes watered and he smiled nicely at the old lady.

"I'm sorry to tell you I haven't gone back through my father's things since I last talked to Leslie," she said, setting the kettle on the burner. "I'm sure she's getting impatient, and I wouldn't blame her one bit. Are you boys her enforcers?"

She tittered. It was like a goose choking to death.

"Ha, no," I deflected. We hadn't discussed whether or not to tell Mrs. Sommer that Leslie was dead, primarily because it hadn't occurred to me whether or not we should. I was too preoccupied with thoughts of my ex-wife, which led me directly to re-experiencing all the anger I ever had had about her. Now I was in the mix and had to make the call, and fast. "Ma'am, do you mind if we sit down at the table for a moment?"

A dark look overcame her jowly face and Mrs. Sommer nodded, gesturing for us to sit down first. The table stood just to the side of the half-kitchen, the top cluttered and stacked high with magazines, unopened mail, and cans of cat food. When she sat across from us, she laced her fingers as a fat orange cat leapt up on the table in front of her. I was startled, but she just petted the animal and waited for me to begin.

"I'm afraid I have some ugly news," I said, wincing at the banality of my wording. "Ms. Wheeler has, well—she's passed away."

"Oh, no," she said, bunching her eyebrows and looking down at the cat.

Jake cleared his throat. "It's a little more serious than that," he said.

I said, "Jake …"

"Look, Graham—this situation is fu—it's dire, man. I mean, isn't it? Now that we're in it?"

"*We're* not in it. *I'm* in it. You're just here."

My heart was starting to pound in my chest. That anger I was harboring toward my missing ex was finding a new target in Jake. As for poor Florence Sommer, her eyes were getting glassy wet and her mouth was hanging open, waiting for the other shoe to drop.

I dropped it.

"Leslie Wheeler was killed yesterday," I said. I said it like we were talking about someone neither of us knew, a third-rate celebrity who we vaguely remembered. Florence Sommer erupted into tears.

"Oh god, oh my god," she sobbed. The kettle screeched. I looked to Jake, and he rushed over to take care of it. "I barely knew her, but god. *God.* What happened?"

Jake was pouring hot water, being domestic. I could have laughed otherwise.

"It's all pretty hazy right now, but it certainly looks like it has everything to do with the film," I said.

"My father's movie? *Angel of the Abyss?*"

"That's the one, yes."

"I don't understand," she said, her voice even more gravelly, if such was possible.

She tamped her smoke out in an empty can of cat chow and immediately fired up another. I pulled the pack from my pocket, shook it and asked, "Do you mind?"

"No, no—go ahead. Smoke up a storm. God's sake."

I lit up. Filtered, which made me feel like second fiddle to her hardcore habits.

"I take it the police haven't come around to talk to you?" I asked her.

"No, nobody. This is news to me. Dreadful news. I'm so sorry about Leslie, but how in the world could this possibly have anything to do with that old movie?"

I tightened my mouth, half-amazed at the cops' ineffectiveness—we'd gotten to Florence Sommer before they did?—and half completely expecting it. Overworked and understaffed, maybe. Hell, it wasn't like they didn't have other murders to contend with. This was Los Angeles, after all.

"That's what I'm trying to figure out. Whatever it is, whoever it is, they're taking it seriously enough to have killed one person already and tried to add me to the list."

"It doesn't make sense."

"Everything makes sense, even if you don't quite get it yet," Jake said, stepping slowly over with two steaming cups. I was impressed with his Zen, even if it was bullshit.

"I think what he means is that there's an answer to all of this, we're just in the dark now."

"It's crazy," she said, accepting her cup from Jake with a small smile. "I've found loads of odds and ends from dad's estate, called all over the city to find people to deal with them. That movie was just one of them—I didn't even know what it was until I looked it up."

"Nobody knowing what it is seems to be a status quo somebody wants to maintain," I said.

"But it's just an old movie," she muttered. It was getting to be a song I was tired of hearing despite the truth in it.

"It's got to be more than that, given what's been happening. I don't know if you read anything about Grace Baron when you looked the picture up, but she disappeared shortly after the movie was made. She was declared legally dead a little while after that."

"What are we talking about here?" she asked me. "The 1920s?"

I nodded. The cat purred loudly.

"Crazy," she said again. Like I didn't know.

"Mrs. Sommer, do you think we could have a look at your father's things?"

"The estate?" she said, eager to be sure we were all on the same page as to the definition of the collection.

"Yes, ma'am."

"I don't keep that stuff here, I haven't got the room. There's a storage unit I rent, in North Hollywood. That's where it all is."

"I'd really like to go check it out," I said. "If you're willing to do that."

"Hell, honey," she said, shaking her head. "Truth is, it's all junk. Most of it, anyway. Half of it's broken and most of the rest worthless to begin with. I was only reminiscing, going through some of it, when I chanced upon that old film can. Far as I'm concerned, you can borrow the key."

Jake said, "That would be very kind." I was surprised by his manners.

Mrs. Sommer rose from her chair, grunting a little, and wobbled back into the short hall by the front door where she rooted through a drawer. The fat orange cat followed, slaloming her legs, and was joined by another cat, this one black and thin. When she came back, she was dangling a bronze key by a plastic fob. She put it in my palm and I looked at the fob. It said JUNIOR'S STORAGE, NORTH HOLLYWOOD. The street address and phone number were printed in gold underneath.

"Thank you."

"I'd go with you, but to be honest, I don't really know you boys, do I?" said the lady who let us into her house and gave me a key to her dead father's personal possessions. I shrugged and forced a smile.

"That's all right," I said. "I promise to bring the key back as soon as I can."

We shook hands and she opened the door for us.

"That poor woman," she said. "I guess I can expect the police to come around with all sorts of questions."

"You can bet on it," I said. "One more question, if I may— what did your late father do for a living?"

"Oh, daddy did all sorts of things, but for a few years he was involved with the picture business, booking theaters and things like that. He even owned a few small ones in the area for a while. Daddy got bored with any one thing after doing it for too long. His family included."

I pursed my mouth and she smiled sadly. We went back to the rental, bound for North Hollywood.

# 12.

## HOLLYWOOD, 1926.

The weekend came and went, replete with drinking and dancing and fighting off suitors like Fairbanks with his stage
sword, and Monday Grace returned to the stage on Saul's little
corner of the kingdom to find Jack Parson back in his chair. She
paused en route to wardrobe to lock eyes with the director; he
looked back, but there was nothing on his face to suggest he was
even aware that he'd been neglecting his duties.

*Saul worked his magic,* she thought. *Or put the fear of god into him.*

The street from which she had been abducted the week
before had been struck, replaced over the shooting break with the
interior of the tavern where she—as Clara, in her living days—
served wine and bread to the same sort of men who came to ruin
her. While she slid into her dress and apron and sat down to have
her hair done, Grace thought over the pages she hadn't bothered
to look at lately, piecing the scene together from memory before it
was time to begin.

"The fly becomes the spider today," Saul roared at her when
she returned, made-up and costumed. He embraced her, filling
her nostrils with his ever-present cloud of cigar smoke. "Until
now you have suffered, my Grace. Now let's have some lovely
revenge, shall we?"

He chuckled and stepped aside, allowing her full view of the
set and the boxy camera already situated atop its three-legged
stand. The cameraman fussed with the contraption while a
heavy man lingered over top, fascinated and intrusive. It was Joe
Sommer.

"I believe you know Mr. Sommer already," Saul said. "And you can thank him for bringing our prodigal director back to us, should you feel so inclined."

"I figured that was you."

"It would have been," he assured her. "And it wouldn't have been quite so smooth, not like Joe did it. I'm a bull in the china shop, but that Joe's got a soft touch."

She looked back to Jack, who was now immersed in his heavily penciled script pages. It was astounding how calm he seemed, how satisfied-looking. She wondered if his creative crisis was finally at an end. She hoped for as much.

"*Bella donna,*" Joe crowed, gliding from the camera to her. "I talked my way in, as you can see. Said I knew the star."

"And they believed you, the rubes," she said.

"Anything for a face like this," he answered, grinning clownishly.

Saul patted his shoulder and wandered back over to Jack. Grace laced her fingers at her waist and arched an eyebrow.

"You'll have to tell me your secret. Last I saw Mr. Parson he was an inch away from a complete breakdown."

"I spoke to him in his own language."

"You don't say. And which language is that, exactly?"

"Why, the language of the cinema, naturally."

"I didn't think the pictures had much in the way of language just yet."

"They will, and soon. But that's not what I mean. I extended Mr. Parson the courtesy of my hospitality, whereby I did what I do best—I exhibited a movie for him."

"You mean to say you showed him a picture and that cleared his head?"

Joe Sommer nodded proudly, rocking on his heels.

"Must have been some picture," Grace said, incredulous.

"Possibly the very best yet made, my dear. Do you know Eisenstein?"

"No …"

"Soviet man, does revolutionary pictures over there in Russia. His newest is called *Battleship Potemkin*, and I just so happen to have a print."

"And a Red movie saved the day."

"More or less."

"Next you know he'll be demanding the crew stand up to Saul, string him up by the rafters."

"We didn't dwell on the politics," Joe said. "More the technique."

"I'll take your word for it, Mr. Sommer."

His face reddened with some secret pride. Grace narrowed her eyes, trying in vain to decode it all, when Jack called across the studio to her.

"Come along, Ms. Baron—your cunning plan is about to commence."

"I shan't delay a rising star," Joe said, and he kissed her gently on the cheek.

She cocked her head a little, then turned for her position on set.

"Ms. Baron, a word?"

Grace lingered in the broad opening from the studio to the warm lot outside, where she lighted a long cigarette and curtsied.

"You may have as many words as you like, Mr. Parson— why settle for only one?"

Jack worried his driving cap between both hands, his face a mask of boyish discomfort.

"I'm afraid I was really quite boorish the other night. I have no excuse, and even if I had, it would remain inexcusable."

"I accept your apology," she said.

"But I haven't apologized yet."

"And what's this 'Ms. Baron' hoodoo? You've never been so formal, and it's not even my real name."

"Establishing boundaries, I suppose."

"Well, knock it off. We're friends. You had a tough night, happens to everybody."

"You're very kind."

Stepping out into the failing daylight, Grace craned her neck back and closed her eyes, luxuriating in the Southern California afternoon.

"What say you buy a girl a drink," she said when she returned to earth, "and tell me what changed your mind?"

"I could write a book."

"Give me the digest version, then."

Jack sniffed. He offered her his elbow.

"It's all a matter of perspective, really," he said, absently stirring his gin with a toothpick.

"That's profoundly vague," Grace responded with a smirk.

Jack took his gin neat, but hers was cut with soda water. They both smoked from the same silver cigarette case: his. All around them the speakeasy was strewn with fake Hawaiian décor, a permanent and technically illegal luau in the middle of the Californian desert. The barman, a Pacific Islander with a thin black moustache, looked appropriately tired of looking at it all.

"I've been a terrible prude, that's all," Jack went on. "What's the saying? I couldn't see the forest for all the damned trees. Every opportunity for art—*real* art, Gracie—right in my hands and I was too stupid to see it."

"It never was the Keystone Kops," she chided. "And thanks for going back to Gracie."

Jack blushed.

"I know it isn't, and the devil knows I've got the finest actress I could hope for on this picture …"

"You flatter me, Jack."

"I mean it. I do, Gracie."

"So what was the forest?"

"I expect I may as well call it my Black Forest," he said.

"Spoken like a true artist—making no sense at all."

"I don't mean to dance around the subject."

He killed off his drink and lifted a finger at the barman.

"Slow down, mister," Grace advised. "You can't just go from teetotaler to sodden in one night."

"I'm … I don't know. Excited, I suppose. I've had the scales knocked out of my eyes, as the apostle says."

"Why Jack, you sound like you've had an epiphany."

"That's a mighty big word for a girl from Idaho," he said,

accepting a fresh drink from the barman.

"I can even read when my mind isn't too muddled on corn whisky," she answered in a faux twang.

"Touché."

"So out with it, already. What does this Russian have to do with it?"

He mulled it over for a moment, swishing the gin in his mouth. When he swallowed, he said, "Darkness."

Grace raised both eyebrows and waited for him to expand. When he didn't, she prompted him: "Darkness?"

"In a word."

"We've been over this, Jack—I've allowed you as many words as you wish."

With a small chuckle, he downed the remainder of his gin, wiped his mouth, and lighted a fresh smoke.

"All right," he began. "I'll set the stage, as it were. About twenty years ago—probably before you were born, you young thing—there was a mutiny aboard a Russian vessel dubbed the Potemkin. Now this is before the Red revolution, you understand, but an event that precipitated it, to be sure. Anyhow, the mutineers went wild, taking the ship from their Tsarist superiors, and as mutinies tend to be, things got rather violent."

"Christ, Jack, you might elaborate a little more and begin at the dawn of time."

She grinned; he crooked his mouth to one side and waggled a finger at her.

"I'm getting to it. From how I understand it, a fellow like Sergei Eisenstein is fairly limited to the kinds of stories he can tell under the reds, so he makes pictures about the revolution. This is his latest, and the thing, this picture ..." He trailed off, savoring the memory.

Grace said, "Jeepers," and finished her drink. She didn't need to request another; the barman set it down the second after she swallowed.

"Here's the thing," Jack continued. "I've seen a great many pictures, pictures from all over the world, but I've never seen anything like *Battleship Potemkin*. It's changed the way I look at cinema, Gracie. It's changed the way I look at *myself*. I guess I have your friend Joe Sommer to thank for that."

"How did he—?"

"He telephoned the studio, simple as that. I guess you mentioned me to him, my, well, problems ..."

"Jack ..."

"No, no—it's perfectly fine, my darling girl. He saved me, your friend. He opened my eyes."

"To what? Darkness?"

"The darkness cinema can offer, yes. Human darkness."

"Gracious, Mr. Parson," she said. "I've seen a few movies myself, and I can't say I've ever had my whole life changed by one."

"*Angel of the Abyss* is going to be that one," Jack said. "Count on it."

Grace Baronsky looked at her director and wondered.

# 13.

## NORTH HOLLYWOOD, 2013.

Junior's was nestled back on Vineland, where I found an actual parking lot where I wouldn't have to worry about getting booted. The flipside of the key fob identified the unit as 13D, which was way at the back of the maze. I unlocked the heavy padlock, pulled it out of the loop, and handed it to Jake so I could heave the shutter door up. Instantly my nose was assaulted with the odor of dust and decay, but at least it was a hundred times better than the old man's daughter's place.

Jake found the light switch, which set a yellow bulb in a wire cage glowing from the ceiling. The light barely illumined a stockpile of crap piled so recklessly on top of itself I could hardly tell what I was looking at. After the initial shock started to wear off, I identified a broken rocking chair, a ping pong table, a pair of carnival fortune teller machines, a rotting moose head, and in the far right corner, an old 35-millimeter film projector that was caked with gray dust.

"Help me move this table," I said to Jake. It was blocking the way to the projector.

"Where to? There isn't enough room in here to swing a dead kitten, let alone a full-grown cat."

"We'll put it outside. I want to look at that projector."

The table was piled high with open boxes made of weak cardboard; we hauled those out first. In one of them Jake found a stockpile of old nudie mags from the 50s, which got him to giggling. I barked at him about the table. He pouted, but we got the damn thing out.

Now that I had a narrow path, I squeezed further into the cramped hothouse and angled around that nasty moose head to get to the projector. There was a Guinness bar towel hanging over the side of a close-by crate, so I snagged it to knock as much dust off the machine as I could. It was an old Keystone Moviegraph, probably upwards of seventy years old. The thing was rusted all to hell and next to worthless on the secondary market, but I marveled at it like it was an original Da Vinci. I was particularly fond of the hand crank: the projector was made for silent films, mostly short subjects. And to my surprise, its reels were loaded up with about eleven feet of sadly decrepit-looking nitrate film stock.

"Jesus Christ," I gasped.

"What is it?"

"Might as well set a bomb in here. This is some irresponsible stuff right here."

"Is that nitrate?"

I made a sound in my throat agreeing that it was. He made a sound of his own and backed out of the unit.

"Get back here, man," I called out to him. "Let's get this out, too."

"What are you going to do, steal it?"

"I'm going to borrow it."

"I don't recall you saying anything to that nice old lady about borrowing anything."

I gave him a look. "Shut up and help me, would you?"

The projector sat on top of a wretched-looking cabinet that even the termites had given up on. I lifted it up and passed it to Jake, who acted like I'd handed him a ticking time bomb. While he edged his way out into the sunlight, I took a peek inside the cabinet. It was filled with cobwebs and dust, a few small black spiders, and by my count seven film canisters.

Paydirt.

I collected the canisters, heavier than they looked, and hauled them out. One of the spiders hitchhiked along. I swept it off to the ground and carried the load to the rental.

"Load it all up. I'm going to poke around to see what else I can find."

"Let me know if you find the Ark of the Covenant in there," Jake scoffed. "Maybe my whole day won't be completely wasted."

I shot up, ramrod straight, and felt the hairs on my necks bristle.

"Who invited you in the first place, you prick?" I growled.

"Hey man," he said, putting his palms out defensively. "I was only joking."

And he was. He was just messing around, and I'd bitten his head off. Now I changed my mind about who the prick was between the two of us.

"Jake ..."

"Forget it," he said. "Getting shot at earns you a little intensity, right?"

"That's a fact."

"Go on. I'll get this shit in the car. But for fuck's sake don't smoke in there, okay?"

I had one before I went back in, far from the car to ease Jake's nerves. The smoke eased mine, too. I didn't find any more film in the storage unit, but I did come across a framed one-sheet for *Angel of the Abyss*, an art deco deal with sharp angles all in sepia tones. Grace Baron's character was naked to the waist and reaching up for a fruit hanging from a branch. She had a weird-looking serpent coiled around the reaching arm and a half-dozen menacing figures in sharp black shadows crowded below her. It was probably worth ten times as much as the projector I was lifting. I admired it for a few minutes, but I left it behind.

As I climbed back into the car, Jake asked, "Where to now?"

"If this thing works, I should be able to project it on any wall, so we might as well go back to my hotel."

The poor guy sweated the whole way back to Hollywood. As for me, I was foaming at the mouth to see those reels in the trunk. And I decided along the way that I'd be giving Barbara Tilitson a call as soon as I did.

It seemed to me the job was back on.

And of course the damn thing didn't work. The bulb was older than my dead grandfather and the plug looked nothing like any plug I'd ever seen. It sure as hell wouldn't fit the outlet in my room, or any other room I'd ever been in. I sat down on the bed and groaned.

History was kicking my ass.

I was inches away from making for the mini-fridge and considering it an insoluble problem for now when Jake said, "I know a guy."

He went for the phone.

Thirty-seven minutes later I found myself smoking in front of a derelict theatre with Jake beside me, bouncing on the balls of his feet and impatient for me to finish. Between us, on the sidewalk, were seven reels of old, flammable nitrate film footage. Some of the cans were marked, others were not. One of them was labeled as reel 5 from *Battleship Potemkin,* strangely enough, but we brought it along just in case.

When I finished my smoke, Jake helped me haul the cans into the lobby, where a sullen looking teenager was sweeping up for the night.

Jake asked him, "Is Franco here?"

The kid jabbed a thumb at a door marked OFFICE. Jake went for the door while I waited, eyeballing the Junior Mints in the concession counter.

Shortly Jake reemerged with a reed-thin guy in a ridiculous red bowtie, who I presumed to be Franco. I wasn't introduced. The three of us carried the cans through the office door, up a flight of stairs, and down a hallway to a projection booth. There we were greeted by a greasy-faced kid who eagerly volunteered to load the film up for our enjoyment. We went back down. Jake directed me to auditorium two of two. We sat in the dead center. I wished I had some of those Junior Mints.

The film was eleven reels long. We were still missing reels 2, 7, and 11—and number 3, which was swiped when Leslie was killed. The result was something of a disjointed mess, but I'd spent my fair share of time in dilapidated grindhouses to piece together a story from a bad print missing key segments.

What we did have was the title card:

SAUL VERITEK PRESENTS A MONUMENTAL PICTURE—
ANGEL OF THE ABYSS

Following that, a vertical list of the key players, Grace Baron at the top. Jack Parson was name-checked after that, and then the picture began.

*The girl hustles from one scarred wooden table to the next, her tattered apron flowing around her. Her arms laden with steins and plates piled high with roasted turkey legs, braised pork giving off curls of white steam. The big men pound the tables with their fists, toothy grins slicing through their beards. Among them a giant with coal dark eyes raises his voice above all the others*—Intertitle: Clara! More beer! More wine! Hurry, girl!—*which sets her scurrying back for another impossible armload.*

*At the bar, a rail thin old man with sunken cheeks touches Clara's elbow, leans in close.*

Serve the Bürgermeister first, child! Do not keep him waiting.

*Indeed the Bürgermeister grows impatient, hollering and standing atop the bench. Clara collects flagons of wine, foaming steins, and rushes from the bar to his table where a booted foot strikes out to catch her ankle. With startled, wide eyes, Clara tumbles forward and sends the libations flying toward an adjacent table where spirits drench a threesome of hunters. The Bürgermeister howls with mirth. The hunters leap to their feet, soaked and enraged.*

*A melee ensues. Plates and flagons shatter. Tables are overturned. Fists the size of hams collide with huge, hairy faces. The thin man snatches at his ears and laments the horror. The Bürgermeister laughs, and laughs, and laughs.*

*Clara erupts into tears and escapes out the back. Waiting for her is the thin man's wife, a bullish woman with a shock of cloud-white hair.*

Intertitle: You needn't ever come back, devil. Black devil!

*From a frosted window in the tavern, the grinning Bürgermeister watches gleefully as Clara scuttles away.*

The next reel, number two, was not among our footage. The picture skipped then to the fourth reel, though I'd already seen the third by way of Leslie Wheeler's cell phone capture. It was much, much better on screen as it was intended to be seen. The film was battered almost to point of unwatchability, but the magic remained—as did the horror of Clara's terrible abduction. While it was running, the phone in my pocket vibrated. I checked the screen and didn't recognize the number. All the same, I bolted for the aisle and answered it on my way out of the auditorium.

I'd barely managed a hello before a froggy voice croaked, "Mr. Woodard? This is Florence Sommer. I do so hate to trouble you, but do you think you could come see me right away? There are a few things I didn't tell you and your associate while you were here, important things."

"We're just watching some of the reels we found among your father's things," I told her. "There were quite a few, as a matter of fact. Can I call you back after we're done?"

"I'd rather talk to you now, if I can," she said, a little breathlessly. "I was reticent before, but to be truthful this simply can't wait."

I narrowed my eyes, stepped out of the lobby to light a Pall Mall.

"What's this all about, Mrs. Sommer?"

"Please do hurry, Mr. Woodard. I'll put some coffee on before you get here."

With that, the phone clicked abruptly in my ear. She'd hung up.

The picture was into the fifth reel when I went back in to explain the situation to Jake. To my surprise, he was almost too engrossed to care what I said to him, when what I said amounted to *I'm going back to Sherman Oaks, take notes.*

As I reluctantly left, poor Clara was being stripped naked on a tomb in a foggy cemetery, surrounded on all sides by cloaked apparitions. I prayed this wouldn't be my last shot at seeing the rest—or most of the rest—of *Angel of the Abyss*.

Mrs. Sommer's cottage was lit up from every window when I pulled the rental back in front of it for the second time that day. I checked the digital clock in the dash before I killed the engine—it was a quarter past eight in the evening.

After I made my way down the path to her door, I knocked all of once before the door opened without any clicking locks and Florence Sommer's substantial frame filled the doorway. Her face was slick with sweat and her chest heaved as though she'd been humping it on a treadmill, a piece of equipment I was willing to bet good money she neither owned nor had ever used.

"Thank you, Mr. Woodard," she wheezed. "Thank you for coming. I'm so sorry to have inconvenienced you this way."

Her voice was monotone, unnatural. Almost robotic. I scrunched one eye half-closed as I pushed into the short hallway, a moment too late to grasp her blatant attempt to alert me. By then it didn't much matter.

The arm that wrapped around the woman's neck yanked back, dragging her violently into the kitchen where two other men waited. It took me a few seconds to register what was happening, for their faces to come into focus. They were regular faces, people you'd see in the street and instantly forget. I thought then that I'd have a hard time describing them to the police later.

Something snapped and a white star of light glinted beneath Florence Sommer's chin. My eyes darted toward it and I saw a clean blade jutting from the hand of the one who was restraining her. She yelped hoarsely. I froze in place, staring like the aliens had just landed.

One of the men nearest the sink fired up a smoke. I wondered if he was trying to assert his dominance by doing so. Old Florence wouldn't have minded.

He said, "Graham Woodard, yes?"

I nodded.

The man sucked deeply from his smoke, sighed the poison back out. He looked to his compatriot with the knife at the woman's throat. Then he nodded, too.

It happened in slow-mo. Sort of. I realized what was going to happen before it happened, a sort of well-informed premonition. Then I tried to lunge for the knife, but my body wasn't on speaking terms with my brain by then. All I managed to do was stumble forward a few paces so I could get a better look at the blade slicing a poor old woman's neck open, right in front of me. The skin parted like a puppet's mouth, exposing red that stayed inside a second too long before it all spilled out at once. The blood formed a curtain that draped down over her cat-hair infused sweater, soaking it in no time at all. Florence Sommer's tongue lolled out of her mouth and she made a wet sound that turned my stomach over twice before it seized like a fist. I wanted more than anything to throw up, but my stomach wasn't cooperating any better than the rest of me. So instead I just screamed.

Somewhere nearby but out of my field of vision, one of her cats hissed.

"Shoulda stayed in Beantown, shit-bird."

That was the guy by the sink again. I turned to him as the killer let Mrs. Sommer's body slump to the dirty linoleum. She slid in her own blood, which smeared up the side of her face. She was dead.

I said, "Hey."

It was all I had time to say in my defense. The third man, a phantom until now, produced a small black gun from the inside of his jacket. The gun went up, pointing at me. I raised my hands. Pointlessly, it seemed at the time, I memorized the gunman's face. Gray eyes, blond hair. Clean shaven. Vertical lines on his cheeks, like some people have. I could pick him out of a line up if I had to.

He squeezed the trigger and the gun barked fire.

# PART TWO

## JAKE

# 14.

## HOLLYWOOD, 1926.

In Boise, at the Knights of Columbus Lodge and, later, for the Elks, and the Masons, and the Buffaloes, little Gracie Baronsky sang, pirouetted, and acted out scenes from popular plays. She brandished an oversized lollipop at her thin audiences, serenaded them with Irving Berlin. Lifted her skirts to reveal plump bloomers in imitation of Gold Rush dancing girls, though she was only nine herself. She earned chortles and smatterings of applause. Aunt Eustace earned twenty dollars a week for her protégée's efforts, when the week was good. And when a given week wasn't so good, Eustace had other means for procuring Idahoan stages for her sister's only child, her meal ticket. Everyone had to make sacrifices when the prospects looked so bright. The stage aunt lifted her skirts, too—and when that wouldn't do, she waited in lobbies, worrying the fray of her shawl, while the starlet-to-be secured her place in another variety or benefit show in the balmy embraces of men who could determine her immediate future.

But Idaho, the elder woman knew, was peanuts. Nobody in Boise would have thought twice about the pictures when little Gracie was prancing around the lodges, but that was before the Empire Theatre opened its doors to reveal the wondrous spectacle that was *Intolerance*. Then they knew, Eustace and Gracie. They knew the heartland was dried up, a dustbowl. It was time to Go West.

It was time to make Grace Baronsky a real star.

Frank stood in the doorway in a threadbare seersucker suit with a wilting dandelion protruding from a buttonhole. He smiled abashedly, and Grace stifled a laugh by covering her mouth.

"I almost never wear it," he said by way of apology. "My ma's funeral was the last time, I guess. Only suit I ever owned."

"I think you look delectable."

"Is that a good thing to look like?"

His cheeks reddened. Grace shook her head, grabbed her bag, and went out to the walkway with him. When they reached the curb, she looked out at the half dozen cars parked on either side of the street and said, "Which one is yours?"

"None of 'em," Frank answered. "I walked here."

"Nobody walks in Hollywood, Frank."

"They do if they don't have a car."

"That's what taxicabs are for."

"I only earn so much, Grace—a taxicab would cut into our entertaining budget."

"God almighty," she said with a small chuckle. "You're really not the Hollywood type, are you?"

"I'm just an apprentice electrician," he said. "I'm no type at all."

She squinted at his square face in the lean light of the streetlamp and tried to find falsehood, a chink in his armor. When she found none, she swung her hip out and walked around him, due west.

"Come along then, Mr. Electrician. I know a grand place to walk to."

Over roast lamb with currant jelly, the imminent star and the apprentice electrician looked to fellow diners like a lady and her valet, but neither of them noticed or cared. Frank devoured his meal with relish, as a man starved, while Grace picked at hers and asked pointed questions of her escort.

"Do you make it a habit," she began, "to invite actresses to dinner in your racket?"

"I have a heap of habits," said Frank, "but no, that ain't one of them."

"What led the charge then, Custer?"

"The truth?"

"Not one of the most seen habits in *my* racket, but sure—why not?"

"You seem lonesome," he said, and he stabbed the second-to-last piece of his lamb into his mouth.

Grace knitted her brow and paused, stricken silent for a moment. When she recovered, she said, "I've heard it said that the bigger the city, the more lonesome its people."

"You weren't lonesome back east?"

"Boise is hardly *back east*...," she said, deflecting. "I guess I was. I guess everybody is, in their own way. Aren't we all just kind of trapped up here?" She tapped her temple with her index finger. "There's a lot of skin and bone between my brain and yours, and all those miscommunications and different perspectives, besides."

"Why, Miss Baron. I didn't know you were a philosopher, to boot."

"I'm a clever old girl, all right."

"A clever, lonesome girl."

"We're back to that."

"I'm sorry," Frank said. "I was only trying to be honest. Maybe it's just the character. The girl you play in the movie, I mean. Seems like I sort of know her a bit better than I know you."

"Poor Clara," Grace lamented. "She *is* a lonely sort, isn't she? But I'd hate to get confused with her."

"You don't come from any abyss," he assured her. "An angel, maybe. But just the regular kind."

"The kind that strums harps on clouds?"

"Oh, I don't know. I never went in for all that Sunday school hocus pocus. Just the pretty kind, I suppose. The good kind."

"I wouldn't want to be any kind of angel," Grace said. She poked at what remained of her supper, moving the pieces around the plate. "I thought angels were what used to be people. The good ones, sure. But, you know. Dead."

"Like Clara."

"Forget Clara. You've got Grace here with you, Frank. I'm real. Alive and real, and yes, a little lonesome. You can't fix that, and I wouldn't think there's anyone who can, but we're here together right now and this is a very lovely meal and for Christ's sake let's not talk about the damned picture."

His eyes blinking, Frank sat up straight, knife and fork still in his hands, and sputtered for a few seconds before he ultimately erupted into a peal of throaty laughter. He laughed so hard that people at the adjacent tables started to pause their own conversations to have a look. When he finally began to catch his breath again, Frank laid his silverware down on the edges of the plate, wiped his mouth with the napkin in his lap, and said, "It's a real horror, isn't it?"

Grace's mouth twitched, turned up into something like a smile.

"Oh, you noticed?"

"All I do is wire the lights, doll. I'm no critic. But I've worked a few shows so far and I've seen a mess of 'em, and by god this one …"

"Jack Parson says he's found the secret to turn it into art."

Frank smirked.

He said, "I thought we weren't going to talk about it."

"Don't you want to know the secret?"

"Tell me."

"Darkness."

"I don't follow."

She showed her palms and shrugged. "There you have it," she said.

"A real horror," Frank repeated.

A colored busboy swept the plates away like a phantom while a girl with a red bowtie appeared to inquire about desert. Frank winked at Grace, letting her in on the code. He ordered a ginger ale, imported. Grace made it two. The girl returned shortly with two Old Fashioneds.

"To your health," Grace toasted.

"And may your star shine in Hollywood forever," said Frank.

"Just keep the lights on me, baby."

On the walk back, Grace hummed "Me and My Shadow"

while Frank kept pace with her small, quick steps. His hands were stuffed in his trouser pockets and a cigarette smoldered between his grinning lips. Her bungalow was still four blocks off, as blocks in Hollywood went, when a hiss sounded between a nickel and dime store and a shuttered diner, in the narrow alley. Frank paused, peered into the shadows.

"That you, Petey?" he called out.

Grace stopped a few feet up, went silent and stared.

"Frank?"

"What's the idea, Petey?"

Frank edged toward the alley and Grace stepped forward as a loud report split the air with a flash of bright white light. The flash only lasted a second but lingered, ghost-like, in Grace's eyes. She screamed and Frank doubled over, rolling away from the alley and backing up against the front of the diner.

"Frank!"

"Get back," he croaked. "Go home, Grace."

"You chasing girls now, Frank?" a voice jeered from the darkness. "Oughtn't be spending money on gashes when you're in the red, boy."

The alley oozed out a squat figure, a fireplug of a man whose face was obscured by the brim of his hat. In his hand was clutched a small revolver. Grace's breath hitched in her breast as she shot her eyes from the gun back to Frank, who was fighting to produce one of his own from the inside pocket of his threadbare coat. The gunman saw Grace first, turned to her so that the revolver was aimed at her. Her neck flushed hot; the lamb and whiskey did somersaults in her gut.

"Don't," she squeaked.

The man Frank called Petey lurched forth, scanning the dark street around her. The shadows seemed to seize Grace by the temples, squeezing in on her like a vise. Then another shot rang out and the gunman grunted. He bent at the knees and threw his torso backward. The gun dropped from his fist and clattered on the sidewalk. The echo of the metal against stone crashed in Grace's ears as loudly as the shot.

The hat fell from the man's head and he stepped awkwardly to the side. His greasy brown hair spilled rivulets of blood down his brow like red ribbons. It ran into his eyes and his jaw fell open with a yawning groan before he collapsed and lay still. Behind him, Frank still held up his own weapon, a jet-black pistol. His free hand grasped his right side. Blood leaked between his fingers.

"Are you all right?" he said, his voice tremulous.

"God, Frank," she said. "You're shot."

"Get home, Grace," Frank said. "Get home. Now."

There was muffled shouting in the middle distance. A dog barked. Grace took one last look at the dead man between her and Frank and spun on her two-inch heel to speed over the four blocks home.

She was behind a double locked door before she realized she must have left her bag at the scene, as it wasn't with her now. Dropped it in her panic, she thought. Her breath came in short, spastic gusts. She didn't dare switch on the lights.

It was the second killing Grace had ever witnessed, and it occurred to her that it didn't get easier to see it.

# 15.

## LOS ANGELES, 2013.

"I need you to wake up, dude," I said. I was trying to sound assertive. In response, all Graham did was beep—or at least that's what all the sci-fi machinery he was plugged into did. "I'm supposed to be your wingman here. The sidekick. I'm Robin, for fuck's sake."

The one eye not mummified by all the bandaging encasing his head stayed closed and disturbingly bluish. I couldn't tell if his chest was rising and falling at all, but it sure didn't look like it was. But the machines kept on beeping and the oxygen pump kept on pumping. I didn't figure they went to all that trouble for a corpse.

Florence Sommer was dead, her throat slashed. Graham was supposed to be dead too, but apparently he hadn't gotten the memo. Somebody went to the trouble of putting a bullet in his head, and from what I gathered that usually got the job done. Not so here. By the time I'd arrived at Good Samaritan he'd been through the worst of it—*it* in this case being a bullet that split his skull and nicked his brain—but the stubborn son of bitch forgot to die. I told him I loved him for that, and I added "no homo" for good measure when I realized one of the nurses was listening in.

That would have gotten a rise out of him if he'd heard me. He didn't.

"Goddamnit, Graham."

He didn't like me much. Like a champ he acted like he did when he didn't have to, but I knew better. I got on his nerves. I got on a lot of people's nerves, and for the most part I couldn't really care less. With Graham I cared. I liked the guy, even if the feeling wasn't mutual. My grandmother would have said he was a good egg, because that was what he was. Somehow, despite it all, I still considered him a friend. Probably the best I had. And here he was, in a coma with tubes in his nose and mouth and veins and head. One in his dick, too; a goddamn catheter. Maybe a vegetable. They didn't know yet. I wanted to break something.

I finished out the old movie after he took off to catch lead with his noggin. It was incomplete, but still pretty long. I never made it a habit to watch movies with no sound, but this was important, so I paid attention. My general analysis was that it was a weird fucking movie. Not just because it was silent, though that added to the jibe. More of a Tarantino man, myself, *Death Proof* notwithstanding.

Anyway, all the sharp angles of the sets, the stark black and white of the costumes, and the performances—I was never one to put much stock into the hammy acting of silent film actors, but with only their faces and bodies with which to transmit the characters, these people did some quality transmitting. When the girl got kidnapped, I felt her fear. And when they killed her … well, I jumped in my seat, honest to god. You get in a certain frame of mind watching movies that old, like you're correcting for the times, for the severe content restrictions. Whoever was overseeing the censorship department for this baby was sleeping on the job that day. That shit was intense.

I got ushered out of the room by a nurse whose weight problem was overruled by her massive cans, a sight I would have loved to tell Graham all about. He would have rolled his eyes, told me I was a pig. He'd have been right. Christ, I was missing him already and he wasn't even dead yet. I made my way past the bacon guarding the room to the elevator and slinked outside to track down a cab.

Since I didn't have any biddies with more money than sense footing the bill for my stay in L.A., I didn't have the good digs Graham got set up with. I was staying at a no-tell Motel six blocks southeast from Mann's Chinese, which was more or less my old stomping grounds before the floor fell out from under me. With no place else to go, that's where I had the cabbie take me. But before I went back to my room, I stopped off at the package store across the street to stock up on middle shelf bourbon. The Egyptian clerk called me "boss." I brought the bottle back to my room and sipped it from a Styrofoam cup in front of a late-night talk show where some lunatic pop star was trying to make her insipid record sound important. Nobody did anything important anymore, even I knew that.

In the next room, somebody was getting some action. I assumed it was bought, but I never begrudged anybody their vices. Hell, I was halfway thinking about calling up Pink Dot for some beer, hot dogs, and porno mags. Thinking about Graham in that terrible state at the hospital put the kibosh on that, but quick.

When the late show was over and the bottle was depleted by half, I was about ready to crash out had it not been for the knock at my door. I don't know about anybody else, but anybody knocking on a motel room door is cause for alarm in my book, triply so at that hour. I didn't have a peep hole, so I cracked the filthy curtains and peered out the window. It was a ginger cop with a sour puss. He wasn't in any kind of uniform, but the guy behind him was, and the redhead showed a badge to me through the glass.

"Detective Shea, Hollywood Police," he said, just like on TV. "Are you Jacob Maitland?"

I unlocked the guard chain and opened the door for him.

I said, "Hiya, Shea," or something like it.

"Mr. Maitland," he answered, putting his badge away. The uniform standing a few feet behind him eyeballed me like I was going to do something. I flashed a goofy grin at him.

"Deputy Pyle," I said.

I don't think he got it.

Shea pressed into the room, not waiting for an invitation. At least I knew he wasn't a vampire.

A *Three's Company* repeat was on the television. Shea switched it off.

"You like movies, don't you, Maitland?"

I tipped my cup to my mouth, disappointed to find it already empty. As I refilled it with a few fingers, I said, "That's kind of our game, Graham and me."

Only half-true—Graham did actually make a living doing something film related. I sat at the front desk for a water company in Worchester writing screenplays that would never see the light of day. Kind of a game, still.

"Y'know how in the movies the cops always tell people to stay in town during an investigation?" Shea asked.

"Sure," I said.

"Well, for one thing, that's bullshit. We can't make you do anything like that. And another thing, I'm going to suggest— strike that, *strongly* suggest—that you go on home. First thing."

"Yeah," I agreed, "I don't recall ever seeing that in a movie."

"Maybe you movie people should come talk to us more often."

"You seem pretty busy as it is."

"You can say that again," Shea groused. He added: "I'm really sorry about your friend."

"He's not dead yet."

"I didn't mean it like that."

"I know you didn't," I said. "I'm a little drunk."

"No law against it."

"Used to be, you know," I slurred. It's hell feeling sober in your brain when your mouth and limbs don't want to act like it. "Back when our girl Gracie shuffled off this mortal coil. You couldn't drink back then, you know. Shit was illegal as hell."

"Seems like I heard about that. Mind if I smoke in here?"

I grimaced, said, "Yes, I do. Sorry, copper. One nice thing about Graham being down and out is I don't have to breathe that filth anymore. Don't you get started, too."

"No harm, no foul," said Shea.

"No foul, no harm," I stammered. I swallowed down the contents of my cup, made a face and hissed.

"You're hitting that sauce pretty hard," Shea said. "I'd like to talk to you some more, but it doesn't seem particularly prudent now. Are you leaving tomorrow, like I suggested? I could interview you by phone, no problem."

"Maybe I'm a suspect," I said stupidly. "You'd want to keep a suspect around, wouldn't you?"

"All right, go ahead and shut up now. I mean it. You don't want to get yourself in trouble, kid."

"I'm thirty-two."

"I'm just telling you."

"You're not the boss of me."

I filled my cup again. Shea sighed. The uniform lingering outside the open door looked ready for anything. I sneered at him.

"We're going before you dig a hole you can't get out of," Shea said. He dug a card out of his pocket and laid it gingerly on top of the television he'd turned off. I wondered what shenanigans Jack Tripper was up to by now. "My info. Call me when you're not falling down drunk, would you? For your buddy."

"For my buddy," I toasted, and that shot went down hot, too. My stomach roiled.

The detective said, "Christ, take it easy."

"Free country, Kojak," was what I said back.

I'm a terrible drunk. Shit, I admit it.

I woke up with a monster headache and no intention to return home whatsoever. It was fifteen past noon and after chugging a cup of gas-station coffee I found a place that sold breakfast greasy enough to take off the edge so I could decide what was next. I wasn't about to leave Graham half-dead in the hospital with Christ-knew-who gunning for his ass, just to go back to my shitty job in Massachusetts like none of this nightmare ever happened. I may have felt a little arrogant for having considered it, but as far as I was concerned this was my problem now. *Angel of the Abyss* and Grace Baron and why nice old ladies had to die because of them.

And my friend with a chunk of skull missing for our trouble.

I was a long sight far from ready, but more than fucking able. I swallowed a pound of eggs, bacon, and pancakes like they were the medicine of the gods and stepped back out onto Hollywood Boulevard like a man reborn, ready for anything. This was my game, now. If only I knew the damn rules.

I paid for my meal, left a chintzy tip. Went outside. I wanted a drink and planned on having one. There were a dozen bars within spitting distance, just like I remembered the old neighborhood. I'd ask the bartender for gin, because gin was my thinking drink. After all, I had some thinking to do. About how to help my friend Graham, who didn't deserve everything that had happened to him.

And the main thing I thought of to help him was finding his ex-wife, Helen.

That one was going to require a few rounds.

# 16.

## HOLLYWOOD, 1926.

"Right before the turn of the century, just a couple years into this crazy game, the State of Maine enacted the first law censoring motion pictures in this country," Jack Parson said, tugging on his bottom lip.

Grace stood behind him, looking at the back of his head with her arms crossed beneath her breasts. She had gone to his temporary office housed in the lot's hinterlands to ask about the apprentice electrician—in the vaguest terms possible—and found her director mesmerized. In front of him, a makeshift screen made from a white sheet flickered brightly and silently as bloody mayhem unfolded atop the staircase ashore of the dreadnought Potemkin.

"It was prizefight pictures they had a problem with. A couple of fellows pummeling the sense out of one another, the oldest sport in history. Too violent, they said. And violence, as anyone knows, begets violence."

Lines of riflemen in white tunics marched down the steps, firing indiscriminately into a fleeing crowd of hundreds. Cripples vied to avoid the running feet whilst a small boy was trampled underneath them to the horror of his screaming mother.

"But those were merely exhibitions," Jack continued as the blood flowed down the Odessa steps. "The real strike came around '15 when Ohio put together a board of censors with the power to arrest anybody who showed a picture they didn't approve of. You know what the court said? They said that pictures 'may be used for evil.' *Evil*, Gracie. Out here in Movieland, most folks didn't like the sound of that. So Mutual Film Corp sued. And they lost. Because pictures are commerce, not art. That was the Supreme Court's ruling by the way. *Pictures aren't art.* Now it's not just far flung Ohio. Now it's the whole of America. And here in Hollywood, we've got that Puritan son of a bitch Will Hayes stirring up the pot. Making sure we aren't inciting loose morals. Mad sex. Murder and the like."

A pretty young woman covered her infant in its perambulator with her body, panicked and faced with the marching horde. The Tsar's men shot her down and the pram went rolling crazily down the steps as an old woman in pince-nez spectacles ran to the scene, desperate to save the child. She was too late: a soldier drew his sword and smashed the blade across her face, leaving a gruesome jumble of broken glass, flowing blood, impotent shrieks.

Grace's gorge rose in her throat, the memory of a man called Petey dead on the street still fresh in her mind. She shut her eyes for a moment and felt the sweat bead on her brow.

"There!" Jack cried, jabbing his finger toward the screen. "Did you see it? Did you see that, Gracie? *That* is the essence of humanity. *That* is the difference between entertainment and art. It shows you something, it holds up a mirror to you own ugliness. The darkness, Gracie. The art is in the darkness."

"It's ghastly, Jack. Shut it off."

He went rigid for a moment, then slowly turned in his chair to look at her for the first time since she entered. His eyebrows were drawn together in a bunch; his upper lip curled into a sneer.

"Haven't you been listening to me?" he said, his voice without inflection. "Don't you understand? What, you'd rather be a chorus girl? Tied to the railroad tracks for Tom Mix to come rescue? Maybe when sound arrives you'll just sing some idiotic song?"

"I sang idiotic songs on the circuit for years, Jack. It's where I got my chops, and I paid for it dearly." A tiny shudder worked its way up her spine. She shook it out. "I've worked my tail to the bone since I was old enough to flash a little leg at a room full

ANGEL OF THE ABYSS

of slavering Shriners and I did it so I could be here, batting my goddamn eyes at a camera and not digging potatoes out of the cold ground like my mother 'til the arthritis turned her hands into claws."

"You won't be batting your eyes at *my* camera," he said gravely. "That's not the picture I'm making. It wasn't before, and it certainly isn't now."

"Now that you've decided you're the Da Vinci of the movies?"

"I'll be the Bosch of the movies. The Dürer of the movies. I'll open up the mouth of Hell and show it to everyone in America. Then we'll see what's commerce and what's art, won't we?"

He nodded curtly and turned back toward the screen. The mutineers were preparing the dreadnought's massive guns against the approaching admiral's ships.

"Take your place, Ms. Baron," he said loudly over the clicking of the projector. "We shoot at nine."

She left for the set without another word.

Frank was nowhere to be seen.

Across the table at FitzGerald's on Sunset sat Eustace and Joe, preening over one another like a pair of kids, whilst Grace studied her aunt's face and thought about killers. Joe Sommer made cheap comments about how Eustace looked a decade younger than her years and Eustace tried to force a girlish blush. Grace squinted her eyes and imagined her aunt when she was ten years younger, with a knife handle in her fist and the blade sunk deep in Billy Francis' gut.

That was Idaho Falls, 1916. A week before Christmas, as she recalled it, where the local Elks put the woman and her young niece up in a hotel packed with all the other performers for the fraternity's annual Christmas variety. There were whites and coloreds, aged Jewish comics and children younger than Grace with blonde ringlets and bleeding feet from the ballet shoes that maimed them. The hallway was a mad circus, replete with dogs and a shrieking rhesus monkey called Charley, which Grace knew because its owner screamed its name as he chased the animal up and down the stairs.

And in the middle of it all were Eustace and Little Gracie Baronsky, the Prodigy of Boise, fifteen years old but billed as ten, which absolutely nobody believed for a second. The plan was to work their way east, earning as much as they could from town to town until at last they'd land in New York where the real action was. Eustace had a letter she kept like an invaluable relic from an agent who wanted to see Gracie for himself. There was talk of Ziegfeld's Follies, who could always use a premium child act—if she was good enough. Auntie Eustace meant to make sure her disciple was better than that. The road to New York was to be the starlet's trial by fire, and if she didn't have 'em on their feet by the end of her every performance Gracie knew perfectly well how much a switch would sting her rear end in the room after.

To ensure a positive reaction, it was Gracie's own idea to capitalize upon the patriotic fervor of a country edging toward war abroad. To that end, she carefully tested the waters amongst locals in taverns and diners the afternoon before a show to see how they felt about America's involvement in Europe. If they were predominantly for it, her song that night would be "Pack Up Your Troubles in Your Old Kit-Bag," the popular British war song. If, however, she found the rubes in favor of isolation, Gracie had a back-up song of her own composition at the ready: "Stay Home, Johnny Boy, Stay Home." She even managed to weep real tears at the song's finale, where she begged her paramour to take care of her rather than a bunch of foreign strangers half a world away. (Her secret was an unhinged pin in her corset that she furtively jabbed into her flesh at the right moment.) If she played her cards right, either one could bring down the house.

The trouble in Idaho City, Gracie found, was that reactions to her innocent inquiries appeared to be split right down the middle. She couldn't decide which song would earn her ovations and which a chorus of boos—and a whipping. To that end, in a state of near panic, Eustace brought the Elk responsible for their booking to their room to confer. The audience would be filled with his brethren, after all, so who better to give them the scoop?

Billy Francis was a big bear of a man, his perpetually slick bald pate unconvincingly swept over with a length of greasy yellow hair he'd grown long on the side. He habitually patted his round belly when he spoke, and his awkward familiarity with Aunt Eustace struck Little Gracie as the ink on the contract that secured them the show. He bounded into the room, shut the door behind him, and immediately sat down on the edge of the narrow trundle bed beside Eustace where he planted a hand at the small of her back.

"The fellows have talked a lot about this," said Billy, his words hidden in a rum-soaked mist. "Fact is, our eldest brother is seventy-two and well remembers the big war in the last century. Brother Jim reminds us that we've bled enough on our own dirt and don't have any need to go traipsing around the globe to bleed on anybody else's."

"Our feelings exactly, Mr. Francis," said Eustace with an eye toward Gracie, who lingered awkwardly by the bureau. "That is quite the sentiment of my little Gracie's performance this evening, so we are relieved to know we are all in agreement."

"It's good to see eye to eye with one's friends," he said, now moving his hand up and down Eustace's back. "I can see we're to be such good friends, all of us. How's about a drink?"

Billy produced a large steel flask from his coat, which he uncapped before taking a deep pull. He said, "Good for what ails you." He handed the flask to Eustace, who also drank with a sour, pinched face.

Taking it back, Billy stood and extended the flask to Gracie. Eustace moved to press down his arm, saying, "Now, Mr. Francis. My Gracie has a performance shortly, and after all she's only a child."

He brushed her hand away like he was shooing a fly, keeping his rheumy eyes on Grace.

"Aw, mother hens always think their fillies are still little children, even when they're budding right well like this one here."

Grace recoiled, her arms instinctively wrapping up around her chest.

Eustace protested, "I said she's only a child."

"No one believes this gal is ten years old, Eustie," Billy said with a chortle. "Hell, even if she was, I'm just a man—who am I to argue with old Mother Nature?"

With a lumbering step, he lunged for Gracie with a rubbery grin and reaching hands. Grace let out a wheezy sigh, sidestepping the man's advance, which only made him laugh. It was a game, and one she was terrified of playing. She squeaked, "Auntie," backed into a corner of the room from which she could not escape. Billy Francis bore down on her, winding a thick arm around her waist and grotesquely tickling her ribs with his other hand.

"Coochie, coochie," he belched.

"Auntie!"

Eustace barked, "Mr. Francis, you'd better stop that."

In lieu of reply, he pressed his rummy mouth against Grace's, pulling her tight to his enormous abdomen. The room seemed to darken around her. All she could do was fight to keep her mouth closed against the probing tongue that worked to part her lips. She didn't know what to make of it when his tongue withdrew and his mouth went slack with a startled shout. Billy's hands flew away from her waist and ribs, went up to the back of his neck as he twirled around, black-red blood spilling down the back of his coat.

"You bitch," he cried, his hands slick with blood. Eustace stood crouched before him, a five-inch blade jutting from her hand. She'd slashed his neck. "For chrissakes, you crazy bitch."

Billy swayed, moaning, and fell into a stumble toward Eustace. The older woman did not hesitate. As soon as he was within reach, she met him halfway and drove the blade deep into his prodigious belly, all the way to the handle.

"You killed me," he croaked. "Holy Jesus, you fucking killed me."

By then Gracie was sobbing, sunk down to the floor and hugging her knees. Eustace appeared frozen, a photograph, one hand supported on Billy's shoulder while the other remained against his gut. When she finally let go, the wooden handle stuck out of him like a branch on a fat tree, sticky and red. He grabbed at it, howling when the blade moved inside him, and whirled toward the bed. The tiny trundle collapsed beneath his weight. He landed with a floor-shaking thud on his stomach and lay still.

Eustace trembled, her eyes fixed to where the body lay. Her lips moved rapidly, but she made no sound. Gracie wiped her eyes and, with no little effort, rose to her feet.

"Is he dead?" she whispered.

Eustace rasped, "We have to get rid of him. Hurry—you're on stage in a couple hours, Gracie."

Joe Sommer erupted in a peal of laughter, snapping Grace back to the present with a small intake of breath.

"Isn't he a *card*?" her aunt said.

Grace agreed, quietly, that he was. Eustace patted her knee and smiled, a genuine smile as broad as it could go, that seemed to say *we're doing all right now, Gracie. Just follow my lead.*

She always did.

# 17.

## LOS ANGELES, 2013.

Two things I didn't have were Graham's cell phone and his wallet. The phone was in an evidence locker somewhere and the wallet was probably still in his hospital room. Neither was any use to me in my quest to find Helen. I couldn't even remember her last name, though I knew Graham must have told me a few times. I'd met her in Boston once or twice and she hadn't made much of an impression on me. Whenever Graham brought her up, I just tuned him out. I wished I hadn't.

One thing I did remember was the number of his hotel room. He'd been staying in room 325, which I happened to notice because it was the same number of the Holiday Inn room I'd lost my virginity in when I was fifteen. I didn't mention it to Graham because I knew he wouldn't find it half as amusing as I did. But hey, it stuck.

It was a long shot, but I hoofed it to the hotel on the off chance that they'd kept his room. I wasn't sure whether or not the police would have notified them as to what happened yet, but I walked up to the front desk like I owned the place and said, "Hi, I'm Graham Woodard, I'm in room 325? I'm afraid I've misplaced my room key."

A young woman with cornrows smiled and set to clacking her fingernails across her keyboard. After a few seconds she glanced up at me and said, "Date of birth?"

"July fifth," I said. I couldn't recall the year so I left it out. She screwed her mouth up to one side for a moment.

"All right, Mr. Woodard, just one moment."

She vanished into the back for a minute, and when she came back she handed me a credit card sized envelope with a key inside. A real key.

"Here you go," she said. "I'm afraid I'll have to charge your account ten dollars for the loss of the previous key, though."

"My fault entirely," I said.

The room was exactly as we'd left it on our way to Franco's theater to watch those reels. Neither of us had been back since. I hung the DO NOT DISTURB sign on the knob and shut the door.

Graham's suitcase lay open on the unmade bed, his clothes half folded and half hanging out like multicolored tongues. I saw that he'd brought a tie and sports jacket, and wondered what for. He was a casual kind of a cat; I'd never even seen him wear a tie. Just being prepared, I thought. Behind the suitcase on the side of the bed nearest the window was his laptop bag. I unzipped it, brought out the computer, and booted it up. First thing up it asked me for the login password. I tried half a dozen guesses, from the title of that dumb movie he wrote to his own name, but I was denied entry every time. I shut it off and returned it to the bag, 0 for 1.

On a more desperate note, I went through the pockets of his extra pair of jeans. There was a receipt for a pack of cigarettes and two squares of nicotine gum in one and a book of matches from the hotel bar in the other. The back pockets were empty. Then I thought of the sports jacket again, and I wondered when was the last time Graham wore the thing. I got an idea about that and hoped to Christ my luck might hold up. It did.

In the inside pocket of the jacket was a single sheet of paper, folded into a small square. I unfolded it and started to read what amounted to the final decree of divorce between Graham Wallace Woodard (*Wallace*—I had to laugh) and Helen Morgan Bryan. I'd guessed he hadn't worn the jacket since he celebrated the finalization of his severance from Helen, and I was right. Hell, I'd been with him that night. Go, Jake, go.

Stuffing the decree in my wallet on the off chance I managed to forget this hard-earned evidence, I picked up the room phone and had the hotel operator connect me with information. An appropriately nasal voice snapped at me to give her the name and city. I told her I wasn't sure about the city, but I needed the number for a Helen Morgan Bryan in Los Angeles County. There were, of course, nine of them. I thanked her anyway and hung up.

1 for 3.

I whispered to myself, "Where are you, Helen?"

My mind clicked. I went back to the laptop, booted it up again, and tried a few iterations of Graham's ex-wife's name. "HelenMorganWoodard" ended up being the golden ticket. That sad bastard.

Now that I was online, I got to searching. I'd done my fair share of ex-stalking in my time so my Google-Fu in that regard wasn't too shabby. It took me about ten minutes to discover that the former Mrs. Woodard had an outstanding warrant for unpaid traffic tickets, and another five minutes to find not only her name but also her picture on a skeezy looking site called modelwarehouse.com. Her page contained six photos, semi-professional, featuring my friend's ex-wife in various stages of undress. She wasn't completely nude in any of them except the last, where she was strategically covering the offending parts whilst looking dumbly at the camera. Behind her was a dilapidated shed with a pair of rusty rakes leaned up against the side. White trash chic. Most of the other models seemed to use obvious stage names, but not Helen. Misplaced pride, I suspected. I wrote down the email address and phone number for the company on a sheet of hotel stationery and continued my search, hoping in vain for an address. I didn't get one.

With my two new documents in tow, I wandered back down to the lobby and found myself back in the hotel bar, where the bartender was thankfully a stranger to me so I could charge my drinks to Graham's room. I sipped Dewar's and worked out a plan of attack. All I had to go on was this dubious modeling agency, so halfway through my second drink I decided it was time to go looking for a model.

# 18.
## HOLLYWOOD, 1926.

She dreamed of shootings and stabbings, of white, bloated bodies and staircases flowing with rivers of blood. In between sleep and wakefulness, the occasional automobile engine or barking dog alerted her to the real world outside of her violent imaginings, which was somehow even worse. Out there, fearsome memories abounded, dancing perilously close to the ominous portents of her immediate future.

Of art and death, buried bodies and those left to bleed out on the street. She rose hours before dawn, a ghost, resurrected but only halfway—the better parts of her left behind, in the cold ground.

# 19.

## L.A., 2013.

The guy behind the desk was jacked in the arms but with a stomach that wasn't necessarily winning its battle against the buttons of his Oxford shirt. The sleeves were rolled up, revealing "tribal" tattoos and barbed wire armbands, the type of tats every frat guy in Boston seemed to have these days, with a greasy black faux-hawk to match. He was pounding an energy drink, his overly caffeinated eyes flitting from me to his computer screen to the framed pictures of half-naked girls that covered his office's walls. This was Ray Warren, CEO of Model Warehouse, and I was sitting across from him in the form of a potential client.

"Tell me about your project," he said, his voice a raspy East Coast drawl. "But listen—no sex stuff, you un'nerstand? Simulated's fine, depending, but I don't do porn."

"No porn," I assured him, playing this by ear. The cat made me a little nervous; those tree trunk arms of his could make quick work of a skinny little puke like me. "What I want is like extras, for an indie film shoot."

Ray chortled and leaned back in his squeaky office chair.

"My girls aren't exactly thespians," he said. "Sure, a few of them have ambitions, but their sizzle reels are only good for the T and A quotient, you know?"

"That's all I'd really need them for. It's sort of a crazy party scene," I improvised. "Eye candy, that sort of thing."

"A movie, huh?" He mulled it over, scratching at the back of his massive neck. "What's it called?"

*"Angel of the Abyss,"* I said, almost immediately regretting it.

"Sounds artsy fartsy," Ray said.

"A little bit arsty, a little bit fartsy. I only really need one girl, to be honest. I'm looking for a type."

"I got all types," he boasted, going for the keyboard. "I even got an amputee, if that's your flavor."

"I've been over your website," I said, watching the sweat gleaming on his forehead. He killed off his energy drink and I hoped to get what I needed before his heart exploded in his chest. "The one I'd really like to hire is Helen Bryan."

Ray's hands retracted from the keyboard and his eyebrows raised, crinkling his forehead.

"Kind of a strange first choice, ain't she?"

"I don't think so. She's perfect for what I need."

"Plain girl," he said. "Nice bust, but not that pretty in the face. I got much better than that."

"I appreciate the suggestion, but if she's available, she's the one I want."

"She's not," he said quickly. "I don't even know why she's still on the site. I need to have her taken off. Helen isn't really with the agency anymore. Sorry, bro."

He shrugged and waved his hands, half-apologetically and half-this-conversation-is-done. I wondered.

"That's a shame," I said. "She's really got the look I'm going for. If she's still in town, I'd sure like to get in touch with her. It's a paying gig, of course. I'd make it worth her while."

"Like I said, she's not one of mine anymore," Ray said, forcefully. "I got models I can hire out to you, anybody else isn't my problem. That one isn't my problem, and I can't help with that. Now, you want to look at another girl, we can talk turkey. Otherwise, I'd say we're done here, wouldn't you?"

I told him I'd think it over and check out some of the profiles on the site, and I thanked him for his time. He watched me cagily as I left the office.

I came back just after seven that evening, hoping to find the place vacant, but the light was still on in Ray's office. The sky was darkening to a dull purple and the parking lot was mostly empty. I parked behind a green dumpster, killed the lights and engine, and listened to a classic rock station at low volume while I watched the window in the office and wished I'd bought something to snack on. It was my first stakeout and I hoped my last. It took a little over an hour for the window to go dark, at which point I switched off the radio and slid down in my seat. I felt like a perfect fool, playing at Junior Detective like I was in some movie, but what else could I do? My only lead to help Graham out was Helen, and Ray was my only way to her.

He came out of the shadows that draped the three covered spots at the other end of the lot and walked over to a late model Taurus, apparently the ride of choice for bottom-feeder agents that preyed on would-be ingénues with stars in their eyes. I waited for another fifteen minutes after he drove away, watching the lot, the street, and the dark second-story window all at the same time. Satisfied that nobody was going to come around wanting to know what the hell I was doing, I got out of Graham's rental and crossed over to where Ray had come out. I found the back door there, a dented steel rectangle with no handle. Exit only.

"Great," I whispered to myself.

Of the three spots under the concrete awning, only the one closest to the door was vacant. The spot on the far right contained a late model sedan and in the middle sat a tan Impala from around the time I was born. I took one look at the relic and decided the thing I loved most about cars from the 70s was their length—the monster was sticking out three feet, forming a perfect stairway to the top of the awning, which stopped right beside Ray Warren's office window.

So I climbed. Maitland-Man, does whatever a Maitland can.

I was completely prepared to bash the window in, but I found it unlatched. All I had to do was push it up and sweep the blinds aside to crawl right in. I didn't know if it was still considered a B & E if no actual B was involved, but I was counting on it. In my head I told Graham he'd damn well better appreciate the lengths I was going to here when he woke up. Maybe he could even bring me a cake with a file in it when they locked me up for this shit.

Instead of the overhead lights he had on when I was legally visiting, I switched on a little lamp on the desk for minimum illumination. I then sat down behind the desk and gave the monitor a glance when something even better caught my eye: Ray's little black book.

"You marvelous Luddite," I said.

If I was at all surprised by how gross his marginal notes in the book were, I was only barely surprised. There was no rhyme or reason to how the names were ordered, just pages and pages of them paired with pseudonyms, phone numbers, addresses, and emails; and every so often, a note to remind himself that he'd already bedded this one or that one. The old casting couch routine, a trick older than Hollywood itself. I cursed the scumbag and got to flipping pages, searching for Helen's name. I was relieved when I found it and there was no corresponding note, though I don't know why I cared. She'd already cheated on Graham twice that I knew of, so what difference would it make? I let it go and tore the page out.

And while I was folding it to stuff in my pocket, a key crunched into the lock in the door.

*Shit.*

I dropped into a crouch behind the desk, chiefly because I panicked and got stupid in a hurry. There was a perfectly good open window directly behind me, but it was too late to worry about it when the door opened and the ceiling lights flickered on. Through the slats on the other side of the desk I could see a pair of legs in black stockings pass by, the heels at the end of the pins click-clacking across the tiles. I wouldn't have held it against Ray if that was his thing, but the legs were much too slender to belong to him. A tattoo of a rose encased in barbed wire peeked out through the nylon on her ankle. I watched it like it was an astronomical event and tried not to breathe.

Of course I had to suck in some air anyway, which I did as slowly and quietly as I could, and when I did I was assaulted by the unmistakable odor of gasoline.

*Double shit.*

The legs crossed over to the far corner of the cramped office where the gas started to splash. The odor grew stronger and the woman started to grumble in a smoky voice.

"Son of a bitch—fuck you, Ray. Fuck you and fuck your fucking office."

I decided then and there that I didn't much want to be burned alive, so I leapt up to my feet and made for the window. The clatter of the blinds brought the woman out of her hateful reverie and she growled, "Hold it!"

I stopped and looked over my shoulder. She had a red gas can dangling from one hand and a pistol in the other. It was pointed at me.

She was a peroxide blonde with rockabilly curls, a gleaming stud in her lip, and drawn-on eyebrows. Her lips were a deep twilight purple and there were sleeves of tattoos on both of her arms. She was beautiful, in a crazy kind of way. She was also crying.

"Who the fuck are you?" she asked.

I said, "I was just leaving."

"Stick around," she said. "Watch the fucking fireworks."

She sure had a mouth on her. I held onto the blinds, let the smoggy evening air from outside wash the gas smell out of my nostrils.

"Would you mind pointing that thing somewhere else?" I asked her. "I got no beef with you and guns make me nervous."

I wasn't lying. I hated the damn things.

She lowered the pistol and narrowed her eyes at me, obscuring the steel gray irises.

"I'm going to burn this place to the ground," she said matter-of-factly. "You can do whatever the hell you want."

With that, she returned the gun to her small handbag and resumed soaking the walls and furniture with gas. I started back out the window, but paused again. We were in an office building that housed a number of other suites in addition to Ray's. There was no telling what—or who—this lady was going to destroy with her little revenge mission. I didn't want to get involved, not after breaking and entering to steal information in the first place, but my conscience was nagging at me. Go figure.

"Listen," I began, keeping an eye on that handbag. "I can see you want to give it to Ray, and that's cool. But if you burn this place you're going to take out a bunch of others that don't have anything to do with you or him. And that's definitely not cool."

"What's it to you, asshole?"

Nice.

"Hey, if it was my office next door, I wouldn't want you to obliterate my livelihood just because you're pissed at some prick I didn't even know."

"You don't even know what that fucker did to me."

"I can guess."

"He a friend of yours? Is that it?"

"No friend of mine. I'm just looking for somebody. He wasn't keen to help, so I helped myself."

"If you got what you need, go ahead and get the fuck out of here, then. You don't want to be here when the place goes up."

She sloshed some more gasoline around.

I said, "Tell you what—don't strike that match. Come along with me, and tell me about it. Maybe I can help you, and I think maybe you help me back. Symbiotic, like."

"Why the hell should I help you?" she barked.

"Quid pro quo."

"Talk English."

"I scratch your back, you scratch mine. I'm not a creep like Ray, I'm just trying to help a friend in need here."

"What friend?"

"You don't know him."

"Then how the fuck could I help?"

"You might know his ex-wife. I'm looking for her."

"Why?"

"She's missing. He's been shot in the head. There's some shit going down."

"Sounds like something I really want to get mixed up with."

"I don't want to mix you up in anything. I just want you to stop what you're doing and tell me if you know anything about Helen Bryan."

"Holy fuckballs," she suddenly boomed. "Helen's missing?"

She set the can down on the floor in a puddle of yellow gas.

# 20.

## HOLLYWOOD, 1926.

Frank lived in a rooming house in the Valley that was raided on a Sunday. He wasn't there, and all of his belongings were gone. Word spread quickly around the set on Monday morning, owing largely to how surprised everyone was that such a quiet, unassuming man like Frank not only had apparent underworld connections, but that he'd shot and killed someone. No one knew that Grace had witnessed the whole grisly spectacle, and she had no intention of putting that forward. She expressed as much shock as everyone else, while remaining largely aloof from anyone with an interest in discussing the matter.

When filming got underway, Jack was a firebrand. They were finishing up a ninth reel sequence in which Clara, Grace's alter ego, faced down one of the men responsible for her murder. Horace, the chief electrician and light man, kept a shimmering lamp on her face with a warped sheet of cellophane to create a ghostly effect. The heat burned her skin, but she worked through it, with it, and stared larger and more menacingly than Theda Bara ever could. Jack was elated, but equally disappointed in her target's level of projected fear. Against Saul's wishes, he reshot the actor's reaction twice before telling the cameraman to keep rolling while he strolled over to the would-be murderer and slapped him hard across the face. As the actor shook from the pain and bewilderment of the thing, Jack called *action* and got the take he wanted.

Privately, Grace resolved to strike back should the director ever elect to slap a reaction out of her.

After the day's shooting, talk re-erupted of Frank, laced with baseless speculations of what sort of trouble he'd gotten himself into. No one had a clue, but everyone had a theory. Grace escaped the studio as though it was on fire, desperate to avoid the nonsense.

On her way out, she was stopped by Horace, a stooped older man with a deeply lined face turned dry and craggy by the Southern California sun.

"Ms. Baron?" he called to her.

"Hello, Horace."

"Don't listen to 'em, what they're saying about Frank. He's a good sort of fellow, I know he is."

"I hope everything turns out all right for him," she said, non-committally.

"I know you're friends, you and Frank," Horace said. Grace broke eye contact and smiled nervously. "I don't know what he's got himself into, but I'm sure it's all a mistake. Frank couldn't do what they said he done."

*You're wrong there, Pops,* she thought but didn't say.

"Thank you, Horace."

"Good night, Ms. Baron."

"Good night."

She walked on, to the automobile Saul Veritek provided for her every morning and afternoon, and climbed into the back without a word to the sullen driver. He navigated the short drive back to her bungalow slowly, carefully, depositing her safely at the walk where she exited and pressed her key into the lock beneath the knob. She did not notice the broken window beside the door, partially obscured by a tangle of bougainvillea, but the glass on the floor was the first thing she saw when she got inside. It sparkled like diamonds in the failing sunlight, and for a moment Grace decided that Jack had finally crossed the line.

But Jack Parson was still at the set when she left; he couldn't possibly have beaten her home. She pursed her mouth and closed the door, scanning the open space for missing items or whoever was harassing her lately.

That was when she noticed the thin smear of red on the floor, forming a sort of arrow pointing vaguely at the washroom. She followed the smear and upon reaching her bed, saw the bag she'd dropped in the street sitting on top of the blankets. She knew then it was Frank even before she pushed the door open to find him passed out in the clawfooted tub, his right eye swollen shut and his shoulder a bloody mess of red and black.

"Christ's sake," she told the insensate man. "Couldn't you have found yourself a doctor, Frank?"

She kicked off her heels and opened up the medicine cabinet for iodine and a fresh washcloth. Nurse Gracie to the rescue.

He came in and out of a sweating coma through the evening and into the night, occasionally shouting out before dropping back into the pitch. The wound in his shoulder was badly infected— scabrous and ringed with yellow crust. The bullet seemed to have passed clean through without hitting bone though, so Grace simply applied liberal amounts of iodine to either side every hour or so with a fresh bandage. And while Frank slept, she tended to him, daubing his brow with a cool, damp cloth and keeping a close eye on his temperature.

It was past noon the next day before he came fully to for the first time. His dark lashes fluttered before opening completely to let the punishing light in. He shielded his face with his hand, whereupon Grace rushed to pull the drapes closed.

"What day is it?" he croaked.

"Tuesday," she answered. "Quarter past noon, or thereabouts."

"Shouldn't you be on set?"

"I phoned the studio and had them tell Saul I'm having trouble with the menses. That'll shut any man up, and quick."

Frank half-grinned, and it looked like it took some effort.

He said, "Thank you, Grace. I mean it."

"Here I came to Old Californy to be the next Mary Pickford and instead you turn me into Florence Nightingale. What do you take me for, anyway?"

"A friend," Frank said. "The best one I got, too."

"If your friends are the type to go shooting at you in the street like it's Dodge City, I can see why. I'm going to put some coffee on the stove, and then how's about you tell your best friend where you've been and what in the name of Wild Bill Hickok happened back there?"

"I've been hiding out," he explained over his coffee, which he took black. "Shacked up with an old pal out in Pomona, but the heat made him nervous so he gave me the short shrift and I ended up in a damn railyard, like a hobo."

"A railyard! Frank, why didn't you come to me if there was no one else?"

"I didn't want to bring that heat down on you, either. You've been through too much with me already. I never meant for any of that mess to happen, Grace—honest, I didn't. You're such a swell gal, I didn't even have any intentions. Just a nice night, you know. And then that rotten bastard ..."

"Petey."

"That's him. God, I'm sorry you had to see that."

"You were defending yourself."

"I never did anything like that before. Shoot a man, I mean. I promise you that, Grace."

"It's all right. I believe you."

"It's not all right," Frank countered, setting his cup down on the table. His hand shook and he spilled some on the floor. "I stumbled into this gig with Horace, but it was supposed to be my way out. I'm supposed to be done with all that."

"With all what?"

"These guys, these fellas I used to run around with. Los Angeles is all tinsel and silver for you folks, you Hollywood people, but it's a pretty rough town, besides. All those flappers and F. Scott Fitzgerald types you read about are having a grand old time in the cities, but then there's a million guys like me with hardly a red cent to our name. It gets hard, real hard. And sometimes when an opportunity comes along your heart and soul tells you it's the wrong thing but you do it anyway because goddamnit, you're hungry and tired of humping it around town with holes in your shoes and not enough in your pocket for a short beer. So you try to be a good Indian, to do everything the right way, the way you'd be proud to tell your mama all about, but what to do when there's nothing left? When it's the bread line or business through the barrel of a .38?"

Grace made a flat, straight line of her mouth and regarded her coffee for a moment. She then set it down beside Frank's, lighted a cigarette, and said evenly, "What did you do for these fellows, Frank?"

"I never hurt nobody, Grace. That's the first thing and it's the truth."

"Okay, what's the rest of it?"

"Dope," he said flatly.

"What, grass?"

"Horse."

"Jesus."

Frank hung his head.

"I never did it and I never sold it. I moved it, and I mean lots of it. Me and another guy, named Jimmy, we'd pick it up in Tijuana and drive it back over the border with a false bottom in the car."

"That's serious, Frank," Grace said. "That's serious time in the pen."

"If you get caught, sure. I never did."

"And you didn't talk?"

"Never."

"Then why Petey? What was his stink?"

"Started back in September. We were picking up a load …"

"You and this Jimmy?"

"That's right. Got the car all rigged up and ready to head back to the Land of the Free. We made it across the border fine, just like always, but along these crummy back country roads to San Diego we got hijacked."

"Hijacked! By whom?"

"Never found out, and I don't guess it matters much now. Point is, these guys—two Mex and a colored fellow—ran us off the road and put the guns to us. I was ripe to give it over, because who wants a belly full of holes? Jimmy figured different. That old kid kept a shooter under his seat, and once he got a hold of it he came up shooting. I went down to the floor, I'm no dummy, and by the time the smoke cleared there were four corpses where there used to be five guys. I was the last one standing, or cowering if you like. Jimmy took care of those bastards, but it cost him his life."

"That wasn't your fault," Grace said with some caution. Neither of them was paying the slightest attention to their coffees, but both of them smoked like chimneys.

"No, it wasn't. What happened next was a different jug of hooch. I got out of there, of course, and I hate to tell you but I left poor old Jimmy with the men he'd killed."

"Right there on the road?"

Frank nodded soberly.

"I veered away from San Diego proper, made it fast as I could to a wide-open field in the Little Landers where I burned the car—horse and all."

"There it is," said Grace. She understood now.

"Yeah," Frank said. "Probably five grand worth, up in smoke along with a swell Bearcat, too. I didn't have too many friends after that."

"Why didn't you leave town, Frank? Head east or someplace safe?"

"I've got cheese for brains, for one. And where's safe, when they're all connected up? The fellas in Los Angeles are linked up with the fellas who run every other town between here and New York. All it takes is a telephone call to set the ball rolling and I'm Public Enemy Number One."

"But they must have been gunning for you all this time."

"They weren't, which is how I got so sloppy. The way I see it now, I must have been watched ever since, to see if I kept on to that heroin. When they finally decided I didn't have it, the order came down to finish me off. It just happened to be the night we were out together. God almighty, Grace, I'm so sorry for that."

Grace sucked in a ragged breath and brought her cup to her lips. She sipped and made a face—cold. Shaking that off, she sat up ramrod straight and said, "The answer to our dilemma seems quite obvious then."

"It's obvious to me, too," Frank said. "I got to get the hell out of here. You've been a regular peach taking care of me, and I'll never forget it, but you don't need this hell. I was plain stupid to think I could hide in plain sight from this mess and the last thing I want is to get you mixed up in it any more than you already are. Just let me get a fresh dressing on this shoulder and I'm gone, Grace."

"You are stupid," she said, "so you should listen to a clever girl for a change. I happen to earn a damned enviable wage acting in this picture, you know. Five grand isn't exactly chicken feed to me, but I can swing it. We're going to pay off these gangsters so they leave you be for the rest of your long, marvelous life."

"You're crazy," he protested, gingerly touching his aching shoulder.

"That's probably the truth, too. And you know, if that Bearcat was theirs, we'll have to cover that, too. Make it seven thousand. I can have that in cash inside a week."

"No, definitely not. I wouldn't allow it."

"Who's asking permission?"

"This would ruin you."

"What, you think this is my last picture? I'm just getting started, Frankie baby. This crummy bungalow will be a distant memory by this time next year. And these rotten gangsters you've been so worried about? Completely forgotten."

"They won't accept it."

"How do you know? Have you tried?"

"These men kill people, Grace. Reason isn't quite among their stronger virtues."

"It's worth a try, Sonny Jim. We *have* to try."

"You don't owe me a thing."

"I take care of my friends. We're friends, aren't we, Frank?"

"You know we are, Grace. I've never known a better friend than you."

She rose to her feet and pranced elfishly to the larder, where she found a decent vintage of pre-prohibition wine and came dancing back with the bottle and a corkscrew.

"That Carrie Nation was still soiling her bloomers about hooch when this was bottled," she said with a devilish grin. "What say we celebrate the end to your little problem?"

"Little is a relative word if I've ever heard one."

Grace popped the cork and filled the coffee cups.

She said, "Salud!"

# 21.

## L.A., 2013.

Her name was Louise, but in Ray Warren's little black book she was listed at Lou-Lou Vanderbilt. I remembered the pseudonym, because it was one of those with a notation beside it from Mr. Charm himself. That alone told me half her story. She told me the rest over burned coffee that tasted like lead at Mel's on Sunset.

"I came out here from fucking Little Rock to be an actress. It's easy to think you can do that shit when you're from nowhere. I wasn't here a month before I found out I'd kidded myself into a goddamned pipe dream. I was waiting tables at a titty bar in Venice and doing two auditions a day. No call backs, no nothing. Maybe I didn't have it. Or maybe I'm just a small fish in a big sea."

"Let me guess," I said. "Ray discovered you at the titty bar."

"Easy guess, but you're right. I had to deal with plenty of fucking creeps, but at least I was dressed. Well, *mostly*. Ray told me I had class and a lot of it. He wasn't even interested in the girls on stage. The son of a bitch gave me his card, told me he had a *system*. He'd made careers for girls like me. He even said I could go ahead and give notice right then and there. I wasn't going to need no damn job anymore."

"Did you?"

"Not that night, but inside a week I did. I made more doing four shoots a week for Ray than six nights a week at the club ever netted me. And nobody touched my ass."

"Not even Ray?"

"Not at first. I know he looks like a total frat bro, but he can charm the panties right off a chick. I'm a fucking retard, but I'm hardly the only one. Besides, I thought I was going to be famous and shit."

"Famous for what?"

"What do you think?"

I raised my eyebrows and sipped my coffee.

"He *says* he's not in the porn business," she continued, "but that's complete bullshit. It's his bread and butter. I don't think there's a thing wrong with it, but he grooms girls to trick them into it."

"Did he do that to Helen?"

"Nah, she never went in for that. Christ knows he tried, but she wouldn't have it. She was only in the game for the drugs, anyway. Half the photographers provide it for free to any model who wants it. I never did, but that Helen was a goddamn Hoover."

"Why'd he ditch her? Because she wouldn't do the porn stuff?"

"That's part of it. That, and she was just too fucked up all the time. Meaner than hell, too."

I chuckled softly, and she read my mind.

"You think I've got an attitude?" she asked me. "You definitely haven't met Helen Bryan."

"Maybe not the real her, no," I said, and remembered the page I'd taken from Ray's book. I pulled it out and flattened it on the table. Louise snatched it up and scrutinized it.

"Yeah, she don't live in Glendale anymore. Good thing you ran into me."

"You know where she lives?"

"I was at her place a few weeks ago. Her and that gorilla she lives with."

"Well, that clinches it," I said, killing off the coffee and making a face appropriate to the flavor or lack thereof. "I'm going tonight. Would you write the address down for me?"

"Don't remember it. But I can get you there."

I stalled. Riding around with a pyromaniac I didn't know from Eve wasn't my first choice for the evening's festivities. I signaled for the check.

"Well?" Louise prompted me, planting her palms on the table.

I sighed—inwardly.

"All right," I relented. "Let's go find her."

The building was right in the heart of Hollywood, right off La Brea between Hollywood and Sunset, spitting distance from Hollywood High. I parked Graham's rental car underneath a towering palm on the street and walked up to the front of the ugly structure with Louise in my wake.

"This is where you went?" I asked.

"About two and a half weeks ago, yeah."

I advanced to the door, which was locked. Beside it an intercom was mounted with two rows of names on handwritten slips. BRYAN was 6C. I pressed the button, and it buzzed obnoxiously. There was no answer, and I didn't really expect one.

"What now, chief?" Louise piped up. "You gonna bust in like you did at Ray's?"

I groaned and said, "Yep."

She grinned. I mashed the buttons, as many as I could. When at last someone answered with a drowsy, "Yeah?" I muttered something about a pizza in a goofy fake accent.

The door buzzed and unlocked. I pulled it open and gestured for Louise to go ahead of me.

"What a fucking gentleman," she commented.

"You're fucking welcome," I said. When in Rome.

We rode the elevator up to the sixth floor. The floors were bare up there, the carpet stripped off, probably awaiting replacement. The concrete was webbed with deep cracks, terrifying remnants of the Northridge quake in '94. I was still feeling the tremors when I moved out there a few years later. I never got used to them.

"6C," Louise reminded me. I nodded and we made our way down to the end of the hall where it turned right and kept going. The next length brought us to the door in question, a big green door with no peep hole or bell. Louise rose her fist to knock but I held her wrist before she could.

"Element of surprise?" I suggested.

She shot me a bemused look. I didn't blame her.

I knocked. The surprise was on me when the door actually opened.

Now I faced a rotund Mexican whose belly bulged over his belt buckle. He regarded me with indifferent eyes and clutched a spackle knife with a sticky white dollop clinging to it. Behind him, every light was on and the place was a shambles. Cardboard boxes were stacked everywhere, half of them overflowing with all manner of junk. Another man was painting a wall opposite the one I supposed the first guy was working on, judging by all the holes that needed fixing.

He said, "Wrong place, man. Nobody lives here now."

"Looks like somebody's still moving out," I said, pointing to the boxes.

"Left behind. They split. You want to look at the place, it'll be ready Monday. Make an appointment."

He started to close the door, but I pressed into the crack.

"Hold up a minute," I said. "I know the people used to live here. I'm trying to get in touch with them."

"Really not my problem, *hermano*," he said. "Unless you're a cop with a warrant, I can't you let you in here."

"That's just the issue," Louise suddenly added, stepping up to the plate. "The woman who lived here is my sister, and she's missing. The cops don't even care, sir. They're barely looking, and I'm scared to death for her."

I had to admit I was impressed—not just with her quick thinking, but by her ability to say twenty-five words in a row and none of them 'fuck.' I didn't think she was up for it.

"*Mierda*," the workman sighed. "That's rough, lady."

"Please," she begged, "just let us have a quick look around. Anything to help us find her and make sure she's safe."

The man screwed up his mouth and glanced back at his partner, who seemed oblivious to our presence. When he returned his gaze to Louise, he groaned out a long breath and nodded his head.

"Okay," he said. "Be quick though, eh? I'm really not supposed to let people up in here."

"Lickety-split," said Louise.

He went back to spackling across from his buddy the painter, and I went first into the big bedroom with Louise. One of the guys switched on a radio playing Tejano, all trumpets and accordions and strident Spanish voices in harmony. We stood in the middle of the room and surveyed the task in front of us. It was Mrs. Sommer's storage unit all over again, a comparison that made the hair prick up on my neck when I recalled what had become of Mrs. Sommer.

"So we're looking for a cokehead with a fidelity problem," Louise said, her hands on her hips. "Most addicts I know keep their connections tighter than a fucking drum, but our girl doesn't seem the type to much care what happens to anybody else, am I right?"

"I thought you knew her better than me," I said.

"I don't think anybody knows Helen as much as they might like to," she said. "Least of all Helen her own damn self."

"So, what—we're looking for another black book, like Ray's?"

"Maybe," she said, unconvinced. "Seems like it depends on whether or not she left in a hurry, or of her own free will. That would make the difference in what she left behind."

"You're good," I said. She winked, sardonically, and dug into one of two dozen boxes scattered around the cluttered room. I followed her lead and opened into one of my own. Louise found stuffed animals and trinkets; I came upon an unorganized mountain of old photos. Graham was in a lot of them.

"That your buddy?" Louise asked over my shoulder.

"Yeah. He's in the hospital right now, out cold. Shot in the head and Helen knows something about it."

"Jesus Christ, Jake," she said.

"It's a doozy of a story," I said.

She stood up, looked me over like a sideshow freak for a moment, then sniffed.

"Why don't you tell it while we look through this shit? I'd like to know how deep I'm getting into this fuckup of yours."

We kept on through the boxes and I told it, all of it, from meeting up with Graham at Bukowski's in Boston to nearly getting barbequed in a low-rent pornographer's office by Louise herself. By then we'd found piles of clothes, dog-eared fantasy paperbacks, a trunk full of tame sex toys, a shoebox packed tight with sales receipts, none of which post-dated Boston. The woman was a packrat, but we weren't any closer to our goal.

Once we'd finished with the bedroom, we sat down on the naked mattress and took stock of the situation so far.

"Here's my take on it," Louise said, twirling her lip ring. "If I didn't know better, I'd want to look into Ray to see if he had anything to do with Helen vanishing on us. I say that because guys like that are total fuck-wits, real scum-nuts, and they go into 'entertainment' to take advantage of chicks like that. I don't really think he has anything to do with it—I know the guy, he's a creep, but this isn't on him—but I *do* think we need a two-prong attack, here."

"What do you mean?"

"I mean while we're looking for Helen, we should be looking into whoever made that fucking movie, the old one that got your ass out here to start with."

"It's just an old movie, though," I said. "Anybody remotely involved with it has died of old age by now."

"Except for the star."

"Except for her," I agreed.

"Think about it," she went on, "something happened to that girl back in the day, right? We don't know what, but *something* did. And that shit got fucking buried, and it was serious enough that all this time later somebody's out there shooting motherfuckers to keep it that way. Am I on target so far, chief?"

"So far, so good."

"Then you start at the beginning. Keep trying to find Helen—fuck, everybody else is already dead or in a fucking coma—but at the same time get back to the good old days and see who made that thing, that Angel of the Whatever."

"*Angel of the Abyss.*"

"Right, and you said you actually have the movie, didn't you?"

"Most of it, in reels."

"Let's give it a watch while we're at it, you and me. You

might see something on the second pass, and an extra set of eyes couldn't hurt."

I said, "I don't want to waste any more time. She's out there somewhere, and the quicker I find her, the closer I am to helping Graham."

"You really dig that guy, huh?"

I knitted my brow, not really up to explaining how a one-way friendship worked. I *did* dig the guy, even if he wasn't really all that fond of me. I wasn't really all that fond of myself, so I didn't really blame him.

"We'll help your friend," Lou said after a moment. "Whatever we got to do."

"This is great and all," I said, giving her a bewildered look, "but why are you so invested? I mean, I appreciate the hell out of everything you've already done, Louise ..."

"Lou, please. Just Lou."

"... but you don't know me, or Graham, or any of us. You've got no stake in this crap."

"The truth? Helen was a fuckup and a bit of a cunt, but I liked the bitch. She stood up to Ray when nobody else would, and I respected that shit."

"Well, that makes one of us."

"And I know a bastard when I see one, too. I've got plenty of practice. You're no bastard."

"Thanks?"

"Don't get any fucking ideas, now," she added with a black-lacquered fingernail in my face. "It ain't like that."

"10-4."

"Come on, let's go check the boxes in the living room."

I followed her, more astounded than ever.


Sandwiched between the two workers, we pored through the remaining boxes, clawing our way through Helen's collection of completely useless ephemera while the painter sang along to each and every song on the radio. The guy had a memory like a steel trap; I couldn't even remember the words to my favorite songs.

In my last box, I found a small but respectable collection of porn on DVD. I slowed to admire her taste when Louise said, "Hey, get a look at this."

She was kneeling over her last box, which was stuffed with cooking magazines and a jumble of mail. In her hand was an open envelope, from which she'd taken the contents and now handed to me. It was a paystub from the Royal Blue Theater on Tremont in Fairfax. Helen M. Bryan was identified as a *concession associate* at the paltry rate of $9.75 an hour.

"I'll be damned," I said. "She got herself a day gig."

"That's a revival house," Lou informed me. "As in, they only play old movies."

She waggled her penciled brows at me while I took a minute for it to sink in. When it did, I gasped.

"Holy crap," I said. "Now we know how Helen knew Leslie Wheeler, don't we?"

"Yes, we do," she agreed with a toothy smile. "Ain't detecting fucking fun?"

"Can you guys get the hell out now?" the burly workman interrupted. "If we get fired it's your asses."

I pocketed the paystub and we got the hell out.

# 22.

## HOLLYWOOD, 1926.

The pair watched Ronald Colman as Beau Geste at the Arcade on Broadway, though neither of them paid the slightest attention to the picture. Rather, they smoked one cigarette after another, slumped in their seats, and waited for the afternoon to drag by as the organ player punched out the musical accompaniment in the least graceful way possible. Grace and Frank had an appointment to keep, and that appointment was with Junior Bassof, a rough customer who might or might not find their terms—*her* terms—acceptable enough to let Frank go on living.

They ate deviled eggs and sipped fountain pops, and when the picture was done they emerged back into the sunlight to light cigarettes and get serious about their rendezvous with destiny. Destiny was billed to come in the form of Junior, Frank's erstwhile boss, who agreed to meet him and his supposed moll at a Jewish delicatessen on Fairfax for the trade-off. They sauntered that way, just a block and a half from the Arcade, with hardly a word between them.

Upon arriving, Frank gestured with his chin at a pair of men seated opposite one another in a corner booth by the window.

"Those are Junior's stooges," he whispered.

"Then let's go say hello," suggested Grace.

"Give me the package," he said. "Let me take care of this. You go on home. No sense in us both ending up in the ground if this thing goes south."

"The *ground*?" Grace gasped. "Don't be dramatic. Come along."

He seized her arm and gave her a bewildered look. Grace just smiled.

"I've dealt with plenty of lowlifes over the years, real low characters on the circuit and elsewhere. These goons don't scare me."

With a wry smirk, she sauntered over the greasy tiles to the booth, where she slid in beside the shorter of the pair like she belonged there. The men glanced her over with appraising leers while Frank lingered several feet away, his face a mask of astonishment.

"You Frank's girl?" asked the man seated across from Grace. His smooth face betrayed a youth he clearly tried to hide behind a put-upon demeanor.

"I thought we were seeing Mr. Bassof," she said.

"You're seeing us."

"All right," she said, beckoning Frank with her hand. He came over slowly and sat down beside the taller one.

"Hi, Frank," the tall youth said. "Petey sends his regards from the morgue."

Frank put his hand on his wounded shoulder. "He shot me. I shot back."

"Guess you're the better shot, then."

"Guess I am."

"So what's it going to be?" Grace put in. "I trust you gentlemen know the terms. We cover the expenses of the car and the—the *shipment*—and we call this whole cowboy game off. So what is it?"

The short man beside her laced his fingers together on the table and exchanged a meaningful look with Frank. Grace caught this, but didn't understand what it meant when Frank pushed out a sigh and said, "The shipment in the car. We're willing to pay for it all, don't you see that?"

The thug said, "All right, sure. The car, the shipment, *and* Petey."

"What about Petey?" Frank asked.

"You knocked him off. That'll cost you, too."

"That was no knock-off," Frank protested. "That was self-defense."

"Either way he's dead, isn't he? So it's another grand on top. No discussion."

"That's garbage," Frank said, making to stand. Grace reached over the table, touched his hand and shook her head.

"We accept that," she said, her eyes boring deep into Frank's.

"Grace …"

"You have it now?" Shorty said.

"I have it," she answered.

"The extra thousand?"

"It's here."

She withdrew the fat package from her bag and handed it to Shorty under the table. He glanced around, making sure he didn't have an audience, and then got to counting. While he did that, the tall one said, "This is contingent on a couple other things."

"What is?" Frank asked.

"Your life, so listen up. You don't talk. To anybody. Ever. If you do, we'll know about it and the deal's off—your head's back on the block."

"He won't talk," Grace said.

"She your mouthpiece, Frank?"

"I won't talk," said Frank. "What's the other thing?"

"You don't live in L.A. anymore. As of today. You can go anywhere you please that isn't here. And you're never coming back."

"That's too much," Grace said.

Ignoring her, Frank said, "That's fine. Are we done here?"

The tall man looked to Shorty, who finished counting, stashed the bills in his coat, and nodded.

"We're done."

The short one said to Grace, "You never saw us in your life, that clear?"

She scooted out to let him pass. "It's clear."

Outside, Frank and Grace found a taxi and climbed into the back. Grace gave her own address and the driver sputtered off in that direction.

Grace said, "Then that's it."

"I'll pay you back, someday. I don't know how, but I will."

"Just do it legitimate like."

"It's all legitimate for me, from here on out."

She smiled. "It's been interesting, Frank. I'll miss you."

"Miss me? I'm not going anyplace. I still have to help light that soon-to-be-famous face of yours, don't I?"

"But that's … no, Frank. You have to leave. You promised."

"You say that like I'm lying to my poor old grandmother. I promised a couple of *gangsters*, darling. Crooks. Who cares what I say to them? As far as they're concerned, I'm already gone. It's finished, all of it. Thanks to you."

He showed his teeth in a broad grin and kissed her on the cheek. The driver looked at them through the rear-view mirror for a moment, until Grace met his gaze. She sat still for a moment, her mouth open, before blinking rapidly and asking the driver if she could smoke in the taxi.

"Help yourself," the driver said.

She helped herself. And while she smoked, she thought about the eighty-five-hundred dollars she'd just wasted on a life she knew she couldn't really save.

# 23.

## L.A., 2013.

The Royal Blue was in a wretched state of disrepair. The marquee didn't look safe to stand under, the concrete façade was crumbling, and the window to the box office was boarded up with a hand-written sign bidding customers to buy their tickets inside. Even the sidewalk was cracked and overrun with tall green weeds. The theater looked like it should be condemned, but sure enough they were in the middle of a late-night revival of *The Elephant Man*. According to the tattered ad pasted to the front door, tomorrow began their three-day Howard Hawks retrospective, only five bucks per show. Slightly worried that the roof was going to fall on me before we were done, I pulled the door open and let Lou walk in ahead of me.

The inside was somehow worse. I felt like I was in one of those 42nd Street grindhouses from the 80s, with the mildewed carpet torn to ribbons and the musty curtains on the walls festooned with cobwebs and thick dust. We went across the lobby, past ripped posters for forthcoming features of past years, to the concession stand where a languid teenager with ironic horn-rimmed glasses raised his substantial eyebrows at me. Below him stood a glass cage filled with stale, radioactive-yellow popcorn. My stomach tightened.

"Is the manager in?"

"I'm the assistant manager."

Lou and I exchanged a look.

She said, "Does Helen Bryan work here?"

"I don't think I have to answer that. Are you cops?"

"We're friends of hers," I said.

"Then you know she don't work here anymore."

"Was she fired?" Lou asked.

"She quit."

I said, "Did she quit, or just stop showing up?"

The kid scrunched up his face.

"You know so much, how come you're asking the questions?"

"I was guessing," I said. "Which was it?"

"Look man, that girl was trouble. I'm not trying to talk about your friend, but she had problems, all right? So when she didn't show, nobody was really all that bugged by it, you know what I mean?"

"When was that?" Lou asked.

"Her last shift, you mean? Thursday, I think. No— Wednesday. About a week ago now. Norm figured he'd let her know she didn't have a job no more when she came in for her last check, only she never came in. Far as I know it's still sitting in his office."

"Nobody thought that was cause for concern?" I said.

"What, she's our problem now? Places like this, we got a high turnover, man. I been here nine months and I'm an old veteran."

"You just like all the old movies, huh?"

"Something like that."

"How about silents?"

"Sometimes. Some of the European ones were okay."

"Ever heard of *Angel of the Abyss*?"

"What about it?" the kid asked. He was losing his patience with me, if there was much there to begin with.

"It's a lost film from the Twenties," I said.

"I know what it is—why're you asking about it?"

"I thought maybe Helen had an interest in it."

"I don't think she would've known about that. She wasn't really all that into film."

"She worked at a theater, didn't she?"

"I used to work at a filling station and I don't give a shit about gas."

"Doesn't everybody like movies?"

"Sure, whatever's new and popular. Something like that, though? Takes a special breed of film geek to have even heard of it."

"Like the Silent Film Appreciation Society?"

"I don't know what that is, but sure."

"Couple of ladies Helen knows, as it turns out."

"Hey, I said she worked here but I never said we were best friends. Maybe she was into old silent films, what do I know? She just never struck me as the type, that's all."

"You never saw her talk to a nice old lady? Leslie Wheeler?"

"How old? There was some really old broad used to come in here to talk to her. Figured she was her grandma. Seventies, maybe eighties."

"This lady was in her fifties," I said.

"Then I don't know. Helen sold Juju Beans and Cokes to a lot of nice old ladies. Some of them were chatty. Best I can give you."

"All right," Lou said, "don't get your panties in a twist. We're just concerned friends, you understand?"

"I hope you find her and I hope she's okay," the kid said, "but that's the end of what I know. She wasn't here long, and then she wasn't here at all. Like I told you, she didn't even pick up her last check—or her street clothes, for that matter."

"Come again?"

"She'd change into her uniform when she got here." He tugged at his dorky red suspenders. "I don't choose to wear this crap, you know."

"And when she left the last time, she was still in uniform?"

"That's what I said, isn't it?"

Lou said, "Can we get a look at those clothes?"

The kid grimaced.

"Come on, man."

I said, "It might help."

"Sure, but I can't just let you poke around the chick's clothes, can I? That's weird."

Lou shrugged her shoulders. I reluctantly took a twenty from my wallet and laid it on the glass counter. The kid snorted.

"Are you kidding?" he said.

"Kids these days," Lou snarked.

I dropped another Hamilton. The kid swiped them both and said, "Right this way, sir."

So hard to find good help.

Helen came to work on what would be her last day in a small lime green tee shirt and ripped blue jeans. I presumed she kept on her underwear and socks, because that was all she'd left in a locker that didn't lock outside the manager's office behind the concession stand. With the kid looming nearby, I turned the shirt inside out while Lou went through the pants. A second later, she said, "Wallet."

I dropped the shirt. Lou opened the wallet.

Inside was a Massachusetts driver's license, a debit card, thirteen bucks, Ray Warren's business card, and a folded-up piece of scrap paper. Lou handed me the wallet and unfolded the scrap. On it was written the name Tim in a childish scrawl, beneath which was a phone number. Lou didn't miss a beat; she whipped out her mobile in a hurry and dialed the number.

"I'm looking for Tim?" she asked in a falsely meek voice when someone picked up. "No one there called Tim? All right, sorry to bother you."

She clicked off and peered at the scrap.

"Maybe it's supposed to say Tom," I offered.

Lou smiled, said, "I think I got it. Come on."

The kid pushed his glasses up to the bridge of his nose. "Wait, you're just going to take her wallet?"

Lou said, "Yep."

The kid shrugged.

Around the corner from Canter's on Fairfax Avenue, Lou stopped in front of an ATM where she stopped and shoved Helen's debit card into the slot.

"Good plan," I said. "Clean out her account and she'll have to come back from wherever she is."

"Not exactly," Lou said, adding, "Fucko."

The display prompted her and she opened up the scrap of paper. I chuckled softly, realizing right away what she was up to.

"I have a pretty terrible memory," she said, plugging in the last four digits of "Tim's" telephone number. "I keep a little list just like this for PIN numbers and shit like that, disguised as phone numbers in case anybody gets a hold of it. It's not a new trick, and since Tim seems to be bullshit—*abrafuckingcadabra, Blackstone.*"

The PIN worked. Lou grinned at me with pride.

"Impressive," I said. "Now what?"

"Let's see what she's got in there."

She navigated a few options until the machine spat out a statement on a small receipt. Lou yanked it out and said, "Holy shitballs."

I looked over her shoulder at the tally at the bottom and said, "You can say that again."

Helen Bryan had three quarters of a million dollars sitting in her savings account.

# 24.

## HOLLYWOOD, 1926.

Looking upon herself in the washroom mirror, Grace beheld the perfect model of the "New Woman": black bob, pixie face of alabaster, small bust and boyish figure. The new Colleen Moore. Tomorrow's in girl. Perhaps even the first new star of the forthcoming talking pictures revolution—why not? Her voice wasn't bad. She had what it took and she had the scars to prove it, though none to show on camera. All of Grace's scars were scored inside, raked deep by the circuit, by the blood she'd seen, by that relentless impulse to conquer the world she was never sure was her own. But she would survive *Angel of the Abyss*, just as she'd survived the vaudeville circuit, and her afternoon meeting with Famous Players people was going to be her first step into a bright new future.

She was to see Joseph March, the director, and Alan Rivers, the Famous Players representative, at March's home on a sprawling, remote strip of Malibu beach. No script had been sent, not even a description of the picture at stake, but by telegram Grace read that March was shown footage from *Angel* by none other than the great Jack Parson himself and was, in his own words, "positively mesmerized."

The trouble, of course, was Frank. He maintained his cloistered presence in her bungalow, forbidden to go out unless absolutely necessary and going stir-crazy day by day. He wanted to go back to work, to buy cigarettes and drink merrily with her at speakeasies as they'd done before. Grace wouldn't have any of it.

"You might as well be a wanted man," she tried to explain. "You'll be killed the moment one of those awful men sees you or hears word you're still in Los Angeles."

"That's all bluster," he countered. "You have to understand it's costly to kill a man for thugs like them. You can't just go around gunning for whomever you please, or else half the town would be bleeding in the streets. It's a calculated thing, and I'm just not worth it."

"Are you willing to stake your life on that?"

"Beats being crammed in a cage," Frank complained.

"Or mine?"

He sighed heavily. "Grace, darling—I wouldn't dare pull you down into something like that, not even on a longshot. What's the percentage in hurting you?"

"I've seen them. I know who they are."

"Practically everybody does. These guys aren't ghosts. They're practically famous in their own right—like you're going to be."

"Oh, no," said Grace, flitting about the bungalow in search of her pearls for the meeting. "I'll be famous, all right—but not like them."

"You know what I mean. And trust me, you're safe as a babe in her crib. We both are."

"Trust," she parroted, rolling her tongue over the word and its meaning. "If that's all I've got to go on, I might as well drop the rest of my vanishing fortune on the races."

She regretted saying it immediately. Frank's mouth tightened, wrinkled. He averted his eyes and rose to pour himself a brandy from Grace's bar.

"Look," she said, "I've got to go to this meeting now. I've lost all faith in Jack Parson and his ridiculous little film, but there's still a chance for me in this business and it starts here. Please don't go anywhere. Take a nap if you want, drink everything in the house, just stay put, will you?"

"I have a better idea," Frank said after a belt of his drink. Grace scrunched up her face, waiting for it. "How about I drive you?"

"Are you crazy?" Grace boomed. "Listen, Frank—I've a

condition letting you stay in my place and that means staying put."

"It's either that, or I hit the nearest speakeasy and take my chances. Your choice, doll."

"I—you ..."

Grace stammered, then stamped her foot.

"You're impossible!" she cried.

Frank said, "I'll get my coat."

It might not have been Mary Pickford and Douglas Fairbanks' Pickfair, but Joseph March's "little house on the beach" remained a sight to behold. Great marble columns supported the roof over the sprawling front porch, which wrapped around one side of the house and became a path to the enormous swimming pool sparkling within view of the Pacific.

"They build the pools first," Frank said as he pulled the car up on the circular drive. "Then they figure out how much space is left for the house."

"What a spread," Grace said.

Frank stopped the automobile in front of a wide set of six marble steps leading up to the front door, which was festooned with stone grapes on the vine. He whistled and killed the motor.

"Now you be a good boy and sit in the car," she said as she opened the door. "That's what drivers do and you, my friend, are a driver. Just as you said."

"Just as I said," Frank repeated with a knowing grin. "Go on. Get famous."

"I very nearly am," she said, and stepped out of the automobile, resplendent in a white silk gown with ruffled sleeves, a string of pearls, and a rosy-pink cloche hat atop her head.

Grace climbed the steps and was met at the top by a tuxedoed colored man who held open the front door and lowered his eyes when she entered the vestibule. She gave him a sharp nod and walked into a white wonderland of stone and glass, twinkling chandeliers and fresh, fragrant flowers in elegant vases. The door shut behind her and the servant vanished from sight just as Jack Parson materialized and exclaimed, "Grace, my dear!"

Jack appeared more refined than ever in a proper suit and tie, and more astonishing yet, he was grinning ear to ear. He stepped lightly over the marble floor to meet her and embraced his starlet with vigor.

"I feel as though I'm about to marry off my own daughter," he said close to her ear. "A proud papa I am, though. Terribly proud."

"I'm here to meet a director," she said with a small laugh, pulling away from his arms. "No one's brought out the blotter yet, Jack."

"You don't know how thrilled he is—*thrilled*, Gracie—with what he's seen of our picture. And to be perfectly honest, I'm thrilled myself. Now that I've cracked it, I feel more alive than I ever have. I can't believe I ever doubted it. *Angel* will never be topped, not by me, anyhow."

"Why, Jack," she said with batting eyes, "you sound almost … human."

"A heartbreaker is what you are. Come, they're in the projection room."

"Projection room?"

"This house is a monstrosity. Pagodas, a sun deck—a pipe organ! And the swimming pool you saw from the drive is only one of two. Pictures pay, pretty baby. Just you wait."

"I'm sick of waiting. Let's go meet the gang."

"You said it," he said with an arm extended for her to follow. "Come on."

She hooked her arm in his and together they crossed over to the farthest door from the front, their steps echoing hollowly throughout the grand marble vestibule. Behind the door was a narrow hallway that ended at another door. And behind that door was Joseph March's projection room.

Two raised rows of four red chairs faced the doorway, in which three men sat in the dark with white faces reflecting the flickering screen before them.

"Hold it," said one among them. "Hold the picture, I said."

The smoky light emanating from the window above them petered out and the lights came on to fully reveal the movie men. From the trio advanced a short man in a tweed suit who squinted at Grace as he offered her his hand.

"Joseph March," he said. "Damn glad to know you, Ms. Baron."

From March's right, a bald man in round spectacles half-bowed and said, "Alan Rivers. That's some picture you and Jack are putting together. I can't say I completely understand it, not with so much left to do I suppose, but it's a corker."

"We were just discussing your eyes," March explained. "One grows so tired of the Pickford model, the *'Papa, what is beer?'* ingénue. That's out—"

"—Bow and Bara have proven that much," Rivers put in.

"Yes, and Louise Brooks. And bankably, reliably, more to the point. This is an industry, after all, and a businessman likes to know what he's getting himself into."

"Naturally," Grace demurred.

Jack cleared his throat and shifted his weight.

"Our boy Jack mightn't agree," March said with a chuckle. "Yes, now of course we're artists in our way, old boy. Don't pop your collar."

"They're a million miles ahead of us in Europe," said Jack. "The Reds, too."

March straightened up and shot a look at Rivers, who pursed his mouth and cleared his throat.

"The Reds," March said. "Well, we'll get to that."

"We still produce eighty percent of the world's pictures," said Rivers. "Right here in Southern California. There must be a reason for that."

"Of course there is," Jack said. "We can shoot three hundred days a year, fourteen hours a day. You can't do that in Moscow. And the land is cheap as dirt. Any man with a nest egg can start a fledgling studio out here if he's got half a brain."

"That's changing," said the third man, lighting a cigar and bouncing on his heels. "We have a system in place here, and we intend to solidify it in such a way that American pictures aren't being made by every Tom, Dick, and Harry—or *Vladimir*, if you prefer—with access to a motion picture camera."

"Permit me to introduce our favorite distributor," Rivers announced, stepping aside to let Grace and Jack see him fully for the first time. "Joe Sommer."

"Why, Joe!" Grace exclaimed, rushing forward to take his hand. "I didn't know you'd be here today."

"Hullo, Gracie."

"Joe here has a hell of a foothold in the hinterlands," Rivers said to Jack. "He could play *Birth of a Nation* to a theater full of Negroes in Michigan and probably fill every seat."

"I leave the high ideals to fellas like Jack and Joseph here," said Joe, smiling down at Grace. "You make the pictures better, and I'll make sure every townie and hick from here to the Catskills gives 'em a gander—and a dime."

"Now that we're all acquainted," said March with a booming clap of his hands, "I suggest we retire poolside for cocktails and negotiation."

Over a crumpled copy of *Spicy Detective*, Frank chain-smoked in the driver's seat and occasionally glanced up at the white crests of the Pacific barely visible over the slight hill before him. Gulls screamed over the water and a mild breeze picked up, floating pleasantly through the car. Movement to his right caught his attention, and as he tossed his spent end out of the window he glanced over at a well-dressed fivesome settling in a semi-circle on the side porch, overlooking the pool. Fine suits and tuxedoes, big cigars and lifted glasses of cut crystal, toasting the day, their success, the brilliant future. *Angel of the Abyss* and beyond, into permanent memory, beyond even death.

He sighed and dropped the magazine on the seat. He had told a ludicrous pack of lies to Grace, a story concocted straight from the pulp pages he was reading and half a dozen regurgitated gangster shows from the movies. Mexico and heroin and fedora-topped badmen. Frank almost had to laugh. He didn't have it in him.

Sliding down in the seat, he peered over the opposite car door at the merry group, hoping Parson didn't recognize him, and angling to see if he recognized any of the others. Two of the other men were strangers to him, but not Joe Sommer. A sharp intake of breath startled him and he realized it was his own. *The hell is that pig doing here?*

It was rapidly becoming evident that his tall tales of Frank the Mule were soon to crack apart.

"As a veteran imbiber," Joseph March said in lieu of a toast, "I happen to love the Volstead Act. We pickled purveyors of spirits and such have never had it better."

With that he downed his glass of brandy in one go and, groaning with satisfaction, snapped his fingers at the colored servant lingering nearby, who trotted over to refill the director's glass.

"The picture," Rivers said, sipping his in a considerably more gentlemanly fashion.

"Of course," said March. "The business at hand. Never give a producer a second to think you're having a good time, boys."

Rivers shook his head, but smiled.

"Now Lasky runs things different than Veritek, you understand," March began. "Saul's a grand old son, he truly is, but the independents are floundering. It's the majors where you want to be—both of you." He pointed first at Jack, then at Grace. "To an outfit like Saul's, it's about the business, like Ford and his automobiles. That's fine. We think that's about right, too. But as Jack here can tell us, it's about the art of the thing, too. Why, you've got to have something to say, and the right way to say it. To film it. And Christ knows, here in the next year or two, to say it out loud, am I right?"

"And there's a third thing," said Joe Sommer.

"Yes," March went on. "And Joe here brought this to our attention. We want to help change the way people see the pictures. What they're all about. Some of them are all for a laugh, or the wonder of something big. That's entertainment, you understand. Or you take Jack's picture, *Angel of the Abyss*, and that's a little something more, which is jake. It's like looking at a complex painting instead of the Sunday funny papers. Both have their place, and both are fine."

"Let me get to the point," Joe Sommer said, edging forward on his chair. "Before the majors started incorporating out here, this business was spread out all over the country. New York mostly, but there were folks making pictures everyplace from

Dubuque to Mobile, and a great many of them were doing it in a dangerous sort of way."

"Dangerous?" Grace said. "In what way?"

"Let me put it this way," Sommer said. "Another great reason the movies set up so well out here is the weakness of the labor unions. They're disorganized here in Los Angeles, and the state simply hasn't got their back. Other places, the Midwest in particular, that's just not so. Out there, especially in the teens, there were—and still are—a lot of dangerous types churning out little pictures seeking to undermine the way we do business in this country. Red types, if you catch my meaning."

"Like Jack's favorite *ar-teest* in Russia," Rivers jeered.

"There's a socialist fire spreading in a lot of quarters of industry," Sommer said gravely. "Rabble rousers like Debs and Darrow are fanning the flames, and some of the pictures that got a little attention in the last decade and picking up steam in this one. One way to combat that is to control distribution."

"That's where the majors come in," said Rivers.

"Right," Sommer agreed. "They're stringing their own theaters across the country, theaters that show their own productions. But as any good distributor knows, that doesn't quite edge out the smaller outfits, some of which get cajoled into showing these socialist movies, garbage like *A Martyr To His Cause* and *What Is To Be Done*. Pictures that rile people up. Pictures that don't do us here in sunny California any favors when we're trying to build a goddamn empire here, pardon my French."

"We want to make a picture that helps put the old kibosh on that nonsense, Ms. Baron," said March. "A tragi-comedy, if you like. A picture that takes the Sinclair Lewis type, the Clarence Darrow, and exposes them for the frauds they are. A capitalist picture."

"An *American* picture," Rivers said.

Grace finished her drink, sighed, and then let loose a raucous laugh.

"Gentlemen, you're not talking to Elizabeth Stanton here. I'm an actress, always have been, and nothing besides. Politics are swell and all, but I'm only here to make pictures."

"And pictures you shall make, my dear," Joe Sommer said, touching her knee. "This one in particular, we hope. It'll pay you plenty—"

"—get you out of that lousy bungalow for certain," Jack muttered.

"—and boy will it be a sensation," Sommer finished.

Grace held up her glass and March's servant filled it from a decanter before slinking off again. "As we used to say back on the old homestead, let's talk turkey, gents."

"There's just one thing," Rivers announced.

"Spill it."

Rivers looked to Jack, who sucked in a deep breath and sat up straight.

"It's about Frank Faehnrich," said Jack.

"Who?" Grace lied.

Alan Rivers arched an eyebrow at her.

"Why don't you ask your driver to come out of that car and join us, Ms. Baron."

"My driver? Why, I don't—"

"Now Grace," Jack said, leaning close. "You're not in any sort of trouble. Neither of you are. But I know you made nice friends with Frank, and I also know he's gotten himself into a terrible spot with those old pals of his …"

"We want to offer him an opportunity," Joe Sommer said.

"He'll help us, and in return we'll help him right back," said Rivers.

"But … he's an electrician, and only an apprentice one at that. What help could he possibly be?"

"*Electrician*," Sommer scoffed.

"Weren't you there when that red stooge plugged him?" Rivers said bluntly.

"Hey, what is this?" Grace set down her drink, splashing some on the table, and stood up from her chair. "I came here to talk about my career, about making a movie, not Frank Faehnrich."

"We *are* talking about your next picture," Joseph March said. "Please, sit down, Ms. Baron. Let me be more clear."

"You had better. This is much too odd, Mr. March. I don't

like where this has gone in the least."

Jack Parson eased her, forcefully, back down to her chair. She furrowed her brow and waited for an explanation.

"Ms. Baron," Rivers started off, "do you know why your friend Frank was shot at that night?"

She shot a look at Joe Sommer, who said, "It's all right, Gracie. These gentlemen and I want to *help* Frank. I promise we do."

"Why can't you just leave him alone? He's reformed. He doesn't want anything to do with those gangsters anymore."

"Gangsters!" Rivers shouted.

Sommer said, "Is that what he told you?"

"I met them myself. I paid them off to let Frank alone."

"Jesus, Mary, and Joseph," Rivers lamented.

"To be fair," Sommer said, "they're gangsters of a kind, just not the underworld sort. Grace, Frank was a sort of spy, for the labor people. Now we don't know whether or not he intended to sabotage your picture, but he helped set fire to a set last year after the crew tried to organize and hold the studio hostage for higher wages."

"A couple of people died in that fire," March told her. "A woman and a child, a young boy. There was a small house—a shack, really—near to where they were filming, and they got caught in the blaze. Burned to death."

"Because of your pal Frank," Sommer added.

"And that's why…?" she asked, trailing off.

The sun tossed a broad swatch of light across her face as she recalled the gruesome scene from the street that night. The man Frank shot—Petey—had said something about *being in the red*. She had taken that at face value at the time, that Frank owed money just as he eventually said he did, but now she turned the phrase over in her mind. Grace wondered now if it wasn't a sort of pun.

"His cronies ordered him out of town," said Rivers. "He wouldn't go, and he wouldn't stick with them. Got a conscience at the last minute, I suppose. A conscience that was a liability to the men he'd been running around with."

"You mean there were no drugs, no smuggling operation?"

"The closest that boy probably ever got to any drugs is quinine," Sommer said. "He fed you a story, and a ridiculous one from the sound of it."

"And it sounds like his old pals in the labor racket used it to squeeze some funds out of you, too," Rivers added.

"This is crazy," she muttered. "Why, this is the craziest thing I've ever heard."

"It's the truth, Gracie," Sommer told her. "Frank isn't anything more than a union thug, the sort who wants to ruin everything we've worked for out here to make a picture business that the people want. To entertain a troubled country. To make a star out of a little country girl like Grace Baronsky."

Lighting a cigarette with a trembling hand, she turned her head until the car was in her field of vision. Frank remained inside, behind the wheel, though curiously slumped in his seat.

"I don't believe he meant to hurt anyone," said Alan Rivers. "That was an accident, and the reason he got out of it. We want to take that newfound conscience of his to its logical end—we want to put Frank in the picture."

"You're kidding," she said, snapping her head back.

"Not in the least," said March with a grin. "I know he's no actor, but the labor crooks know him, and when they see him make a turnaround, to come around to the right way of thinking right there on the silver screen …"

"You want to make an example out of him."

"In a manner of speaking, yes."

She pinched the bridge of her nose and envisioned herself standing up, walking calmly from there to the automobile in the drive, climbing inside, and telling Frank to get them both the hell out of there. Which, she instantly knew, would signal the end of her career in pictures before it ever got the chance to start. Her first picture still unfinished, she'd never make another. The boozy businessmen around her would undoubtedly turn the tables on Frank, turn him in for his part in the set fire. She could go with him, back to Idaho or further still—she'd already changed her name once, why not again? Go back into the vaudeville circuit. He could be her manager. Grow a beard, perhaps. Never set foot in California again …

But he lied to her. Took advantage of her charity, her friendship. All the while a red thug who sought to destroy the very thing she loved most, needed most. Her very livelihood, her dreams, her destiny.

*Petey crumpled on the street, soaking the ground with blood …*

*The knife in Billy Francis' gut, leaking blood …*

*Blood on the Odessa steps …*

*Blood, blood, blood …*

Grace emitted a small sound as she stood up again, the cigarette falling from her fingers. She didn't notice.

"What about the other men?" she said breathlessly. "The ones I paid off? They said they'd kill him if he didn't leave town."

"That's the beauty of it," Rivers answered, picking up her smoke and tamping it out in the ashtray. "I know the Assistant D.A. personally. All Frank has to do is write down their names and they'll never be able to touch him. They'll be too busy pacing in their cells."

"You'd do that for him?"

"If he agrees to our terms, absolutely."

"Go get him, Gracie," Sommer said, gently. "Everybody wins."

She paused, stalling. Joe Sommer grinned up at her. Rivers checked his wristwatch.

"All right," she said at length. "All right."

With a deep breath she left the four men on the veranda and went 'round the house, to the front, where she descended the marble steps to the drive. Frank peered up at her from his slumped position behind the steering wheel. When she was near enough, he hissed, "What in god's name is going on over there, Grace?"

"A meeting," she said. "And they want to talk to you."

"Christ," he growled. "Come on, get in. We've got to go."

"It's not like that, Frank. They want to help you. They told me everything. I'm sore, I won't lie to you, but it's going to work in everyone's favor, including yours."

"Do you even know who Joe Sommer is?" he shot back. "That muckamuck—that goddamn fink."

"He happens to be a friend of my aunt's, if you must know …"

"He's a strike-breaker, or used to be. Cracked skulls for some of the production outfits when the crews wouldn't work. Got on swell with those boys, protecting the profits and all. Guess now he rides high with the tuxedo brigade."

"God, Frank—none of that means a thing to me. I'm just trying to help you, and so are they, Joe included. They want to offer you a chance to dig yourself out of this grave you got yourself into."

"Grave nothing. I believed in worker's rights at one time. In fact, I still do, just not the way we were doing it. I care a lot about pictures, Grace, which is why I wanted to see them work the way every industry ought to work. And this one so new, it had a chance, but that chance is shot. It's lost. I'm done with all that, but a guy like Joe Sommer wouldn't ever let me forget it. A better company man never lived, and he's got it out for the little man and baby, I'm as little as they come."

"You're not so small," she said. "And besides, all they want to do is talk. I can't say it isn't a strange proposition, but it's sure an interesting one."

"I've heard a lot of propositions from finks like Sommer. I don't want to hear another one. I'll be straight with you, Grace—get in or don't, but I'm leaving and I mean right now."

She stood still as a statue, her face without expression. Behind her, the men on the veranda watched in silence.

"They're using you," Frank said. "Or at least trying to. Can't you see that? They couldn't care less what happens to you. There's always another girl with feet just as bloody as yours from the circuit stages to take your place."

"That's some cynical way to look at things," she said.

"You should try it," he replied. "Open your eyes a little. See what's going on around you. You're a commodity. I'm the enemy. Nobody has our best interests in mind but ourselves, and it's about time you realized that. Now are you coming or shall I leave the car in front of your place?"

"You lied to me," she said sharply.

"I thought I had to. To protect you."

"From what?"

"From thinking the wrong thing about me."

"I think the right thing now. And it's still wrong."

Frank narrowed his eyes and started the motor. The automobile shuddered, rumbled to life. Back at the house, Joe Sommer stood up quickly.

"It's time, Grace," Frank said.

She reached in through the window, retrieved her bag on the backseat, and turned back for the veranda. While she climbed back up the steps, the car rolled away, sputtering into the distance as Frank drove.

Joe came running toward her, panting, "What happened?"

"He rejected your offer," she said matter-of-factly as she rejoined the group. "I, however, would like to do what I came here to do: talk about my next picture."

# 25.

## L.A., 2013.

"The solution," Lou said over coffee across Fairfax from the ATM, "is as fucking easy as A-B-C, my friend."

"Let's hear it," I said.

"We make a withdrawal. A *big* one."

"You mean steal Helen's money?"

"Temporarily. Most banks only let you take so much out at a time, and there's no way we can con a teller into giving us anything, so my plan is to hit as many ATMs as we can in as short a time as possible and take out the maximum every fucking time."

"Okay, so we start a rip-off spree until the bank catches on and freezes the account …"

"Exactly."

"Maybe—*maybe*—get, what? A few thousand bucks?"

"If we're lucky."

"And then what?"

"Wait."

"Wait?"

"Fucking wait."

"For what?"

"For her—or *somebody*—to come to us."

"Brilliant."

Lou brightened. "You think so?"

"No," I said. "I don't think so. I think it's stupid. And probably dangerous."

"Since when was any of this not dangerous?"

"You have a point, but I still don't see the use. There's three quarters of a mil in that account. Who's going to notice a couple thousand right away?"

"Whoever has access to the account. The bank is going to call them and fucking quick. 'Somebody's jacked your card and they're stealing your fucking funds, bitch.'"

"I'm sure that will be their words exactly."

"I'm serious, Jake. If it's Helen's money, she'll get the call and want to find out what the fuck's going on."

"And if it's somebody else's?"

"Same deal, and hopefully they'll lead us to her."

"And what do we do, advertise in the *LA Weekly*?"

"That would take too long," she said, completely missing my sarcasm.

A chick from Lou's school of fashion came around to ask if we wanted another round of joe. Lou said we did, and a pair of crullers to match.

"It's on him," she added, gesturing towards me.

"I'm not rich, you know," I said as the waitress sauntered off.

"Here's an idea," Lou said, ignoring that. "We only know of two places that Helen is associated with, right?"

"The apartment and Ray's office."

"Right."

"But she doesn't live there anymore and Ray fired her."

"Oh," Lou said. "Right."

The coffee and crullers came, and after the waitress vanished again I said, "Okay, let me go back to the beginning here. Here's what we know: when Helen was working at the theater, she met Leslie Wheeler and got well enough acquainted with her to suggest Graham for the *Angel* restoration."

"Yep."

"Graham—and I—came out here for that, whereupon Leslie ended up dead, Helen missing, and Graham shot at twice, the second time successfully, or semi-successfully."

"Don't forget that other lady, too."

"Yeah, Florence Sommer. Also dead."

"That's pretty much everybody involved in this clusterfuck except one ..."

"The Wheeler lady's friend."

"Right. Barbara Tilitson."

"So how does she figure in?"

"I don't know, but I can't think of anything else to go on. Assuming she hasn't been knocked off too, I say we look in her direction."

"And forget about the money?"

"I'm not sure that has anything to do with this yet, but I wouldn't discount it. I'm suggesting a bit of both plans—we make the withdrawals like you said, then track down this Tilitson woman and see if anything comes together."

"Vague hunch, Kojak."

"You got something better?"

She took a huge bite of her cruller and shrugged.

With her mouth full, she said, "Let's make it happen, Cap'n."

We were locked out after our third withdrawal. Each ATM yielded a max of three hundred, so we managed nine hundred before our fourth attempt went south. The screen politely informed us that the account was unavailable, pending inquiries, and to contact the branch manager as soon as possible. The fact that each machine came equipped with a surveillance camera that transmitted our pictures back to whatever security agency the bank used was on my mind, but the least of my worries. We took the nine Cs and went directly back to Hollywood, to the office of the Silent Film Appreciation Society where this whole shindig got underway.

And there, we found Barbara Tilitson, who was three sheets to the wind, which is to say piss drunk.

The office was mostly picked up from the last time I saw it, with Graham, and the yellow police tape was gone, informing me that the cops were done with the place. We found the door open a crack and when I knocked, Barbara hollered something unintelligible that I choose to interpret as an invitation to come inside. So we went inside. And there was that nice old tea-sipping lady sitting on the floor with her legs splayed and a mostly empty bottle of crème de menthe between them.

"We're not open," she slurred, "but if you've got something

to drink you're welcome to join me."

"You're in a state," Lou said.

"And you've got metal in your face," Barbara came back with a throaty laugh. "Sit down. Get a cup from the kitchen or drink straight from the bottle, I don't care."

"Do you remember me, Ms. Tilitson?" I tried.

"Sure, sure," she said. "That boy from Boston."

"One of 'em. I'm Jake."

"Sure, Jake. And Graham? The other one's Graham."

"That's right. He's in the hospital. In a bad way, actually. He was shot in the head, Ms. Tilitson."

Her eyebrows shot up near her hairline, though her eyelids remained drunkenly droopy.

"Oh, oh, my. That was bound to happen, I expect. Yes, that was bound to happen."

Lou said, "Why do you say that?"

Barbara Tilitson chuckled darkly.

"When you kick a tiger in the balls, it's bound to bite you, sweetheart."

I felt my neck get hot and struggled to contain myself. "What tiger, Ms. Tilitson?"

"Oh for Christ's sake, call me Barbara. I'm not your *grandmother* …"

"Fine," I said. "Barbara. What tiger are we talking about here?"

"'Tiger, tiger, burning bright,'" she recited, "'in the forests of the night …'"

Lou moved for the kitchenette, said, "I'll make some coffee."

"Better Irish that up, dear," Barbara said.

I thought, *This is going to be a long night.*

Barbara insisted on finishing her crème de menthe before she'd touch the coffee Lou made. Neither of us argued. After we managed to get a couple cups in her, she lolled on the chair Leslie Wheeler died in, looking gray and defeated. After a while she drowsed for thirty or forty-five minutes and we let her. When she came back to, she seemed more than a little confused that we were there. I poured her another cup and Lou started some oatmeal she found in the cupboard to fill the old gal's stomach.

"Lord, I never do this," Barbara mewled after a few bites of the oatmeal. "The bottle was just there, a celebratory sort of thing. I'm sure Leslie must have bought it. I never go in liquor stores, god knows."

"No judgment here," Lou assured her.

"I don't even … I don't even know what day it is," Barbara said with a choked laugh. The laughter descended quickly into small, heaving sobs. I was paralyzed. Lou hurried to her side and held her close. I was terribly grateful and not a little impressed.

I stayed quiet and still, waiting for Barbara to calm down a bit. There were a couple of near-misses, but she eventually stopped crying and wiped her eyes on the sleeve of her sweater. She then took a deep breath and said evenly, "I just miss her so much."

"I know," Lou said. I was dumbstruck by how genuinely sweet she was being. With me it was all toughness and swear words. I decided it wasn't the mystery I was going to solve this time out.

"Barbara, what did you mean when you said Graham was bound to be shot?"

Her face flushed. "Oh," she said, "I did say that, didn't I?"

"We're just trying to get to the bottom of this," Lou told her, pulling her in for a sideways hug on the chair. "Before anybody else gets hurt."

"Good god," Barbara said, shaking her head. "We were just so excited, finding that reel. Leslie and I, I mean. I'd never had imagined in a hundred years all the trouble it's brought. She might have, but not me."

"Why?" I asked. "What did Leslie know that would make her think that?"

"That woman …"

"Who? What woman?"

"That awful old …" She cut herself off before she was forced to swear again. Quite the contrast with Lou, I realized.

And it was Lou who got the lightbulb over her head. She said, "Wait—didn't that kid at the theater say something about an old woman? He thought she might'a been Helen's grandma, remember?"

I hadn't made anything of that. But Lou tucked it away, the clever girl.

"I didn't tell the police," Barbara went on, stretching it out painfully. "I suppose I'll get in trouble for that. But Leslie, my dear Leslie ... she didn't want anyone to know."

"Know *what*, Barbara?"

She wrinkled her nose and covered her mouth. I was losing what little patience I had left. I said, "Look, we've been running all over the county trying to find Graham's ex-wife, thinking she might lead us to the end of this bullshit, and you're dangling the carrot right in front of us."

"I'm starting to think we wasted our time taking that damn money," Lou said.

"Money?" Barbara said, looking up with wet eyes at Lou. "What money?"

"Helen Bryan's money—that's Graham's ex. It's kind of a complicated mess, didn't really go anywhere ..."

"Oh, no," Barbara whispered. "Oh, Jesus ... you didn't."

"It's not like we robbed her," Lou said in defense. "The idea was to lure her out, like."

"Listen to me," Barbara said between harsh breaths, "Helen Bryan is probably dead by now. That's how she works, how that terrible ... listen to me. That isn't her money. It belongs to some people, awful people, and when they find out you've taken it—"

"Wait a minute," I barked. "What the hell do you mean, Helen's dead? How would you even know that?"

"Leslie shouldn't have involved her. She shouldn't have involved any of you."

"Hey, I'm just along for the ride," Lou said.

Barbara was getting manic, starting to hyperventilate. I wondered if I should look for a paper bag she could breathe into—wasn't that what you're supposed to do?—when a thin, papery voice startled me from behind.

"Ah, you must be the two who went around town stealing from me this evening."

Barbara muttered, "Mrs. Parson ..."

I turned around quickly to see an old woman, deeply wrinkled and white as a sheet, her silver hair done up in a large old-fashioned bun. She was leaning on one of those canes with four legs and peering through hazy gray eyes. I guessed she was pushing eighty and there were a pair of mean looking dudes flanking her right and left.

The old woman rasped, "Did you put these hoodlums up to it, Barbara?"

Barbara could only stare. The woman hissed a weak laugh.

"How about this one?" she asked, waggling an arthritic finger at Lou. "Your new conquest, I suppose? A bit young for you, isn't she? But I don't suppose your kind have much in the way of limits."

"Watch it," I growled at her. I wasn't above putting an elderly homophobe in her place, never mind the heavies she brought with her. That is, until the one on her left moved his jacket to show me the gun in his waistband.

Lou stood up slowly and showed her palms. I wished she hadn't. I remembered the little pistol in her purse, but I guessed the shock of the moment made her forget. She'd been hell bent for leather to do some damage that night, but now was when we really needed her verve.

"Barbara didn't have anything to do with it," she said calmly. "We're just trying to find a friend, not steal anything."

I balked at her use of the term "friend," not to mention at the fact that these were very likely the people who killed Helen, if what Barbara said was true. But I stayed quiet, frozen. And I wondered if I'd survive a bullet to the dome the same way Graham had. Maybe they'd put me in the next bed over and we could be coma buddies. It almost sounded relaxing.

Lou dug out the money, nine hundred-dollar bills, and reached it out as far as she could without stepping forward.

"Take it," she said. "It was a stupid fucking idea, anyway."

"It certainly was," the woman Barbara called Mrs. Parson said. Then: "David."

The guy with the gun had it out of his pants and aimed across the room quicker than my eye could follow. It was sleek and silver and it looked heavy, especially when it kicked and belched fire, sending a bullet spinning inches from my shoulder and directly into Lou's chest. She made a high-pitched squealing sound, like a kitten, and bared her teeth as she spun awkwardly toward Barbara. The money went flying, fluttering like nine tiny green kites in the smoky air between her and the gunman.

If I expected a lot of blood, I was surprised not to see any at all. Just a small black hole in her top, right between her breasts, which she touched with a look of sad astonishment as she collapsed on top of Barbara. I think I must have yelled. I *heard* a yell, and my throat felt raw, but everything seemed to be happening apart from me, like an out of body experience. Barbara was crying again and the gun was still out, though the other man was now helping the old woman out of the office and into the shadows of the musty hallway. She called back, "Take care of it, David. Make sure."

Lou was down and Barbara was more or less incapacitated, so the barrel bore down on me next. In that fraction of a second it occurred to me that for Graham to have survived a gunshot to the head was so statistically improbable it ranked as miraculous. There just wasn't any way that was going to happen twice in a row, probably from the same gun. So I went limp the way kids do sometimes when you pick them up, like a marionette whose puppeteer dropped the strings, and fell to the floor the moment David squeezed the trigger. Glass shattered behind me at the same time the gun barked, one of those framed movie posters they had on the walls, and I rolled away from it, toward David's legs. The gun followed my movement. I bit down on his ankle as hard as I could. He roared and the gun went up. He fired it at the ceiling. I hoped no one above us caught the bullet and reached up to grab the bastard's beanbag, which I squeezed as hard as I was biting the ankle.

The gun clattered to the floor. David's fist crashed down on the crown of my head and fireworks exploded in my brain. I released his balls but bit down harder still. He screamed and grabbed a handful of my shirt, lifted me off the ground. Next thing there was another shot and I squeezed my eyes shut, certain beyond a doubt that I'd caught a bullet and just didn't feel it yet. I gave a good fight. Did the best I could. I was only sorry I never really found Helen for Graham and that Barbara was probably the next to go.

You can't win all the time.

What a goddamned clusterfuck.

I opened my eyes and waited for the pain or, failing that, the end. Instead David fell into a heap beside me and lay still. His hair was a matted mess dribbling red. A few feet away, Barbara Tilitson stood trembling with the dead man's pistol shaking in both hands. Her eyes streamed tears and her mouth jabbered silently, senselessly.

Behind her, bent over the Queen Anne chair, Lou said, "Oh, fuck."

I scrambled for the phone and dialed 911.

Looked to me like Lou's idea about withdrawing the money worked, to an extent. And to enormous cost, too.

She was still swearing at the paramedics when they rushed in to work on her. They tried to look at my head too, but I brushed them off. Lou was loaded up on a gurney and taken downstairs to the ambulance waiting in the street with dizzying lights.

She was dead before she reached the hospital.

I was weeping like a baby when I found out, sitting in the sterile waiting room with a bevy of cops around me. The police were not moved by my feelings and started into me right away. I said I wanted a lawyer and that I wanted to talk to Detective Shea. As luck had it, he was already in the hospital. When he finally made it down to see me, I learned why.

"Your buddy's awake," he told me. "Lucky son of a bitch. He's going to be all right."

I sighed with relief, but I was still crying. Poor Lou. I never bought her story about why she did it, why she came along with me. I never was going to find out. One last adventure for a lost soul, I guessed. It was going to have to do.

"What about the guy who killed Louise?" I asked.

"Dead, but I guess you knew that. It's quite a trail of bodies you and your pal leave behind you, isn't it?"

"And all over a damn silent movie."

"About that," Shea said, fishing a pair of reading glasses

out of his shirt pocket and putting them on. He squinted at his notepad and continued, "I've been digging around a lot, looking into that movie. The Internet's a hell of a thing, don't know how we ever got by without it."

I raised my brows and waited for him to get to the point.

He said, "You're the movie buff. Ever heard of Jack Parson?"

"No," I said. "That old stuff is Graham's department. Bores me to tears."

"He's the fella who directed your *Angel of the Abyss* back in the day. Turns out his son was a bigwig in the biz, too. Bigger than his old man. Exec type, money guy. Made a run for Congress, lost by a wide margin."

"I don't know any of this, detective."

"Well, Junior's gone to his reward, too, but he married a young woman who appears to still be kicking around, though she's older than dirt now if she is. Name of Cora. But it looks like you wouldn't know about her, either."

I swallowed hard. "Holy shit."

"Something coming to mind?"

"The old woman …"

"Mrs. Tilitson said something about an old woman. She's pretty out of it, though. What was she talking about?"

"Jesus—the guy who shot Louise, the one Barbara killed— he came with another guy and an old woman. And Barbara *knew* her. She called her Mrs. Parson."

Detective Shea cocked his head to one side and said, "And Bingo was his name-o."

# PART THREE

## GRAHAM

# 26.

## HOLLYWOOD, 1926.

Saul Veritek's heart attack happened on a Sunday. The press reported he was home alone at the time, preparing for bed, when the attack struck. People in the know were well aware that he was in the company of a pair of aspiring actresses, without whom he would never have survived. All of this information came to Grace's ears that Monday morning, when she arrived at the lot for the day's shooting. Someone suggested a moment of silent prayer for Saul's full recovery, and though few likely prayed in earnest, everyone remained quiet for a few minutes before Jack took up his bullhorn to address the company.

"We will continue our work," he told the sullen group of two dozen cast and crew. "Saul would have another heart attack if he thought we were wasting time here. There are only about twenty-five pages left to film, and I think we can do it before the end of the week. In fact, I know we can, and we will. That's all. Let's get to work."

He set the bullhorn on his chair and ran his fingers through his hair. Grace approached, script in hand. He smiled awkwardly, and she wondered if it was her imagination or if he looked a little jittery.

"I'd like to tell you I'm sorry for that mess at March's," he said, sounding genuine. "You know I hadn't any horse in that race, I just wanted to help facilitate your next step."

"No Frank, no deal," she said with a half-hearted shrug. "That's no kind of picture I want to work on, anyhow. All it amounts to is a wasted afternoon."

"I don't suppose you've heard from the old red himself?"

"No, and I'd tell you if I had. After March's driver took me home, my car was waiting right there in front, just like Frank said it would be. My guess is he finally skipped town. That Joe Sommer seems to have it out for him and bad."

"Joe's a bit of a bulldog, all right. Used to be a Pinkerton man, way I hear it. Helped the major studios get their footing out here, away from all that labor craziness back east."

"Well, I won't be used—not by Joe, Frank, or anybody else. I'll make the pictures I want to make, the right kind, and not so some red chaser can make a point to people I don't even know."

"That's fair enough, Grace," said Jack.

She maintained a hard face, a face designed to express her general distaste for liars and conmen, despite the hurt Frank had caused her. In all the time Grace had spent in Los Angeles she had yet to find a single person she could honestly call a friend. Not a colleague, not someone who could help propel her career or who wanted her to lift up theirs, but a sincere human connection. For a time she thought Frank was going to be that person. Now that she knew different, the sting of disappointment was difficult to mask.

"Say, Jack," she said, eager to get off the subject of Frank Faehnrich. "Before we get started, a question about your little speech a moment ago."

"What's that?"

She flipped through the dog-eared script in her hands, knitting her brow at the dull blue mimeographed pages. "You said we've got twenty-five more pages to shoot. By my count there are only nineteen."

"That's because I mean to do a little re-shooting. Not much, just a few scenes I wasn't happy with when we were looking them over in March's projection room."

"Oh? Which scenes?"

Jack laughed softly and tussled her hair. "Don't worry, we'll get around to it. Keep your mind on Billy Goat Gruff over there for now, will you?"

He stabbed his thumb at the graveyard set, where Bob

Scaife was being fitted with a grotesque goat's head. Grace gritted her teeth.

*Living death, for Clara, does not come cheap. She may roam the earth, and she may seek her vengeance, but not for free. The same entity to whom she was sacrificed demands recompense for her second iteration, the New Clara, and for this she must now return to the scene of her death, and the scene of her resurrection.*

*And there, among the moldering tombstones and iron fence posts encrusted with verdigris, he waits—a towering figure with arms outspread from the billowing sleeves of his cloak and massive horns coiled atop its shaggy head. She draws nearer to him, her bare legs swept with lazy mist, and the moonlight reveals the beast's awful face, the face of a goat with grinning teeth and soulless black slits for pupils.*

Intertitle: "Two more!"

*The goatman beckons to the sepulchral bed, to consummate their unholy union, and Clara, sneering, slips free from her burial gown and complies …*

Much of the cast and crew—Rob Scaife, the goatman, included—planned to descend en masse upon Saul in his hospital room after the day's filming. Grace needed no time to decide upon a round of drinks at the nearest blind pig instead. She waved off her driver in the lot, hitched the strap of her bag over her shoulder, and walked the quarter mile to Anthony's, which was reputed to be run by a Chicago syndicate man snaking his fingers into Los Angeles. But the booze was no bathtub moonshine to give anyone seizures and the place never got raided, so who was Grace to complain?

She found a nice dark table in the back and ordered a waitress to set them up—a glass of beer, a shot of whiskey, and a cup of hot, black coffee to keep the motor running. The round came back in good time, and Grace dumped the whiskey down with the sharp image of Jack Parson's leering look as she writhed beneath the Satanic figure of his goatman.

"Hold on a minute," she gasped at the waitress with her first post-hooch breath. "Another one of those."

The girl nodded and went back for the bar. Grace started in on her beer and closed her eyes, trying in vain to think of anything apart from the awkward humiliation of that dreadful scene. She'd known it was coming, she'd read the pages weeks ago. But she'd also dreaded it all those weeks, and now that it was done she wondered how Jack would ever get it past the censors, what theaters would dare book a picture like that. And worse still, what studio would stoop to hire the girl who fucked the devil in *Angel of the Abyss*.

"Thanks," she said to the waitress upon delivery of another whiskey. It went down as quickly as the first one and the girl vanished before Grace could request yet a third. It didn't matter. She was feeling it, the burn in her breast and the slowly approaching fog in her brain. She nursed the beer and the coffee in equal measure, bought a package of Chesterfields from the cigarette girl, and watched a mixed-race band starting to set up on a stage barely big enough to hold them and their instruments. By the time the waitress finally returned, she pointed to each empty vessel and said, "And how about a pencil and something to write on, huh?"

# 27.

## L.A., 2013.

"An individual's chances of surviving a thing like this depends upon a number of variables," the doctor said, his voice even and without much inflection. "It depends on where in the brain the point of impact is, which part of the brain is affected. Also the velocity of the bullet is key, as is whether or not the bullet then exits the brain or stays inside, even in fragments. You lucked out on all counts, Mr. Woodard."

"Except for the part where he got shot in the head," Jake said. He was sitting on an unoccupied hospital bed beside me, listening intently. I was surprised he was still in Los Angeles, much less there in the hospital. But I didn't yet know how long I'd been out.

It was only a couple of days. I'd been awake for most of a third.

One of my eyes was still swollen and my vision was hazy, like I was drunk. Equally impaired were my motor skills and speech. Inside my brain everything seemed fine, but my body and mouth were slow to get the message.

"In your case," the doctor continued, "your recovery is going to rely much more on physical therapy than the surgery. Your speech is slurred, and your right side appears mildly impaired."

Almost instinctively I tried to make a fist with my right hand. All I managed to do was smash my fingers together in a weak lobster claw imitation.

"Now whether or not you feel up to speaking with the police is your decision, Mr. Woodard. I've given it my okay, provided that it's brief and not too stressful. But if you feel the need for more time—more rest, really—then that is what I'll tell him."

"Shea?" I asked. It sounded like *Thay.*

"That's the detective, yes."

Jake leaned forward. "He wants to see if the guys who shot you are the same ones who came after us."

"Us?" I wondered aloud.

"Long story, but I'll fill you in."

I blinked my good eye and swallowed, or tried to. My throat felt like it was coated with wax paper.

"I'll talk to him," I said.

"You're sure?"

I nodded. The doctor left and Jake stood up, patted me gently on the shoulder. He said, "This is going to be the best drinking story you ever had."

"I get all the best breaks," I said.

"Listen," he said, "I'm just glad you're going to be all right."

Shea came in then, tugging at his lower lip. His shirt was untucked and he hadn't shaved in a day or two. All things considered, I didn't feel too sorry for him.

"How are you feeling, Graham?"

I gave a thumbs up. I was being sarcastic, but he didn't seem to catch on.

"Mind if I talk to you for a few minutes?"

"No," I said.

He sat down where Jake had been. Jake remained standing beside me as though he was my defense attorney or something. His protectiveness was more than a little baffling to me, but I tried to keep my focus on the cop.

"I'll try to make this as quick as I can," he began. "How many individuals attacked you?"

"Three."

"All men? Were any of them women?"

"Men," I said.

"No Mrs. Parson," Jake cut in.

Shea shot him a look. "Mr. Maitland …"

"Sorry."

To me, Shea asked, "Can you describe these men?"

I took in a slow breath, thinking it over. "Ordinary," I said. "White guys. 30s, maybe early 40s. Dressed sort of casual preppy. Polo shirts, suit jackets."

"Any names?"

"No."

"David doesn't ring a bell?"

"No."

"Ever heard of Cora Parson?"

"No, who's that?"

"I'll get to it. What else about these guys? Identifying marks—scars or tattoos?"

"Don't think so. One of them cut Florence Sommer's throat." I groaned, remembering it. All that blood. "Right in front of me."

"What did they say to you?"

"Not much. They were ready to do it. Just kill us, her and me both."

"Well, they can't get to you in here. You're perfectly safe now, don't worry about that."

I said, "Thank you."

A nurse floated in silent as a ghost and got to futzing with the wires stuck to me and the machine they led to. I mostly ignored her. She did us the same favor.

"Now Mr. Maitland describes his assailant as a man named David, about five foot ten, with a stocky build and short, salt-and-pepper hair."

Jake nodded, said, "Also a big fucking hole in his skull, but he wouldn't have had that if you saw him."

I tried to make a face, but all I really did was drool a little. The nurse wiped my chin.

"Could be," I said. "Yeah, one of 'em."

"The one who shot you?"

I thought about it, though I really didn't want to. I was only conscious for a few seconds after the bullet struck, it all happened lightning fast—but in those seconds I knew for a fact that I was about to die. I saw the guy's face all right, a stoic expression to put Harold Lloyd to shame, but the moment he fired his gun all I was concerned with was the tiny projectile ending my life right then and there. It's a mind-fuck, dying like that and coming back when you never expected to.

"I think so," I told Shea. The shooter was the stocky one, all right. And neither of the other guys had salt-and-pepper hair. *David.* Such an innocuous name for a cold-blooded murderer.

Shea made some notes on his little pad and said, "Okay. All right. Thank you, Graham. I'm sorry to bust your chops at a time like this."

He then stood and turned to face Jake.

"As for you, Mr. Maitland—no more Junior Detective bullshit, you hear me? I appreciate your willingness to help your buddy and I'm sure he does, too, but there's a reason for police departments."

At that moment Jake's normally smug face sank into a deep, sorrowful frown. I'd never seen him like that and it startled me a little. The detective slapped him lightly on the arm and started for the door. Jake followed him out, and in the hallway muttered something I couldn't clearly hear, though I was certain I heard my ex-wife's name. He returned to the room after that, and I kept my one seeing eye on him as he rounded my bed.

"The hell was that about?" I slurred.

The nurse straightened up and told Jake he was going to have to let me get some rest.

"Just a minute," Jake pleaded. "Please."

She sighed and left us alone for the moment. Jake sat down on the side of my bed and put his hand on my knee.

And he caught me up.

Sleep was temperamental that night, and when it did come it was fraught with nightmares. Nightmares about this David bastard, about being shot over and over. Nightmares about a girl I never met named Louise, who didn't fare as well as me. And nightmares about Helen, appearing in my hospital room in the night, telling me she'd never see me again in the same words I once said to her, but with a terribly different meaning—and consequence. At one point my heart rate spiked and a crew of technicians rushed into the room to check on me. For my trouble I was given a sedative and a juice box. Apple. My least favorite of the fruit juice family.

When I was alone again I remained awake for a long while. Footsteps and muted voices filled the hall outside my shut door. I stared at the soft white glow of the curtained window and thought about everything Jake told me, about four dead women and almost a million dollars and an old woman with a direct, living connection to Grace Baron's movie.

As for the movie, or what was left of it, Jake said the police intended to impound the reels we found for evidence. I wished I could watch them again, watch more closely for anything I might have missed. And I was seriously nervous about how a bunch of unskilled people were going to handle the nitrate stock, which I'd never had the opportunity to digitize, much less restore. Moreover, it nagged at my brain—you know, the one a bullet passed through?—that Florence Sommer's father had most, but not *all*, of the film's reels. It seemed to me the rest had to be somewhere. And if the late Mr. Sommer was less careful with how he stored some than others, perhaps the ones still missing would offer some insight into what this horror show was really all about.

If only I had the slightest clue as to where they might be.

# 28.

## HOLLYWOOD, 1926.

Grace slept with no dreams at all.

When in the morning the telephone jangled, she came awake with a start and grumbled, "Damn it, Saul." Her skull felt too small for its contents and the sunlight spilling through the slats of the blinds stung her eyes.

She ignored the telephone as she always did, but as the hard hooch-induced sleep melted agonizingly away, she recalled that Saul was in the hospital still. Reaching for the watch on the nightstand she checked the time and saw that she was terribly late for the day's work.

Then the sunlight disappeared all at once and darkness was restored to the bungalow. She blinked and wondered had she misread the time? Or had her watch stopped? She'd thought it read two o'clock.

The telephone fell silent and the horn of an automobile sounded outside. Grace sat up and squinted at the window when the glaring white light reappeared, forcing her to squeeze her eyes shut and look away. It hadn't been sunlight at all. It was the headlamps of the automobile with the blaring horn.

It was two o'clock in the morning.

She pulled the sheet up to her chin and waited, listening to her own breath.

The engine rumbled, and the headlights swept the bungalow before vanishing altogether. The automobile sputtered away, its chugging noise diminishing to silence.

Grace sat still for half an hour, her knees pressed against her breasts. And she stayed awake until her driver arrived to take her to work.

# 29.

## L.A., 2013.

My second day post-resurrection Jake returned to visit me. He told me he was heading back to Boston first thing in the morning. I didn't blame him, and I told him as much.

"I never invited you out here in the first place," I said, only half-joking.

"I'm not sure if I'm glad I came or not," he said. He'd been uncharacteristically sad and introspective since my return to the land of the living. I couldn't blame him for that either, considering what had happened. We had both watched helplessly as women were murdered before our eyes. Well, me more helpless than him—Jake and Barbara took the bastard down. All I did was catch a bullet with my head.

After a slow moment of quiet, I said, "Do you really think Helen's gone?"

The truth was I hadn't given the question anywhere near as much consideration as I should have. I pinned it on my injury, on the trauma of my experience. I didn't need to think about it, so I didn't. But that didn't push it out of my mind. For all the anger and near-hatred I felt for my ex-wife, the thought that she might really be dead tore me up inside. Nothing could take away the years we spent together, for better or for worse, despite it being mostly for the worst. Even if I didn't know exactly how I was supposed to feel about something like that, what I felt was deep sorrow.

"I don't know," Jake said, staring at the floor. "Coming from that old psycho, who can tell?"

"Jack Parson's daughter-in-law," I said, thinking aloud.

"At least something finally ties it all together. This shitshow and that goddamn movie, I mean."

I tried to relax, despite the pain in my head and the pit in my stomach. It didn't take. I made a fist with my left hand and squeezed it tight. My right just twitched.

I said, "I need to get out of here."

"You got shot, Graham."

"This isn't over."

"For you it is. You're safe here. There's a cop right outside the door. It's a miracle you're even alive, not to mention not drooling all over the place and crapping your pants. You're the luckiest son of a bitch ever got shot in the head, and now you're acting like you're sorry you didn't get killed."

"Maybe I am," I moped.

Jake's face darkened and his jaw twitched.

"Fuck you," he said. "Fuck you, Graham. I saw a girl die because of this. You saw Mrs. Sommer get her throat cut. A shitload of people are already fucking dead but you—you made it. I made it, too. Neither of us should ever have come out here in the first place and by all rights we should both be dead but we aren't. So *fuck* you. I'm going home, and as soon as they let you leave—*let* you leave, you selfish prick—so are you."

He was breathing hard after that and staring me down. I didn't say anything. I didn't know *what* to say. I might have apologized, told him he was right, but he left after that. The sentry in the hall wished him a good afternoon. Jake just grunted and then he was gone.

The most excruciatingly long days of my life dragged by in Jake's wake. I didn't hear a word from him, but I took him at his word and assumed he went back east. Shea dropped around once, but only to tell me there was nothing new to tell me. Helen was still classified as a missing person. I couldn't help but make the connection to Grace Baron—another missing person, and one who was never found. The connection made my stomach churn.

As for Cora Parson, she too was missing, in a way. Which is

to say David's botched triple murder had likely driven her into hiding.

"The woman is seventy-seven years old," Shea told me. "One doesn't imagine she's gone very far."

"Olivia de Havilland is almost a hundred and still makes appearances," I said.

Shea just raised one eyebrow. I didn't bother explaining.

"Look," he said, "in a couple of weeks you'll be out of this bed and into physical therapy, hopefully in Boston. Where you belong. By then we should have caught up with this woman and I'll personally phone you to tell you all about it. Until then, if something happens, you'll be among the first to know. So just get your rest, eat your lousy hospital food, and continue sitting this one out, Ms. Marple."

That last bit he said with a smile. He was not an unkind man, for all his bluster and subterfuge. I smiled back, though mostly on the left side.

"10-4, chief," I said.

I snuck out of the place the next night.

It was nowhere near the great escape I initially imagined, however. I waited for my police protection to waddle off for a cup of coffee and simply walked out of the room, down the hall, and into the first open room I found. Inside it, a man I judged to be about my size was snoring loudly in his bed with the wall-mounted television on. I rooted through a drawer across from the bed while Richard Boone swaggered on an episode of *Have Gun, Will Travel*. One blue tee shirt, a pair of shorts, and a couple of flip-flops later, I waltzed right back into the hall and took the elevator down to the lobby. Anywhere else the bandages cocooning my head might have drawn stares, but here I looked more or less in place. There was a different cop hanging around the front desk. He nodded to me on my way out. I gave him a weak salute.

At the end of the circular drive in front of the sliding glass doors, I sat down on a green metal bench and took stock. I'd been limping, my right side functional but drowsy, uncoordinated. Whether or not this was a permanent condition, I didn't know.

But it didn't seem as though it was going to get any worse. I decided I could live with that, chiefly because I was probably going to have to.

I took my wallet out of the stolen shorts and counted my available funds, which turned out to be enough to catch a taxi back to Hollywood. The driver wasn't the chatty type, and that suited me fine. I was too busy thinking about what a reckless imbecile I was being, and how nothing was going to change my mind.

# 30.

## HOLLYWOOD, 1926.

A spotlight illumined the broad stage beneath the screen, into which walked a grinning man in a tuxedo and enormous cowboy hat. The audience erupted with applause, and Grace followed suit. This, she knew, was Hoot Gibson, the star of the night's premiere, *The Man in the Saddle*. Hoot's cowboy pictures had been playing for years, but unlike William Hart they continued to bring them in. Hoot was doing just fine, as his goofy ear-to-ear smile attested.

Beside her Saul Veritek clapped and smiled, too. He leaned close to her and whispered, "I can't stand these dismal oaters."

"Oh, it was all right."

"Dismal," he repeated, still clapping.

When the applause died down, Hoot waved both hands at the assembled colleagues and started in on a drawling message of thanks. Grace tuned him out. She had not been able to stop thinking about her late-night visitor, the lights and noise, who it was and what they wanted. Frank Faehnrich was her best guess, but her mind turned blank when she tried to suss out the reason Frank would have to harass and frighten her in that way.

Was he angry that she didn't get into the car with him that day? Did he consider her a traitor now? Would he burn down her bungalow like he burned that set, with her asleep inside?

Grace shuddered.

Saul said, "Bit chilly in here."

"Yes," she said.

In front of the theater, well-dressed men and women shook hands and congratulated one another and themselves for their successes and conquests. The preponderance of the attention was focused on Hoot Gibson—it was his night after all—but Grace couldn't help but gawk at the bevy of recognizable faces surrounding her: Tom Mix, Blanche Sweet, Billy Bletcher, Antonio Moreno. Phantoms of Hollywood she had never seen so small, so real. She managed to keep her mouth closed but stared all the same.

"Don't look like such a star-struck bumpkin," came a voice beside her. Grace shook it off and turned to find Jack Parson at her side. "These are your peers, or soon shall be."

"It's so odd seeing them in the flesh," Grace said. "Smaller in real life."

"In full color and sound, too. They're not just people, though. They're stars. It's another level altogether."

"Aren't they artists?" she asked, her voice tinged with sarcasm.

"Some, yes. Not most. Art requires suffering. I think so, yes. Nobody suffers in Hollywood. This country is riding much too high, all this post-war giddiness. We've forgotten about the dead, about the lean times."

"Isn't that what we're here for? To help people forget?"

"Hmn," Jack grunted. "It'll be worse when sound comes. Cinema should trump vaudeville, the Follies and all that nonsense. But that's all it will be. All singing, all dancing. The pictures won't be *pictures* anymore. This will all degenerate into just another low entertainment. Watch."

"You're the biggest cynic I ever knew, Jack. There will be enough room for everything under the sun. Don't throw the baby out with the bathwater yet. You'll be able to say a lot more with talking pictures, won't you?"

Jack lighted a cigarette and narrowed his eyes at the bright marquee.

"I may just say everything I need with *Angel of the Abyss*," he said. A faint smile played at his mouth.

Grace studied him for a moment, failing to decipher his

meaning, when Saul came out of the milling throng to shake Jack's hand and bring him back to earth.

"I hear you haven't ruined our picture yet," Saul said.

"The ship's still sailing, captain," Jack told him.

"Never doubted it for a moment, my boy. Never for a moment. I didn't bring you on for your good looks."

Jack's face was inscrutable. A near poker face with a Mona Lisa smile. Saul continued talking, gesticulating as though the heart attack never happened at all, but all the while Jack's eyes remained on Grace.

"There's a party starting up at the Brown Derby," Saul said to Grace, touching her on the arm. "Why don't you two come along? Only the best and brightest there—well, and me."

He chuckled again and Jack assumed a stern frown.

To Grace, he said, "That new place on Wilshire, shaped like a *hat*."

"Oh, for Christ's sake, Parson," Saul groused, though he still grinned. "Let some air out once in a while, would you?"

He jammed a fresh cigar between his teeth, slapped Grace on the behind, and sauntered back off into the throng.

"Listen, Grace?" Jack said, rocking on his heels and sniffing the warm evening air. She snapped her attention back to him— she'd been staring at Richard Dix. "Let's skip the revelry for once, shall we? I'm not much in the mood for it. And besides, I'd like to talk to you."

She raised one eyebrow and found a cigarette in her handbag, which she slid between her lips.

"About the picture?"

Jack lighted the smoke and said, "What else is there?"

Grace sucked deeply at the cigarette and rolled her eyes over the crowd one last time.

"FitzGerald's?" she asked when they refocused on her director.

"No, the studio. There's something I'd like you see."

# 31.

## L.A., 2013.

It was weird how much I missed sitting in my swivel chair and feeding old film stock through a computer. All I ever wanted to do since I was seven years old was make movies myself, my own stories on my own terms, but one sour experience made me slam the door on that old dream forever. Still, in spite of everything, there was nothing in the world I loved and desired more than cinema. Even during those turbulent years with Helen—and this was something I never admitted to myself until she was gone—my wife was always going to come in second to my one true love.

These were my thoughts when I limped up to the front desk of the Wilson Arms and introduced myself to the startled attendant, to whom I probably looked like a refugee from a B horror picture. Half-Igor and half-Invisible Man, with a liberal sprinkling of Frankenstein to enhance the whole deal. I told her I'd had a room there, paid for by the Silent Film Appreciation Society, and I wanted to know if I could re-claim it.

No dice.

And the place was well beyond the realm of my price range, so I had her wheel out my luggage and line up another taxi for me, and I rode downtown until I found a place wretched looking enough for me to afford. The roof sagged in front of its tiny office and there was an aging prostitute just standing out front, smoking and picking a scab on her lip, like it didn't make any difference, which it pretty much didn't. I checked in on my own credit card, got the key, and when I came out again the working girl was still there. I bummed one of her smokes and she made a sad joke about how she doesn't usually give anything away for free. I guessed she felt sorry for me, the way I looked, and that made it a little sadder still.

I went to my room and lay down on the musty bedspread, where I finished the smoke despite the state's strict laws on that sort of thing. I didn't figure anyone would give a damn. I put it out in the sink.

Then I checked my old-school horror-show appearance in the mirror, heaved a sigh, and went for the telephone. It was bolted down like everything else in the room. Nothing was attached in my old room. That place was plush enough they could afford a few stolen items. I picked up the phone and dialed information, asked for the number for Cora Parson. Unlisted, but I counted on it. It was a long shot.

The old lady was probably still riding pretty high on her family fortune, and in some quarters the name still meant something. She wasn't going to be like the rest of us plebes and keep a public listing. Nevertheless, I wanted to find out where she lived and fast. She might have skipped out somewhere to hide, but she was also an elderly woman and couldn't have gone terribly far. I was betting she was still in L.A., or at least very close by. Her residence would be my first point of contact to get anything more to go on, if I could find it.

I leaned against the wall and listened to the people going at it in the next room, longing for another cigarette and thinking about what Shea had told Jake—*no more junior detective bullshit.*

But hell: he hadn't said it to me.

When I was in Hollywood in the 90s, there was a place near the old Tower Records where actors and filmmakers and, more than they, dreamy wannabes could go to file their resumes and headshots. It was a small office in an ugly 70s-era office building and the way it ended up working was producers low on cash or just plain sleazy would track down crew and bit players desperate for work so they didn't have to pay them. For about two months I was bouncing around this notion about making a short film with this Jordanian guy I'd met; it fell apart before it went anyplace but he was the one who sent me to this office to get some names of people who might work on the cheap. I remembered how surprised I was to see more than few familiar names and faces among the dozens of three-ring binders I went through that day. The joint was like an archive for everybody working in the movie business below the superstar level.

There was no telling if the place would still be around all these years later—there's nothing like turnaround in Los Angeles—but for once my luck held and I found the office still going strong, though now most of the shelves full of notebooks were gone and there was a bank of five computer monitors crowded around a small plastic table.

A smarmy looking kid with retro glasses and a too-tight sweater vest asked me if I needed some help. I wondered if I was ever going to get used to the pity/disgust stare, and wondered about toning down the whole giant-bandage-on-my-head look before my next step. Whatever that was.

"I'm looking for information on a producer," I said, leaning against the doorjamb to give my right side a chance to rest. "Used to work with the guy and I'm getting a small production together."

"This isn't really an information bureau," he snarled, rudely. "If you're looking for talent, that's where we can help. But if you're looking for someone to bankroll your little movie …"

I wanted to slap him, but I knew if I did I'd probably end up on my ass. So instead I cut him off and said, "Actually, my little movie is funded. I only wanted to bring somebody in on it since he'd done me a favor before. We've got some major talent attached and I think he'll be very excited to hear about it."

My words were beginning to slur again and I worried the kid was going to assume I was some drunk or junkie off the street, which would have been a pretty safe bet from his perspective. That I was a miraculous survivor of a gunshot wound to the head would probably not even be his second guess. At least I'd been able to change into my own clothes.

"What might be this gentleman's name?" the snotty bastard asked.

"Parson. John Parson." I remembered it from the bio I read on the plane.

Of course, I knew the younger Parson was as dead as his father. I just hoped this kid didn't.

"All right, let's take a look, then."

He went to the nearest monitor and sat down in front of it. After hunt-and-pecking his way through the username and password, he brought up an ancient interface that looked like it could have run on DOS. Still, there was a row of tabs at the top labeled with professions, and among them was *producer*. He clicked the tab and scrolled down the list, some of which appeared in red for some reason.

"P, P, P," he mumbled until he reached that letter. "No, sir. No John Parson. I'm sorry we couldn't have been more help."

*I'm sure you are*, I thought, again fantasizing about whacking him across the jaw. My daydream was interrupted by another young person, a girl with Lucy-red hair, who leaned back in her chair two monitors over and said, "Did you try the old notebooks, Shawn?"

I raised my left eyebrow at him and said, "Did you try that, Shawn?"

Shawn groaned.

The girl rose from her chair and walked over to one of the remaining shelves, sagging from the weight of its contents. I followed her over and she selected a particularly thick white one, flipped to the back and ran her finger down the columns until she found what she was looking for. What *I* was looking for.

"Parson, John. This lists him on the board for a company called Monumental Pictures in Culver City. Think it could be the same person?"

Monumental was the name of the production company behind *Angel of the Abyss*. It went under before my parents were born, but it certainly wasn't unheard of to resurrect old names for new uses. Then again, I had no idea how long Parson had been dead, or if this second iteration of Monumental was still a going concern.

I said, "That's John, all right."

"I'm afraid all this has is that and the web address. MonumentalPictures.net. This is a pretty old book, though—at least eight years, I think. I'd say visit the site and hopefully it will have all the info you need."

She gave me a caring look, her eyes unable to stay away from my bandages for too long.

"Thank you so much for your help," I said to her. To the other little shit, I said nothing at all.

I left and found a pharmacy where I bought some gauze and other items to redress my head. I also bought a cotton beanie to cover most of it up. From there I took my bounty to the nearest copy center, which in the post-Internet-café age were just about the only places other than libraries where you could find a computer for public use. I paid for an hour but I only needed five minutes.

The website was so old it had frames and clip art, but there was an address and a phone number. I copied them down and rushed back to my motel room where I dialed the number before the door slammed shut behind me. Out of order.

But I still had an address.

The next half hour I spent carefully unwrapping my mummified head to redress before I went back out again. It was the first time I'd seen the wound, and it was horrific. My right eye was still swollen shut and the entry point was black and crusted. There was some kind of cotton or cloth stent lodged in the tiny hole, but I didn't go prodding at it to find out more. I developed a fear of exposing it too long and, after wiping my half-shaved head down with some antiseptic wipes, wrapped it quickly and cinched it with metal teeth. Then the beanie went on and I looked less like a horror creature and more like a derelict who lost a battle with a baseball bat in some back alley.

I couldn't decide which was worse.

West of the 405 and not too far from the Mar Vista Projects there stood on South Slauson a large gray obelisk of a warehouse. There was no signage to identify its purpose, no windows on the street-facing side. The place could have been used for anything, or nothing at all. Either seemed equally dangerous to me. There was no telling who was in a place like that and what they were doing there. Possibly something perfectly innocuous and above-board, but given the way my little working vacation to L.A. had turned out so far, I wasn't interested in putting any money on that.

Not that I had much in the way of money—once again I'd charged my taxi ride out there, forty bucks. It was a miracle my credit card company hadn't cut me off yet, decided the damn thing was stolen. As things stood, I was going to be looking at one hell of a bill, assuming I lived long enough to be shocked by it.

I stood on the sidewalk as the cab drove off, listening to the city and the dull roar of the 405, and tried to imagine whether or not the junior Parson did anything remotely related to movie making in this place, once upon a time. I had my doubts. Monumental Pictures folded in the year between the disastrous premiere of *Angel of the Abyss* and Grace Baron's official "death." I didn't know exactly when John Parson decided to resurrect the name, nor why, but it seemed a good bet to me whatever it was, it was something his widow was willing to kill just about anybody to conceal.

At the front door I found a small button, presumably a doorbell. I didn't touch it, but I tried the handle. Locked. From there I walked around the side, past a rickety looking ladder leading up to the roof, and around to the back. There was an empty parking lot back there, the macadam cracked to hell and the cracks filled with tall weeds and crab grass. The back of the warehouse sported two steel doors just like the one in front and a loading dock situated atop a broad concrete slab. I tried both back doors with the same result.

I was just about to start weighing the pros and cons of trying that ladder when the left side door crunched open and a hairy face poked out. I jumped a little, startled.

The face, almost all beard, said, "Jinx, that you?"

The temptation to run popped into my head, but then I remembered that running was off the menu for me for the foreseeable future. Instead, I said, "No, sorry."

"You need to sleep here, man? It's cool. It's safe."

The door opened the rest of the way and a thin, pale man stepped out. His long hair was brown and gray, matted like his beard. He didn't seem particularly dirty, but he was clearly homeless. He looked at me with watery blue eyes that said he could tell I was in dire straits, that he knew a lot about that.

I said, "I kinda … just wanted to look around, actually."

"No trouble?" He seemed skeptical. I couldn't blame him.

"No trouble," I agreed.

He bit his thumbnail and traded glances with me and whatever was behind the door. While he thought it over, I decided to introduce myself.

"My name's Graham. I've been looking for somebody, and I think maybe she's been here. Maybe not for a while." I didn't know if I meant Helen or Cora Parson. Or both. It didn't really seem to make a difference.

"I been squatting here off and on about a year," the man told me. "A couple guys a little longer. I guess the place shut down 'round 2000. S'what I hear, anyway."

"What was it before that?"

"I dunno. Marky would know. You should ask him."

"Is he here?"

"Marky's always here."

The guy pressed the door all the way to the wall and stepped aside to let me by. As I passed him, he squinted one eye and reminded me: "No trouble, man."

I showed him my palms and smiled, and I walked into the dark, musty space.

There were no fires burning in barrels as I might have expected, and in fact most of the open area was completely dark and vacant, apart from rows of empty metal shelves and cardboard boxes here and there. The residents—the squatters—were concentrated in a smaller space walled off with particle board and strung with multicolored Christmas lights. The man, my friend, went toward it and motioned for me to follow. The guy seemed a lot more the hippie type than the murderer type, so I followed and tried not to think about the Manson Family.

Seated on a surprisingly decent looking loveseat were a man and woman, both in their 30s or early 40s. She was black and he was Hispanic. Both were smoking cigarettes, or what I assumed to be cigarettes. When my guide approached, the man sat up straight.

"Who's that, Duff—Jinx?"

"Nah, it ain't Jinx. This guy's called Graham."

Now both of them perked up as I emerged from the shadows behind Duff. The man, who I gathered was Marky, stood up to assess me. I smiled stupidly at him.

"Graham," he said, spreading it out so it sounded like *Gray-um*.

"Hi," I said.

"I got no problem with you, Graham," he said, as though that were an issue already raised. "No problem at all. But we do got a couple rules here before you can set down and rest."

"He said he won't make no trouble," Duff assured him.

"Junkies lie all the time, bro," Marky countered. "You know that."

I sighed and said, "I'm not a junky and I don't need to rest here. Marky—you're Marky, right?"

"That's right."

"Marky: I'd like to be straight with you."

"I like that," he said.

"I'm here because this place used to be run by a man, a man who's dead now, but his widow has caused me and my friends a lot of trouble."

"Trouble like that bandage up on your head?"

"That and worse. I want to find this lady and put an end to it before anybody else gets hurt, and this place is the only lead I got."

"This place used to store old movies," Marky told me, matter-of-factly. My ears pricked up. "Still some of them old movie cans around, too. This one time a dude dumped one of 'em on a fire and that shit blew up—no lie, just like a bomb."

"Nitrate," I said.

"I dunno, but we hauled his ass right on out of here, I tell you that."

"Can you show me some of those cans?"

"Look bro, you said you wasn't going to cause no trouble. You're talkin' about people getting hurt and you look like you already been worked over good. That's against the rules, man. I told you, we got rules."

I wished I'd only been worked over, but I kept that much to myself.

I said, "Nobody's after me, at least not at the moment. I'm supposed to still be in the hospital, actually, and the folks who did this to me still think I'm dead, as far as I know. All I need is a little information, and I promise you it won't break any of your rules for me to get it, if it's here."

He wrinkled his nose and mulled it over. While he was thinking, the woman passed a bottle up to him and he took a long pull. Then, without a word or even looking me in the eye, he passed the bottle to me. Its contents were radioactive green and the label read MD 20/20—KIWI-LEMON. It felt like a moment of truth, or a test of courage, or something. I didn't want to offend my gracious host, so I took a belt and gagged the stuff down. I coughed hard after that and Marky took the bottle back, laughing his ass off.

"Shit bro," he said, "you didn't *have* to drink it."

Now the woman and Duff joined in on the hilarity and, once my retching coughs were under control, I chuckled a little too.

"Come on," Marky said then. "Lemme show you something."

# 32.

## HOLLYWOOD, 1926.

"Give me a minute."

Grace waited in the doorway while Jack went into the darkness of the studio, his footsteps echoing loudly throughout the shadowed stages. A few moments later she heard a metallic crunch and a row of lights hanging from the rafters burned on.

"And God said," Jack boomed from the opposite end of the broad space, his arms outstretched.

Grace walked in, her heels clacking a different tempo from the director's shoes, and paused between the city street and the cemetery. The rafter lights illumined the fake gravestones like sunlight after a storm, streaming through the dissipating clouds.

Only the sacrificial tomb evaded the light, masked by the length of her own shadow.

# 33.

## CULVER CITY, 2013.

Some of the titles on the decaying labels I recognized. A few I didn't. Part of me was looking for *Convention City*, despite the urgency of the situation. Mostly I just wanted to see if there was anything among the three towers of dusty silver cans that would lead me where I needed to go.

The reels were stacked as far away from where Marky and his cohorts resided as possible and, like their little area on the other side of the warehouse, they had built walls around them. Unlike the particle board from their apartment, however, these walls were wooden and cut into odd shapes, and blanketed with dust.

"After that film blowed up the way it did, I didn't wanna be any too close," he explained.

I gritted my teeth, hating to think what that guy might have destroyed. Some years earlier I'd read a story about a conservative church group in Florida who bought an old, defunct drive-in and held a nice little Nazi burning party in the parking lot when they found a closet full of films. I raged about that for weeks.

"Why didn't you just get rid of them?" I asked him.

"One of these days I'll find somebody wants to buy 'em, I figure. You interested?"

I squinted in the low glow of his flashlight at an almost illegible label that read *What Has To Be Done*.

"Well," I stalled. "Possibly."

I set *What Has To Be Done* aside and kept sifting through the stacks. Just when I finished the second and started in on the third, Marky said, "There's an old office, too. Way over there, on the street side. Kind of a dressing room and office, I guess. Big mirror in it, all broke up."

"I'll want to see that," I started, when I saw I was holding a missing reel from *Angel of the Abyss* in my hand. The hand shook and my heartbeat quickened. I went through the next few reels in a hurry, and two more were from *Angel*. Another just had TEST written on the label, the ink so faded it was almost gone. *Screen test?* I wondered. I planned on finding out.

"Looks like you found you something good," Marky said. "I saved 'em, though. They mine, man."

"Please tell me there's a projector in here someplace."

"What's that?"

"The thing you feed the film through, to show it up on a screen."

"Oh, right, right. Like at the movie theater."

I clutched one of the *Angel* reels to my chest like it was my own baby and widened my eyes, awaiting a response.

"Yeah," he said at last. "Yeah, there's one of them. Back in that office. Or dressing room. Or whatever the hell it's supposed to be."

"God, I hope it works," I moaned, and in my shaken state I brushed up against one of the diving walls, nearly knocking it over. Marky rushed forward to right it, and between the two of us we kicked up quite a dust cloud. Once again I was coughing my lungs up in front of this man, who didn't seem fazed by it at all. And when the glare of his flashlight settled upon the oddly shaped platform, my heart almost stopped dead.

That first reel, the third, that I saw when Leslie Wheeler emailed me the video of it, had been playing and re-playing in my mind ever since I first got into this mess. Even when I was unconscious in the hospital I saw Grace Baron emerging from the fog on that crazy, avant-garde street lined with painted backdrops of bricked facades and shop fronts.

There was no doubt in my mind that I was standing two feet from one of those backdrops now, a piece of *Angel of the Abyss*.

"Jesus," I gasped.

"You wanta see that project-a-thing or what?" Marky barked.

I swallowed hard and gathered up all four of the reels I wanted.

"Yeah … yes. Lead the way, Marky."

"Them damn things best not blow my head off."

I grunted to signify that I'd heard him, but my attention was focused on the oldest damn film projector I'd ever put my hands on.

It was a Twenties model Zenith safety projector, in astonishingly good shape. The lamp house was brown with rust but there was a relatively new bulb in it; the diffuser and lens were either restored or just remarkably well looked after. I snaked the cord up from the floor, covered in woven cloth as they were in those days, and sighed with relief to find the plug was suitable to a modern outlet.

"You've got some power," I said to Marky. "To get those Christmas lights going. Is the whole place wired?"

"I guess I could run the extension cord over," he said. "We juicing off the city, actually."

I nodded and he ran over to start pulling up the cord. When he came back, I gently fit the plug into the cord's outlet and held my breath as I switched the antique on. And glory hallelujah, the damn thing worked.

Marky said, "Don't make 'em like they used to."

"You got that right."

*About everything*, I thought, feeling sentimental for a past I never knew. Common pitfall in my profession.

Duff and the woman got to singing back in their corner of the warehouse, drunk as lords on that foul green stuff, and though Marky's eyes shot that way he stayed with me. He kept the flash on my hands while I fed the first of the reels into the sprockets. Once it was ready, I turned the machine to face the dirty gray wall and started the show.

# 34.

## HOLLYWOOD, 1926.

Hugging herself, Grace turned her gaze from the faux tombstones to Jack and forced herself to smile. The liberally flowing booze from the premiere was starting to wear off as she started to question why she agreed to come to the studio in the first place.

"What's doing, Jack?" she asked with a small, artificial laugh.

He laughed back and went directly to the camera, which he heaved up by its wooden tripod. Grace narrowed her eyes, watching him carefully as he carried the equipment over to where she stood.

"Don't tell me you're this overworked," she half-jested. "Surely the next scene can wait 'til morning."

"No," he said. "Not this one."

His smile and laughter had faded. Now he set to arranging the camera, peering through the viewfinder at the cemetery, muttering quietly to himself.

"Jack?"

"Just a minute. Say—would you stand beside the tomb? Just to the left."

"What was it you wanted to talk about, Jack?"

"Just to the left of it," he repeated. "I'll need to set the lights."

"Come off that," Grace said with as much force as she could muster. "We're not really going to film anything—at this hour? Alone, and without Saul?"

"We worked a week without Saul."

"He was ill. He's back now."

"We don't *need* him," Jack hissed. "Who's making this picture, anyway? Jack Parson and Grace Baron, that's who. All that tubby Jew does is interfere. And this—*this*—is something he could never wrap his dry little mind around, anyhow. No siree."

She stepped back, away from him, and rubbed her bare arms despite the muggy warmth of the studio.

"You're frightening me, Jack."

His grin returned and he paused for a moment, shaking his head. He then looked up at her, his face in shadow behind the rafter lights.

"That's only because you don't listen, dearheart. Dear, sweet Grace. You haven't listened to me at all, not from the start."

"I'm listening now. I'm here, Jack, and I'm listening. What was it you wanted to say?"

A small tremor worked its way up her back. She tried to shiver it out.

"Don't you remember? The steps? The soldiers? *Potemkin?*"

Grace nodded vigorously, feigning comprehension she did not have.

"Yes, yes I remember."

"What did I say? That day, Gracie. About art—the key. The secret."

She recalled the troubling scene as clearly as though it were playing before her now; the screams, the blood, the terror. And she recalled her director's words, too—words that puzzled her then and terrified her now.

"Darkness," she whispered. "You said, 'human darkness.'"

Jack Parson wiped the sweat from his brow with the sleeve of his topcoat and sighed loudly.

"That's right, Grace. Gracie Baronsky. My star. You understand. Oh, thank God! You understand."

He left the camera and walked stiffly toward her. She flinched, but he did not appear to notice as he wrapped his arms around her and squeezed her tightly.

Into her ear, he softly whispered, "What we do here tonight is the end of cinema, my lovely girl. Talkies will never top what we're about to give them."

Her eyes spilled over, tears falling in dark spots on his shoulder.

# 35.

## CULVER CITY, 2013.

Having watched *Angel of the Abyss* with three missing reels alongside Jake before my little accident, I was now finally putting the film together by way of memory added to the remaining footage glimmering on the wall before me.

Marky murmured, "Shit man, this flick's so old it's silent."

I shushed him as politely as I could and fell back in step with the nightmare beauty of Grace Baron's Clara, a murdered woman returned from the grave to wreak vengeance on the men who wronged her. She slinked through densely fog-laden alleys in a sheer garment, her alabaster body barely concealed and her jet-black bob a stunning mess atop her scowling face. Even in rage—in death—she was astonishing. Not just her looks, but her range; even without intertitles her every thought was communicated through her eyes, through her flaring nostrils and small, dark mouth.

The world would have fallen in love with her, had it ever been given the chance.

I went through the three reels quickly. At about ten minutes apiece, they went by too quickly, and I sat in silence for several minutes absorbing them. Clara got them, of course, all the men who took her and made her their victim. And when that was done, the goat-headed beast with whom she'd made her carnal pact took her into its arms, enveloping her in its great, dark cloak, and she vanished with him in a wisp of smoke. The picture was harrowing and gorgeous, and much too sinister for its time. Even now it jarred me—me, who went through every

stomach-churning 1970s Euro-horror film in my college days—
even as it bewildered me with its breadth of design and the
depth of Baron's extraordinary performance. As sure as I was
that Parson and his heirs had everything to do with the violence
and secrecy taking hold of my life at that moment, I had no
other choice but to admit the man had made a masterpiece.

So why must it be kept secret?

That question was answered by the fourth and final reel.
The one that had only TEST on it.

I fed it into the projector, and in the horrible minutes that
followed, I understood everything completely.

# 36.

## HOLLYWOOD, 1926.

Squirming in his strong grasp, Grace sniffed and fought the
cloud that seemed to envelope her senses.

"Jack," she said, "listen to me. I have an idea."

His fingers dug into her ribs and he shook slightly. As if
weeping. She exhaled sharply and continued: "We're going to
make an astounding picture together. You and me. Like nothing
anyone's ever seen, or done. Because you're an artist, not like
these Hollywood types. You're not one of them, Jack. You're our
Eisenstein, and you're going to prove it to everybody."

"I am," he rasped. "I will."

"But not tonight," she said, her tone motherly. "It's not the
right time, Jack. We'll need more crew, won't we? To get the
lights just right? To keep your mind on the direction? Why, you
can't run it all. You're the *mind*, Jacky. Not some mean crewman.
Let's do it tomorrow."

Jack groaned sorrowfully and leaned away while still
grasping her at the waist. His eyes were pink, puffy. He looked
devastated, sad.

"You never understood this picture at all, did you?" he
asked.

"What do you mean? Of course I—"

"No one does. It's a nightmare. Someday, Lord willing, they
will see what I've done, and they'll see that I closed the gap.
That pictures don't have to exist on the other side of the screen,
separate from the people who see them. That the darkness in
them—in all of us, Gracie, in you and me—is what binds us to

art."

He squeezed his eyes shut for a moment and shuddered. The movement went from his hands into her body, and she stifled a cry.

"Only we can do this, Grace," he said, opening his eyes and staring hard into hers. "You, and I. The artist and his subject. No one else can help us. And no one else can know."

"Know? Know what, Jack?" She struggled and he moved to grasp her roughly by the arm. "Know what?"

# 37.

## CULVER CITY, 2013.

I said, "Oh my God."

"What the shit, man?" Marky responded. "What the shit is this?"

I couldn't answer him. I was choked on my own quiet sobs.

Probably I knew it all along, or at least suspected it. I'd read that she was present at the film's abysmal premiere, but I knew now that could not have been true. Because Grace Baron was dead by then. There could be no doubt about it. I was watching her die.

Not Clara—Grace. I was watching Grace Baronsky die.

The thing was so clumsy it looked more like behind-the-scenes footage or a home movie than a scene from the brilliant production I'd just seen. The camera shook as it was positioned, already rolling, and in flashes bodies moved in the periphery of the frame. I longed for impossible sound, to hear what was happening just off camera, but it became clear soon enough.

Though the framing was off and the lighting bright and ill-designed, if indeed designed at all, once the camera was steady I watched as a man in a rumpled tuxedo dragged a struggling woman to the same cemetery set from *Angel of the Abyss* and threw her down, violently, upon the sacrificial tomb. Her gown was torn and her makeup streaming down her still unbelievably angelic face—Grace. Grace Baronsky from Idaho, the starlet who never was.

She lunged up, swinging at the man with an open hand, but he was quicker than her and put down her rebellion with a close-fisted punch to the jaw. Grace rocked back and the man climbed atop of her, planting a knee on her chest. He tore her gown open, right down the front, and when he moved aside again she was exposed to the waist.

"Is this for real, bro?" Marky said, his voice uncharacteristically quiet.

I said, "It's for real."

Grace lolled on the fake tomb, raised her hand to her face and stretched her mouth open wide. Whether or not she was screaming, or crying, or making any noise at all, I couldn't tell. I cried for her. I think maybe Marky did a little, too.

The man went off screen for a moment while she lay there, stunned. When he returned, he was pulling himself into one of the long cloaks, the costume of the sect who killed Clara in the picture. He then went back to the camera, his body filling and darkening the frame for several seconds. When the light came back, he had moved it, set it up to angle down at Grace, at her anguished face and exposed torso. He tore the gown the rest of the way down, and off. I felt awful watching—disgusting, down to the pit of my stomach—but I somehow knew I had to. I had to bear witness to this. It was eighty-seven years too late, but it had to be me.

I wiped my eyes on the back of my hand and forced myself to keep looking. And that was when the man showed the dagger to the camera.

# 38.

## HOLLYWOOD, 1926.

"Jack," she pleaded, her voice wet and slurred with pain. "Please don't. Please, Jack."

"Clara doesn't speak in this scene," he said. "You know that. Be quiet."

"I'm not Clara. Jack—*I'm not Clara*. It's Grace. Please, it's Grace you're hurting. I'm real. This is all real ..."

He spun around, the hood of the cloak falling from his head and his teeth grinding with anger.

"Of course it's fucking real!" he roared. "Don't you think I know that? Why else would I bother? Can't you even try to imagine the impact had Eisenstein actually shot those people on the stairs? Had he actually had them slashed and stomped down? The curtain would be torn down, damn it! Art and life! Cinema and death! Human darkness, just as I've been saying all along. For Christ's sake, Clara—*Grace*—can you see now? Can't you finally see?"

Jack moaned and swung around to kick over an adjacent gravestone. Grace whimpered, started to rise from the tomb. Her vision blurred and her jaw throbbed, but she pushed past it, lifted her weight and tried to focus on the door leading out. It seemed miles away.

"No, Clara!" Jack shrieked.

Grace cried out and tumbled off the tomb, rolling away from the set. The cold floor of the studio slammed against her naked body, and she got to her knees, ready to leap up for the door, for escape. But he was upon her before she could move another inch, slinking his arm around her neck and dragging her back. Back to the set. Back to the tomb. To her final performance.

Fighting for breath, Jack Parson lifted her kicking from the floor and threw her down, a second time, on the tomb. She yelled out and he drove his fist into her diaphragm, knocking the wind out of her lungs in a prolonged gasp. The studio spun like a merry-go-round and she saw the glint of the blade and she knew it wasn't a prop, it wasn't the spring-loaded, retractable dagger the day players used to act out her demise weeks ago.

No fake knives. No more acting. After all she'd done, all she'd survived for the privilege to perform on celluloid, Grace Baron was going to die for art.

Jack snapped his head to look at the camera. The machine was still rolling, with only a few minutes left in the reel. He turned back to Grace, wheezing under him, her eyes wide and mouth set tight.

"For history," he said, calmly. "Thank you."

And then he raised the blade.

# 39.

## CULVER CITY, 2013.

The blood welled up, impossibly dark and thick, like oil. The dagger only sank so deep, about three-quarters of the blade, where it stopped. And the man—Parson himself, of that I was sure now—held fast to the handle, permitting the wound to pour, Grace's life to leak out from between her breasts in what was now scratchy, flickering black and white. It spilled down her side, following the groove of her ribs, and pooled beneath her still, white body on the fake tomb. And there the reel ended, leaving nothing on the warehouse wall but a bright square of light as the projector continued to turn and click, the only thing making my soft, hitching sobs inaudible.

"Turn it off," Marky said, his voice low and grim. "Turn that thing off, man."

"I think it happened here," I said, half to him and half to myself.

"What'choo mean, it happened here? That murder? That's what that was, isn't it? A murder?"

"It was. And I think this place used to be the movie studio where that happened. The movie before, and then that. Grace Baron's killing. It happened right here, and ... Jesus. That's what this has been about all along."

"What, bro? What kinda shit is this, anyway?"

"That old woman was just protecting her good family name," I said, knowing I wasn't making any sense to him. In the far corner, the woman was no longer singing, but Duff still was. Completely oblivious to the horror Marky and I had just seen. I envied the hell out of him for that.

I dragged a deep breath into my chest, my mind racing from the moment I got the phone call from Leslie Wheeler to waking up in a Los Angeles hospital with a hole in my head, wondering if it was even remotely possible that I could explain any of it to this homeless man who trusted me enough to permit me into his safe place. Somehow it seemed I owed him some kind of explanation, if only to calm his obviously rattled nerves—but that wasn't something either of us were much concerned about when the gunshots started.

The woman shrieked and I hit the floor, knocking the projector to the ground where it broke apart noisily. Duff shouted something I couldn't understand and then there were rapid footsteps, followed by another pair of popping shots. Marky cried out, scrambling toward the noise.

"Marky, don't!" I called after him.

He sped out of the back-office area, just barely clearing the doorway before another report sounded and he dropped backward like a brick. His flashlight clattered to the floor and the light went out. The shooter was close enough that I could smell the cordite. My ears rang slightly from the shots, but all I could hear now were slow, deliberate steps drawing near to the doorway. As quietly as I could, I picked up the empty can from which I'd taken that awful reel of nitrate film. Rust flaked off on my fingers.

The office and warehouse were almost pitch black; only the faintest glow emanated from the Christmas lights across the building, but it was enough to illumine the shape that appeared in the doorway and bent over Marky. I held my breath and tried to keep from shaking, scared as I was. Any second this guy was going to come in the room, and I wanted to be as focused and ready as I could.

Next thing I knew, Marky coughed. It startled me and it sounded bad. The shooter made a surprised sound and then grunted. I jumped to my feet, took two long strides toward the door, and threw the can as hard as I could at the guy. It struck him in the neck and he shouted, turning and grasping at his neck as his gun went off. The muzzle flashed brightly in the air, and I was thankful it hadn't been pointed at Marky. Or me.

The gunman roared, "Goddamnit!" I flung myself at Marky, seized a handful of his shirt and dragged him roughly back into the office where I slid him across the floor and up against the inside wall. My hands were tacky with his blood. I couldn't tell where he'd been hit, but he was wheezing and moving lazily about, dazed.

"Fuckin' bums," the shooter yelled. "Fuckin' shit-birds!"

*Shit-bird.* I'd heard one of the goons at Florence Sommer's house say that, moments before they killed her and shot me. I guessed this guy had to be on cleanup duty—hit the warehouse, get rid of everything, kill anyone you see. Old Cora Parson must not have known the place was being used by squatters. I'd never have gotten in had they not been there, but now it seemed like my interfering with their quiet corner of L.A. had gotten most of them killed. And that really pissed me off.

I gently patted Marky on the shoulder, hoping to Christ he was going to make it through this shitstorm, and then did probably the stupidest thing of my life thus far: I rushed out of the office and lunged right for the guy with the gun. He made a noise in his throat, spinning to get the drop on me, but I threw a left-handed punch at his throat that left him sputtering for air instead. My knuckles throbbed and the way my brain was going, the pain only served to make me angrier. So I punched him again, same place, and felt his windpipe collapse like rice paper. For my trouble my right leg turned to Jell-O and I went careening toward the hard cement floor.

It was the worst violence I'd ever committed, which wasn't saying much, me being a generally pretty peaceful guy. With his air supply cut off, the man forgot all about his gun, which he just dropped so he could claw at his throat. I couldn't make out his face very well in the nearly non-existent light, but the flat, dry gulping noise he made in his mouth was enough to turn my stomach. It was almost enough to make me feel bad for what I'd done too, but not quite. Not after what he'd done to Marky and what I imagined he must have done to the other two. So when he dropped to his knees beside me, I didn't shed any tears about lifting my left foot and kicking the son of a bitch over. I didn't stick around to watch him suffocate to death either; I stumbled around to find his gun and Marky's flashlight, got both, and hurried back to the office.

After screwing the flashlight back together, I switched it on and turned it at Marky. He squinted and grumbled, "Man, get that damn thing out my eyes."

"Where are you hit?"

"My goddamn arm," he complained. I shone the light on his right arm, which was soaked with blood, the nucleus of which was a dark hole in the bicep. "Hurts like hell, man. Shit, I never got shot before. It *hurts*."

"Trust me," I said. "I know."

"The hell was that dude?"

"Somebody who doesn't want that film to ever get out."

"What about Duff? And Shawna?"

"I don't know," I said honestly. "But I don't think it's good."

He squeezed his eyes shut and said, "Damn."

"Hang tight," I told him. "I'm going to find a phone and call 911. But listen, I'm getting out of here. I just—Jesus, I just killed that guy."

"Good," was all he said about that.

Duff was dead, shot in the chest, but Shawna was gone. It was a gruesome sight made worse by the cheerful glow of the colorful Christmas lights. Pangs of guilt ripped through me when I found him, though I tried to convince myself it wasn't really my fault. I didn't exactly believe that.

The gunman hadn't forced his way in through the front door, wouldn't have needed to; he had a key. Outside I found a late model Saab parked at the curb. There was no doubt in my mind whatsoever that it was the same car I saw racing down Hollywood Boulevard after somebody took a couple of potshots at me in front of the Wilson Arms. I ran back inside and snatched the keys from the dead man's pants pocket. I snagged his wallet while I was at it. For good measure, I shone the flashlight on his face.

It was the piece of shit who cut Florence Sommer's throat.

From the office, Marky called out to me, so I went back in one last time.

"They gone?" he said.

I nodded somberly. "Duff is. I'm sorry. I—I don't know what happened to Shawna. She's not here."

"Why'd you bring this shit to us, man? You wasn't supposed to be no trouble. You said you wouldn't."

My chest felt too tight for what was in it and my neck burned at the back. I said I was sorry again and felt horrible for repeating something that didn't help at all.

"We was safe," Marky said. "We was safe here."

I wanted to puke. I wanted to puke all over the floor until there was nothing left inside and I could just lie down and die. Everything was finally coming to a head but it was too much, more than I could handle. I couldn't even stick out the movie business when I tried, how the hell was I supposed to deal with all of this?

"I'm going to get help for you," I said. "I never wanted any of this to happen. I hope you know that."

The last thing he ever said to me was "Go."

I went.

The Saab was his, the killer's. Cora Parson's man. Started up easy, the radio softly playing the classical station. Goddamn Bach. Real relaxing stuff to get in your head before you go murder a bunch of strangers. I slammed the button to turn it off.

It took me a minute to regain what little composure I had left. Once I was calm enough to function, I saw the cell phone in the cup holder, with which I dialed 911 and said enough to get somebody out there before abruptly hanging up. Marky was going to be okay, or at least as okay as possible, considering. That accomplished, I dug into that dead bastard's wallet to see what it could tell me. And the first thing it told me was that I'd just killed Jack Parson's grandson.

Gary Alan Parson, to be precise. Height, 5'9". Eyes, brown. Hair, brown. Age, 44. He was never going to be 45. I could hardly wait to tell that to his mother's face.

The address listed on the dead man's license was in El Centro, in Imperial Valley. Luck was with me insofar as there was a roadmap in the glovebox that would get me there. The needle on the gas gauge indicated three quarters of a tank in the Saab. I looked at my hands on the wheel in the dim green light of the dash and they looked like they were only dirty, rather than sticky with Marky's blood. I felt my gorge rise a little. I didn't want to see any more blood, mine or anybody else's.

But I was damn ready to end this. I jerked the stick into drive and hit the gas.

# 40.

## HOLLYWOOD, 1926.

*A*ngel of the Abyss wrapped after four more shooting days. They were tense and largely quiet days. They were days without Grace.

Saul and Jack scrambled to shoot around a double, hastily hired through an agency. The girl had a vague resemblance once her hair was cut to match Grace's bob, but there wouldn't be another close-up, another frame to capture Grace's emotive face. She was gone.

Saul kept a key to her bungalow, since he paid for it, and wasted no time letting himself in on the afternoon of her first missed day. Nothing was missing, nothing amiss. The watch he'd given her, her wardrobe, the telephone he installed for her. And not so much as a note to thank him for all he'd done, for his exhaustive efforts to make her more than merely Gracie Baronsky. More than just a girl. All those weeks it was Jack he worried about, but somehow along the way he'd managed to straighten up and fly right. In the end, it was Saul's protégée who failed him.

He ordered the bungalow cleaned out by the end of the week.

The pressure of incumbent stardom deemed too much for the poor thing, went one of the hushed rumors blazing around the set and through somber speakeasy conversations at night. Hiding out back home—where was it? Iowa? Maybe under an assumed name.

Others cast the blame on the communist apprentice

electrician. Privately, such was Saul Veritek's assumption. Eloped … or worse. Who could say? They had a production to finish. The picture business didn't wait around for anybody.

Such were the vagaries of Hollywood.

# 41.

## EL CENTRO, 2013.

Imperial Valley was about 220 miles from Culver City, which made for a four-hour drive. I drove south along the coast and the sun was just starting to come up over the horizon, burning down over the Pacific from mountains in the east, when I was north of San Diego. The water sparkled blue and orange and the air was so fresh I realized how bad it had been up in L.A. From there I went east on I-8 with the sun in my rearview mirror.

I filled the tank back up west of La Mesa and used the sanitary wipes by the pump to finally get the blood off my hands. The knuckles on my left hand were red and raw from where I'd twice punched the late Gary Parson to death. I idly wondered how much trouble I was going to be looking at once this was all finished, for his death and the theft of his car. And for whatever I was going to have to do once I reached El Centro. I got a couple packs of Parliaments and a tall cup of crappy, convenience-store coffee for the road, and then I went to find out what that was.

In front of a mid-sized Spanish style house a few blocks south of the town's country club, I sat in the idling Saab and waited for someone to notice me. The curtains were all drawn and there weren't any cars in the drive. The yard was impeccably manicured, the grass greener than any real grass, perfectly squared hedges bordering the small property. I smoked three cigarettes in a row while I watched the house, hoping Gary didn't permit it in his ride, and even took the time to put one of them out on the upholstery, just for kicks.

As I lit a fourth I started to worry I'd come all this way for nothing, though I'd known that was a risk. It was the only lead I had so I ran with it. And since nobody saw fit to come out to me—if in fact anyone was in the house at all—I killed the engine, left the key in the ignition, and limped out of the car so I could go to them.

Rather than ring the bell, I went around the side of the house, edging up against the hedges, and came into the equally well-kempt backyard. A red and yellow plastic tricycle was turned over on its side on the grass. I didn't like that, but I took the gun from my pocket anyway. I'd come all the way across the country to work with a stranger's equipment, and it seemed like that was just what I was about to do. It was just a different kind of machine than I was used to. My machines back in Boston restored the dead to their former glory; the one in my hand now was purposed for quite the opposite effect.

A box window in the kitchen jutted out with potted plants pressing against the glass. There was also a small patio extending away from a clean plate-glass sliding door. I couldn't see through the glass; the morning sun threw a glare that made it impenetrable. My left hand tightened around the grip of the gun and I wondered how well I'd be able to shoot with my southpaw. Trouble was, I'd never fired a gun with my right hand, either. And my right still wasn't in the mood to make a proper fist, much less squeeze a trigger.

I lingered at the corner, out of view of the windows, mulling this over. My aim was going to be shit, my visibility was nil, and I hadn't the slightest idea who was inside or what they were going to do when they saw me. I was sweating beneath my bandage and my right foot was starting to tingle like it does when it falls asleep. A one-man army I was not.

My solution was simple and, I guess, a bit on the dramatic side: I lurched into the backyard, took aim at the sliding glass door, and fired a shot that obliterated it in a noisy explosion of glass.

Ta-da.

I wanted to create confusion and panic, and judging by the

frenzied shouts that came from within the house I decided I was successful. As fast as I could, I moved past the destroyed door and pushed up against the siding. I was waiting for someone to come out to investigate or, failing that, to kill me. I'd had enough time on the drive down to give some thought to my feelings about killing, and I came to the conclusion that I didn't care for it. As worthless a human being that murdering bastard in the warehouse was, it still disturbed me that I was responsible for somebody's death. For that reason my plan was clear in my otherwise foggy head—the second I saw someone come through that door, I was going to shoot them in the leg.

Only nobody came through the door. And in the aftermath of the shot, the shattering glass, and the shouts from inside, all I could hear was a woman crying.

*Oh for Christ's sake, Graham,* I scolded myself. *Don't tell me you went to the wrong goddamn house.*

I felt like running away, or limping as the case would have been. Like getting back in the Saab and getting the hell out of Imperial Valley. Another four damn hours, sure, but I'd go directly to the Hollywood Police, march right into Detective Shea's office, and explain everything. And hope to God I wasn't looking at some kind of serious charge.

Then I heard the weeping woman say, "What's happening, Cora? Why is this happening to us?" This was punctuated by the shrill wail of a small child.

*Cora.*

I went inside, gun first.

Though I saw the old woman, my attention was focused entirely on the other woman, who cowered on a suede loveseat shaking, and clutching a weeping toddler in her arms. The woman was around thirty-five or so—my age—with curly brown hair and a plain but pleasant freckled face. She wore an oversized tee shirt and sweat pants, casual clothes for relaxing at home, but she was anything but relaxed. Rather, her wide, ice-blue eyes stared me down with equal parts horror and hatred, leaking tears and shimmering in the light of the faux Tiffany lamp between her and the old woman.

Gary Parson's gun was more or less pointed at the lamp. I couldn't aim it at any of the unarmed people in the room—two women and a child—but I wasn't quite prepared to put it away, either. And despite the fact that I'd never laid eyes on Cora Parson, the still, scowling woman in the Queen Anne chair beside the loveseat struck me as the very person I'd come looking for.

"What do you want from us?" the younger woman cried. Her outburst set the little girl into a fresh bout of screaming and sobbing. "My husband is dead! Do you understand me? *Dead!*"

David, I supposed. The thug Cora left to kill Jake and Barbara. The human monster who *did* kill Jake's friend, or whatever she was. I narrowed my eyes and turned them on the old woman. She neither trembled nor cried. Her veiny hands curled like talons over the arms of the chair and her clear gray eyes regarded me with steely revulsion.

"Cora Parson?" I asked her.

"Mr. Woodard," she answered me. It wasn't a question.

"Cora," the woman said, "who is this? Is this the man who killed David?"

Cora pursed her papery lips and said, "No, Sarah. This is not the man."

"Then who is he?" She pressed the child's head tight against her breast and redirected the question at me: "Who are you? What do you want from us?"

"My name is Graham Woodard," I said. My voice was steady, but my heart was pounding out of my chest. This was not the scene I anticipated. "I was hired by a woman named Leslie Wheeler to help restore a motion picture—a very old motion picture that was thought lost for a very long time. That film was made by Mrs. Parson's father-in-law, back in 1926."

Cora shot me a bemused, smug look. Sarah knitted her brow and snarled, "I know what my husband's grandfather did for a living, damn you. What has that to do with anything?"

"Then let me tell you something you don't know. In fact, I can tell you a lot of things you probably don't know, from the looks of it."

"Don't listen to this man," Cora cut in. "He is clearly a lunatic. He may not be the one who murdered our poor David, but he is most assuredly allied with the killer."

"Oh, don't worry about that, Mrs. Parson," I growled. "I've become a killer too, now. Your boy Gary paid a visit to me and some of my friends. This is his gun, as a matter of fact. I took it from him. I took his shiny car, too. He won't be needing either of them anymore."

"Oh, god!" David's widow wailed. "Oh, my god!"

"But I've gotten ahead of myself," I continued. I changed my mind about the gun and angled it to point directly at Cora. She didn't change her expression one bit. "You see, Miss—it's Sarah, right?"

"Go to hell," she said.

"Right. You see, Sarah, Jack Parson—the elder Jack Parson—was apparently something of a sadist. I mean a real goddamned psycho."

"You shut your lying mouth," Cora snapped. "Don't you dare come into my house and disparage my husband's father."

I shook the gun at her. "Be quiet, Cora," I said. "I'm nowhere near finished yet."

"Jack Parson died before you were born!" Sarah said. "This is goddamn crazy."

"Oh, it's crazy all right. And I suspect Parson was pretty damn crazy, too. Christ, runs in the family, from what I can see. Maybe he was a genius, as well—I saw *Angel of the Abyss*, Cora. All of it, every reel. It's a masterpiece. An honest-to-Christ work of art. It's just such a crying shame a young woman had to die for it, which is why you've gone to such insane lengths to keep it buried, am I right?"

She only glared.

"Very few people ever saw it, but in Europe your father made a name for himself after Monumental folded—though that's not why he left the country, is it? He's well remembered, and that name still means something, doesn't it? Your name. Parson. Your husband traded on it and so do you. It would be a hell of a blow should the world find out that the great Jack Parson murdered Grace Baronsky on film to satisfy whatever monkeyfuck crazy bloodlust he had eating away at his brain, don't you think?"

"My father-in-law was an artist!" Cora shouted suddenly,

lurching forward in the chair, her face twisting with impotent rage. "And my husband revived Monumental from the ashes when nobody else gave a damn. My family does have a good name in this business, Mr. Woodard, in this state. And I intend to make absolutely certain it remains that way."

"Even if it means murdering anybody who threatens you with the bloody truth."

"M-murder?" Sarah screwed up her mouth and looked at me as though I'd just dropped my pants.

"That's right," I said evenly. "Leslie Wheeler was the first. I took a bullet in the head that was supposed to kill me—I think that must have been your husband who pulled the trigger there. Then there was Florence Sommer, and a girl named Lou, and tonight two people who had nothing at all to do with any of it. Their names were Duff and Shawna, if you're interested."

"You're lying," she muttered. "What an awful thing to say. You're a goddamn liar."

"I didn't leave the hospital with a fucking hole in my head and drive four hours to El Centro to tell you lies, lady. I came here to put an end to this nightmare, to stop your horrible mother-in-law from causing any more damage to me and my friends. I am a goddamned film restoration technician, for Christ's sake. All I ever wanted out of this was to see Grace Baron's only performance, and I sure as hell did. And by seeing it, I opened up Pandora's Box and unleashed *this* piece of shit on half of Southern California." I gestured at Cora with her dead son's gun.

The child continued to quietly whimper, but thankfully she did so in her sleep. The trauma and excitement had been too much for her and she crashed right out. Her mother kept looking at me with those huge wet eyes for another minute before turning them on Cora.

She said, "Cora? What is he talking about?"

"I'm sure I don't know. But certainly someone has called the police by now. That shot couldn't have gone unnoticed. Not here."

"I hope you're right, you nasty old bag," I said. "The Hollywood Police Department has been looking for you, Mrs.

Parson. Showing up at Leslie and Barbara's office was not a wise decision on your part."

"What is this, Cora?" Sarah repeated.

Cora drew a breath in through flared nostrils and her right eye twitched. I guess she was imagining the tables turned, maybe one of her sons putting another bullet in my skull. It didn't really matter. Not anymore.

"I loved my father-in-law," she said after a while. "I loved him better than my own father. He was a great man. Can you understand that, Mr. Woodard? Only one in a million men are truly great, and Jack Parson was one of them. He was a visionary artist. And had the world been in any intellectual position to comprehend it, he would have changed the face of cinema while it was still in its infant state."

"By sticking a knife in a girl's heart? Is that what passes for genius in your family?"

Her daughter-in-law's eyes remained fixed on her, and for a brief moment Cora exchanged glances with her before coming back to me.

"He was a passionate man, Jack Parson. Something of an *enfant terrible*, I suppose. In Europe he saw many dreadful things, as anyone there did in those days. I think that was what finally calmed him, brought him back down to solid earth. Only then did he fully see how far he'd taken things. Before, with that film."

"You mean with that *murder*."

"If that's what you prefer. I believe he regretted deeply what he had done, for what it's worth to you. But he could not very well bring her back, could he? And should the world be deprived of the many important films he made after, just because of some low, midwestern vaudeville slut?"

With that, the old bitch smirked. She actually *smirked* at me, daring me to make something of it. For a fraction of a second, I considered it. I considered pulling that trigger and putting that inhuman woman down like you would a rabid dog. But that would have been too easy and too much trouble for me. Instead, I switched gears to what I'd really come to know.

"Your time is running out, Mrs. Parson," I said, my voice

finally breaking as I prepared myself for what I was about to say. "Probably you're right about the cops. I made quite a racket coming in here and I doubt the nice people you live around are used to that sort of thing. So you might as well tell me now, and damnit, don't make me ask twice—what did you do with Helen?"

Almost beyond my control the gun in my hand inched closer to her pale, stolid face. She blinked and said, "Nothing at all."

Police sirens wailed in the middle distance. There was no question where they were heading.

"Here they come, Mrs. Parson. You're done and you damn well know it. They already know what you've done. Why lie about one more killing?"

"I've told you, Mr. Woodard. I haven't harmed a hair on her drug-addled little head."

"She was my *wife*, you old bitch. Jake said she's dead. *What did you do?*"

A small, wry grin formed at her white lips and she emitted a throaty little laugh.

"I met her in what I gather was the same way Ms. Wheeler met her, at that little theater where she worked. She proved useful to me, keeping me informed of that homosexual woman's plans, and when I grew worried that there might be police involvement I convinced her to hold a significant amount of money for me. Lest it be seized, of course. It's extraordinary what you can persuade an addict to do with a little help from their chosen vices, Mr. Woodard. Though I suspect you already know that perfectly well."

"Cora," the other woman whispered, astonished and horrified. Finally she got it. She believed and she understood. She'd married into a family of monsters. I felt sorry for her. "Cora, my *god*."

"Oh *shut* up," Cora answered her. "We've all suffered here. I've lost both of my sons."

"And you seem so broken up about it, too," I hissed. "You're a real piece of work, Cora Parson."

The sirens pierced the air as they came onto the street. Through the drawn curtains of the window behind the women

I could see the blue and red lights pulsing right in front of the house. As soon as I heard the shuffle of approaching footsteps, I gently set the gun down on an end table—away from Cora.

And before the police reached the door, I turned back to the old woman and looked deep into her soulless eyes, and I said, "Where is she, Cora?"

The old hen half-grinned, her age-worn lips all but cracking at the strain. She said, "For the record, that colored girl isn't dead. Shawna, you said? Yes, I think that's right. It isn't as though I didn't know my building had squatters. How did you suppose Gary found you there?"

My stomach dropped, half-turned over at the thought that Shawna's willingness to tattle to Cora had gotten Duff—her friend—killed. I wondered if she would be able to live with herself when she found out, but pushed the thought away in favor of getting my question answered.

"Where, Cora?" I persisted. "Where is she?"

"I haven't the faintest idea where your wife is, Mr. Woodard. In some gutter, I'd imagine."

"Not Helen. Grace. Where is Grace Baronsky?"

Fists pounded on the front door and a deep male voice shouted, "El Centro Police Department—open up."

Cora met my gaze and raised her eyebrows.

"Oh," she said. "Grace."

She told me.

# EPILOGUE

## GRAHAM AND JAKE

## L.A., 2013.

Two things I learned upon my return to Los Angeles knocked me on my ass. The first was that Jake never left town. He was waiting at the station when Shea brought me in, having gone to a hell of a lot of trouble keeping me out of jail back in El Centro. I even got a police escort the whole 220 miles back, since the cops weren't too keen on letting me drive a technically stolen vehicle used in the commissions of numerous crimes. Jake had already heard all of it and, to my surprise, didn't have an obnoxiously snarky comment for me when I came into Shea's office that afternoon. He gave me a hug.

"I wasn't going to give up on you, man," he said in my ear, squeezing me tighter than any man ever had. "But I'd never thought you'd escape from the frigging hospital, you moron."

"He'll be going back, too," Shea put in. "The smart money says you haven't done your well-being any favors with this little adventure of yours, Graham. You're going to have to pay the piper for that crap."

"I know," I said. I felt like I was in the principal's office just then. It didn't help that I was leaning awkwardly to the side with my knees pressed together like a scolded kid. Actually, I was just in a lot of pain and my coordination was shot to hell.

"And that's not even mentioning the inquest," Shea said. "You'll be fine, but you're going to want to get yourself a lawyer."

"I've already been cleared," Jake beamed. Like we were

thug-killer brothers now, or something. I sighed and decided not to dwell on it.

An officer brought in some more of that lovely police station coffee for the three of us and, after Shea thanked the kid and politely kicked him out, he asked both of us to sit down. I sipped at the sludge and waited for bombshell number two, though I didn't know it at that exact minute.

"Graham, Helen has been located, and she's alive."

I froze and the office tilted a little as my stomach plummeted and then righted itself again. I said, "Oh, my god."

And I erupted into tears.

There's nothing in the world wrong with a man crying when it's called for, but the amount of tears I'd shed between Grace Baron and my ex-wife, who I'd believed dead for much too long, was enough to fill my quota for a lifetime. Jake squeezed my shoulder and both he and Shea waited me out. I was a good deal embarrassed to break down like that in front of them, but goddamn, it felt good.

Once I managed to stop blubbering, Shea gave me the not-so-good news.

"She was picked up in Venice. She, uh, she had half an ounce of coke on her and she was so blitzed she could hardly see straight. She'll be doing a little time for that, I'm sure. I'm sorry."

"Christ, Helen," I murmured.

"It's better than what you thought, bud," Jake said.

He was right. But still.

We talked, the three of us, for most of the afternoon. A lot of it covered everything that had happened, from each of our perspectives and experiences, and though Detective Shea couldn't express enough how much he wanted to slap Jake and me for getting in so deep, he proved himself to be a genuinely warm and upright guy as far as I was concerned. He assured me that Cora Parson would never live to see the outside of a prison again, and though it couldn't undo the unholy wreckage she'd left in her wake, it was good to hear. I liked Donny Shea. Maybe that was why I felt so guilty for keeping one little bit of information from him. At least for the time being.

Jake, on the other hand—my partner in all of this, for better or worse—came along for the ride on this one. I might have expected the coordinates to some remote spot in the San Gabriel Mountains when I asked Cora Parson where Grace Baron was hidden, but to finally find her all we had to do was take a cab out to the crumbling remains of a once grand mansion.

"Joseph March's house," she'd said simply in the moments before I let the El Centro police in and, temporarily, experienced handcuffs for the first time in my life. "That is where you will find Grace. Where she belongs."

The name was vaguely familiar, but a quick Internet search filled me in on the finer details. Joseph March was a minor director in the silent era whose career tanked once the Talkie came around. At the height of his success he occupied the mansion in Malibu, which had passed from owner to owner over the years, eventually left to rot by the dawn of the 80s. It was prime Oceanside real estate, though, so by the mid-90s the entire property was scooped up for a song by someone with more money than I'd ever see with plans to restore the house to its original condition. One look at the place upon our arrival was all we needed to know those plans had been greatly delayed.

"Christ, what a dump," Jake opined.

I was inclined to agree. The place looked like a haunted house from some old B horror picture with its sagging roof and rotting eaves. The overstated columns in front were choked by creepers and the steps were falling to pieces. A swimming pool on the side facing the Pacific was filled almost to the top with dirt and tall, intersecting weeds. I figured the guy who bought the place must have had second thoughts about restoration; the house was wrecked and probably just needed to be knocked down. But not before we did what we came to do.

"I don't know, Graham," Jake said as the cab pulled away. "It doesn't look exactly safe."

"You can wait out here," I told him. "I don't mind."

"Forget that," he countered. "In for a penny, man."

"All right."

I climbed the ruined steps with Jake's help, using my cane to knock aside chunks of the broken stone to keep from tripping on them. The front door, a massive hunk of oak going green from rot, wasn't locked. I pushed it open to reveal a dark, rank foyer overgrown with vegetation. Our steps echoed loudly against the walls as we went inside. Jake kept his hand at the small of my back, like he was worried I'd fall over. It wasn't the first time it occurred to me what a decent human being he'd turned out to be. I still thought he was annoying as all hell, but I was starting to tolerate the guy.

"Big joint," he said, his voice bouncing all over the place like a museum. "Where to?"

I heaved a sigh and went forward, stepping lightly in spite of my limp, working to avoid the weeds and detritus covering the marble floor. There was an open doorway in front of me and a closed door to my right. I looked first through the open one, which led into a large empty room lined with what once were bookshelves, but now wouldn't even serve as useful firewood. I looked back in time to see Jake trying the closed door. It didn't budge, so he threw his shoulder into it and fell right through. He yelled out, startled, and I came to him as quickly as I could.

"You all right?"

"Goddamn thing," he groused. I decided he was all right.

We were in a dark hallway that smelled like a jungle and a locker room rolled up in an old rug. I helped Jake up and we peered into the darkness together, our eyes adjusting to the light. We saw the door at the end of the hall at the same time, and neither of us said a word. We just walked side by side right up to it, and this time it opened up without a problem.

I flicked my disposable lighter to see what fresh hell we'd stumbled into. Once the flame leapt up and gave a faint glow to the metal frames of tiered seats and the small window in the center of the wall behind them, I understood everything perfectly.

"Oh," I said. "Oh, Jesus."

"What?"

"Where she belongs."

"What is all this?"

"A private screening room," I told him. "A mini movie theater. Because that's where Grace belongs. It's where she always belonged. On the screen."

"So—she's here?"

"She has to be."

The flame burned my thumb and I released the button. We were plunged back into darkness, but I remembered seeing an old sconce on the wall of the library. I told Jake about it and he rushed to get it. When he returned, we were both relieved to find it still held some fuel and the wick actually caught. Now we had light to work by.

It didn't take long. Together, we pulled up the moldy old carpet to reveal a floor comprised of wood slats. Like everything else in the house they were half rotted away, so Jake passed the light over the sundry gaps between the seats and the facing wall where the screen once hung until he gasped and shouted out, "Here! She's here. Oh my god."

I hobbled over and peered down through the broad, jagged cracks. Looking back up at me was the hollow eye socket of a human skull.

"Jesus," Jake whispered. "All these years?"

"Most of a century," I said. He held the light steady so I could look at her, or what was left of her. Just a gray-white skull, only bones left barely concealed in the threadbare ruins of an ancient gown.

"I've got my phone," Jake said, his voice unexpectedly choked with emotion. "I'll call Shea."

I nodded and he left the screening room. Left me and the light and the remains of the doomed girl who should have been the most enduring name and talent of her time, but was instead forgotten, lost to history. I'd been through so much to see her sit where she belonged, among the royalty of silent cinema to whom she truly, rightfully belonged. And I knew, now that the ordeal was really done, that the job I'd come to do in the first place was finally going to be done. I was going to make damn certain *Angel of the Abyss*, for all its beauty and horror, was finally brought back from the grave.

On my hands and knees in the tremulous light of the sconce, I smiled down through the holes in the floor at the bones underneath, and I said, "Hello, Grace. I'm Graham Woodard. I think I've been looking for you for a long time.".

# ABOUT THE AUTHOR

Ed Kurtz is the author of The Rib From Which I Remake the World, Bleed, and other novels. His short fiction has appeared in numerous magazines and anthologies, including Best American Mystery Stories and Best Gay Stories. Ed lives in Connecticut, and can be found online at www.edkurtzbooks.com.

## Bibliography

*Angel of the Abyss*
*At the Mercy of Beasts* (forthcoming 2018)
*Bleed*
*Caliban* (forthcoming 2019)
*Control*
*Dead Trash*
*Nausea*
*Nothing You Can Do: Stories*
*Sawbones*
*The Forty-Two*
*The Rib From Which I Remake the World*

Curious about other Crossroad Press books?
Stop by our site:
http://store.crossroadpress.com
We offer quality writing
in digital, audio, and print formats.

Enter the code FIRSTBOOK
to get 20% off your first order from our store!
Stop by today!

www.ingramcontent.com/pod-product-compliance
Lightning Source LLC
Chambersburg PA
CBHW071131200626
46817CB00018B/2701